Vernon stood at the washstand, shirtless, his back to her as he bent over the bowl.

The candlelight danced across unblemished skin and she watched, fascinated by the play of muscles across his shoulders and back, as he continued his ablutions. Her hands itched to touch, to stroke, to discover if his skin was as smooth as it looked. His breeches were stretched tight, outlining taut buttocks— thrust temptingly in her direction—and long, lean thighs. Her mouth dried as her skin heated. A thrilling sense of anticipation swirled in her belly, then slowed, arrowing in to the juncture of her thighs and provoking a strange restlessness.

An insistent need.

Thea resisted the urge to move, to turn onto her back, to push aside the covers, to extend her arms and invite him to hold her. How would it feel to throw aside morals and caution and pride and follow that craving? She lay motionless, still watching as Vernon hummed a tune she did not recognise under his breath, seemingly perfectly relaxed.

Desire.

Sh⬚⬚⬚⬚⬚⬚⬚⬚⬚⬚⬚⬚⬚⬚⬚⬚he
ha⬚

Author Note

Scandal and Miss Markham is the second of
The Beauchamp Betrothals linked books, but it is
a stand-alone story and it's not essential to read
Cinderella and the Duke first.

It is time for Lord Vernon Beauchamp—handsome,
wealthy, darling of the *ton* and younger brother of
Leo, Duke of Cheriton—to meet his match. But his
life seems almost too perfect. A man like him—and
he has featured in other books of mine, apart from
Cinderella and the Duke—would surely just need to
snap his fingers to win any woman he chose? But then
I thought a bit more about his life and I realised he
has always been Leo's sidekick, always the second in
command, and he is bored. He needs shaking out of
his perfect life, and I knew just the woman to do it.

Enter Dorothea Markham, a glass manufacturer's
daughter with fascinating springy copper curls, a
stubborn streak a mile wide and a penchant for acting
first and repenting later—or not, as the case may
be. She doesn't need help from anyone when her
brother fails to return home—least of all from a spoilt,
wealthy aristocrat with a tendency to tease her…and to
make her pulse leap alarmingly.

Enjoy the trip as Vernon and Thea embark on an
adventure to find her missing brother and end up
finding more than they bargained for.

SCANDAL AND MISS MARKHAM

Janice Preston

HarperCollins

PUBLISHERS — *Since 1817* —

Published in Great Britain 2017
by Mills & Boon, an imprint of HarperCollins*Publishers*
1 London Bridge Street, London, SE1 9GF

© 2017 Janice Preston

ISBN: 978-0-263-92610-1

Printed and bound in Spain
by CPI, Barcelona

Janice Preston grew up in Wembley, North London, with a love of reading, writing stories and animals. In the past she has worked as a farmer, a police call-handler and a university administrator. She now lives in the West Midlands with her husband and two cats, and has a part-time job as a weight management counsellor—vainly trying to control her own weight despite her love of chocolate!

Books by Janice Preston

Mills & Boon Historical Romance

The Beauchamp Betrothals

Cinderella and the Duke
Scandal and Miss Markham

The Governess Tales

The Governess's Secret Baby

Men About Town

Return of Scandal's Son
Saved by Scandal's Heir

Linked by Character
to *Men About Town* duet

Mary and the Marquis
From Wallflower to Countess

Visit the Author Profile page at millsandboon.co.uk.

To Mum.
I like to think you would be proud.

Chapter One

Thea's head snapped up at the sound of wheels crunching across the gravel outside Stourwell Court.

Daniel!

Hope erupted through her…it had been five days since her brother had gone out one day and not returned. She leapt to her feet and hurried to the salon window. A glimpse of a curricle drawn by a pair of blacks set her heart racing, and she flung her embroidery aside, gathered her skirts and ran for the door. Across the hall and through the front door she sped.

Please. Let it be him.

Doubts nipped at her as she sprinted down the steps to the now stationary conveyance, but she ignored them. She could not bear to let that prayer of hope fizzle and die. She shut her mind against the evidence of her eyes as she reached the foot of the steps and hurried to the curricle.

'Daniel—'

Her eyes met those of the driver—a stranger—and she skidded to a halt, gravel spinning from beneath her feet.

'Who are you? Where is Daniel?' She raked the driver with her eyes and then switched her gaze to the horses. 'Those are his—'

Her jaw snapped shut and her cheeks scorched. 'Oh!' Those doubts had caught up with her and knocked her flat. She bit her lip as sick disappointment flooded her, followed by the fear that had dogged her ever since her brother had failed to come home.

'I beg your pardon, sir. I mistook your horses for those of my brother's but I see, upon closer examination, they are not his.'

They were a pair of blacks, yes, but of far superior quality to Daniel's, and a groom—another stranger—perched on the back of the curricle. And besides...

Fool! Daniel didn't even take his curricle. He was on horseback.

And that had been her one ray of hope in this desperate mess, one that she clung to with all her heart: her brother had ridden away and not returned, but neither had Bullet, his grey gelding, whose homing instinct was powerful and who in the past had often carried his foxed rider safely home after a night spent drinking. Thankfully, though, Daniel had soon outgrown that wild behaviour.

And now Thea clung to her belief that whilst Bullet was missing, there was still hope.

The stranger appraised her with raised brows and she scowled back at him, irritated by the amused curl of his lips. She quashed the tug of attraction she recognised deep in her core. It was a very long time since she had allowed herself to be attracted to any man.

'Your brother being Mr Daniel Markham?'

His voice was deep and cultured—that of a gentleman born. Thea had been subjected to enough elocution lessons to recognise that aristocratic drawl. She studied the driver, from the brim of his tall beaver hat to the toes of his shiny boots. What business could a man like this have with Daniel? Suspicions swirled. Did this stranger have something to do with Daniel's disappearance? Daniel had been troubled before he disappeared, that much she did know. But, unusually, he had refused to confide in her.

'He is,' she said. 'And you are?'

He frowned, clearly put out by such a brusque demand. Well, Thea had more pressing concerns than a strange gentleman's sense of his own importance.

'I am Lord Vernon Beauchamp, here to speak to your brother.'

'A *lord*? What on earth do you want with *Daniel*?'

A muscle leapt at the side of his jaw. 'Bickling, hold the horses.'

He tied off the reins and the groom jumped down and ran to the horses' heads. Lord Vernon Beauchamp climbed in a leisurely fashion from his curricle and walked across the gravel to Thea, not stopping until he was so close he towered over her, radiating confidence and power. Thea set her jaw and stood her ground, refusing to be intimidated even though his commanding air and his raw masculinity rattled her from her head to her toes.

'I suggest that is a matter between your brother and me, madam. Am I to understand he is not here?'

'No, he is not.'

She glanced back at the house. No sign of her mother. Good…no doubt she was with Papa; she often read to him in the morning after he awoke. Heaven knew how much longer Thea could protect them from knowing the full truth of Daniel's absence. She looked up at Lord Vernon.

'If it concerns Stour Crystal, I assure you that I am perfectly able either to assist you myself, or to refer any query to the appropriate individual at the manufactory.'

'Stour Crystal?' Lord Vernon surveyed the frontage of Stourwell Court before looking back along the carriageway, to the wrought-iron entrance gates in the distance. Thea bridled as she fancied she detected a slight curl of his upper lip as he stripped off his driving gloves. 'Your family manufacture lead-crystal glassware?'

'We do.'

And I am proud of it.

Her father had built the business from scratch, manufacturing some of the finest quality cut lead crystal in the land. *His Lordship* might have been born into the aristocracy but that did not give him the right to look down upon her. But with that defiant pride came the realisation that she had not offered her visitor the customary hospitality due a visitor. She had allowed her disappointment he was not Daniel to override her manners and that would surely only add to his lordship's low impression of her and her family. She bit back any further comment and moved away from Lord Vernon to smooth her hand over the haunch of the nearest horse. She smiled at the groom.

'He is hot,' she said, 'and you must be tired and in need of refreshment.' After the heavy rains of a week ago, the weather had turned unseasonably warm. 'Take the horses around the back—you will see the way to the stable yard and you may care for them there. Come to the kitchen afterwards. Cook will give you some food and something to drink.'

The groom waited until his master gave him permission—granted by a flick of the head—to proceed before leading the horses away. Lord Vernon, a look of irritation on his face, swished his driving gloves against his palm. No doubt he was unhappy at his groom and horses' needs being considered before his own: yet more evidence of his sense of entitlement. Mentally, Thea shrugged but she took care to conceal her scorn. She had neither the strength nor the heart to engage in a verbal sparring session.

'You, too, must be weary, my lord. Shall we continue this discussion indoors?'

As the scrunch of hooves faded, his lordship inscribed an arc through the air with his arm and then bowed.

'After you.'

Thea marched to the front porch, feeling much like a cat whose fur had been rubbed the wrong way, but she vowed to remain polite; she had no wish to reinforce his prejudices. The man had been neither rude nor derogatory, but—she pictured again that subtle curl of his lip—she knew how his sort viewed ordinary business folk who must work for their living.

She led him across the hall and into the study.

'Would you prefer ale or wine, sir?'

'Tea,' he said.

She was certain he was being deliberately awkward. Their aversion was mutual then. So be it. She had more pressing concerns than how some spoilt aristocrat viewed her and a handsome face and a manly physique meant nothing to a woman who had forsworn all men. She jerked at the bell and a footman soon attended.

'Bring tea for the gentleman, please, George, and a glass of Madeira for me. And some of Cook's fruit cake.'

As George turned to leave, Thea said, 'Is Mama with Papa?'

'She is, miss. Shall I inform her we have a visitor?'

Thea glanced at Lord Vernon, who had removed his hat to reveal a full head of auburn hair that curled around his ears. A little flutter deep in her stomach taunted her: perhaps she wasn't as immune to an attractive man as she thought. She wrenched her attention away from her treacherous body.

'No. That will not be necessary, George.'

'Very well, miss.'

Thea then sat in a chair by the window and gestured to a nearby chair.

'Please, take a seat, sir.'

She waited until he was settled, her thoughts whirling. She knew from past experience, through her dealings with other men, that he would be reluctant to discuss business with her simply because of her sex. If she were to learn the truth of his visit, she must try to annoy him into indiscretion and she knew the perfect way to aggravate him: men often found it hard to deal with females who were direct.

'Is it money?'

His brows lowered into a thunderous frown. 'Is *what* money?' His question almost a growl.

'Does Daniel owe you money? Are you here to collect on a debt?'

'I do not—' He snapped his jaw shut, abruptly cutting off his heated response. His eyes—an arresting shade of green that sparkled in the light of a stray sunbeam filtering through the window pane—narrowed. When he spoke again, his voice was level. 'Why should you jump to such a conclusion? Is your Daniel a gambler?'

Thea frowned in her turn. This man was clearly not to be easily manipulated.

'He is not.'

'Then I ask again, why do you jump to the conclusion I am here to collect on a debt?'

Thea shrugged, stood up and paced to the fireplace. She swung around, to see that her visitor had risen to his feet. She huffed a silent laugh. A lord and a gentleman, trained from birth in correct etiquette. When a lady stands—even a lowly born lady such as she—a gentleman, too, must stand.

'Please. Sit down.' She crossed the room to sit in her own chair and his lordship—with a supercilious lift of one brow—followed suit.

He folded his arms. 'I am waiting.'

His voice was soft. Almost menacing. Thea shivered at her sudden mental image of a wolf: crouching, watching, patient. She thrust aside that picture, silently castigating herself for such a fanciful thought. He was a man…a powerful lord, maybe, but a man none the less.

His question…what was it again? About debt. 'We are in business, my lord. I wondered if Daniel had overlooked a bill.'

His lips twitched. Thea searched his expression and felt her tension ease and her sense of foreboding lift as she realised he was trying not to laugh. No sign of a menacing predator now. She really must try to curtail her imagination.

'I cannot decide whether to be amused or offended that you could even suspect I am a debt collector,' he said. His smile now surfaced fully, his lips parting to reveal white, even teeth.

Heavens, he is a handsome devil.

She quashed that thought and dismissed the accompanying trip of her pulse.

'Might we, do you think, start this conversation anew and dispense with the suspicion on both sides?'

Thea inclined her head by way of reply. A truce would speed this meeting along and give her the opportunity to discover if Lord Vernon Beauchamp knew anything that might shed light on Daniel's disappearance.

George came in with the refreshments and Thea poured a cup of tea for her visitor before handing him the cup and saucer. He captured her gaze as he murmured his thanks, his deep voice vibrating through her. Then he brushed her fingers as she handed him a plate with a slice of cake. A whiff of cologne arose to tease at her senses: spicy, with notes of cinnamon. Musky and expensive. The resulting flicker of desire deep in her stomach exasperated Thea all over again.

She recognised his tactic. This was an attempt to use his charisma to wheedle information from her. He was a handsome aristocrat, experienced in the art of flirtation and accustomed to having his own way…well, he would soon find she was too shrewd to allow weasel words and admiring glances to fool *her*.

She had been burned before.

Never again.

Besides, she had neither the time nor the inclination to engage with him in this particular game. There was far too much at stake.

'I do not know your name.'

His statement startled her. 'But…of course you know my name. Daniel is my brother. I, therefore, am Miss Markham.'

He cocked his head to one side. 'But I did not know whether or not you were married, Miss Markham. For all I knew, you could be Mrs Wilful, or Lady Copper Curls.'

He smiled. Charmingly. A fan of crinkles formed at the outer corner of each eye. Thea raised her chin and directed a stern look at him.

'You were about to tell me your business with my brother, sir.'

Lord Vernon set his teacup and saucer on to a side table and settled back into his chair, his elbows propped on the arms as he placed his hands fingertip to fingertip beneath his chin.

'My business is with your brother. It is not proper that I should discuss it with you.'

'Because I am a female?' No matter how many times she was told she was unable to understand business matters, it became no easier hearing the same sentiment from yet another male. 'As I said before—my brother and I collaborate in our father's business. We do not have secrets.'

'And yet you have no idea why I am here.'

Thea swallowed past the painful lump in her throat. 'That is entirely different. I cannot be privy to your whims and fancies in deciding to call upon Daniel.'

'Whims and fancies,' he murmured. 'I cannot say I am flattered at being thought a man subject to whims and fancies.' His expression hardened and again she was reminded that, beneath his urbane exterior, there lurked an altogether different beast. 'You boast there are no secrets between yourself and your brother and yet you are unaware it was your brother who wrote to *me* to request a meeting.'

'For what purpose?'

He raised a brow. 'Perhaps *you* can enlighten *me*?'

Thea shook her head and a lock of hair sprang loose to dangle in front of her eye. She clicked her tongue in irritation, swept the curl from her forehead and hooked it behind a hairpin, then sipped at her Madeira, her mind working furiously. This conversation was not going the way she intended. She was desperate to find out if this man had any information that might tell her where Daniel had gone.

'I have not the first idea why Daniel wrote to you. Was it connected with the business?'

'I can safely say he did not summon me to discuss a matter of business. The only knowledge I have of lead-crystal glassware is the quality of the liquid contained therein.'

'That comes as no surprise.'

Heavens! When will I learn to curb my tongue?

A muscle bunched in his jaw. 'And such a riposte is entirely predictable. You clearly suffer under the illusion that the idle aristocracy are fit for little other than frittering their fortunes away upon their own pleasures and depravities.'

She couldn't decide if she felt shame at having insulted him, albeit indirectly, or pride that she could stand her own against such a man.

'They are your words,' she responded, raising her brows. '*Your* interpretation of my expressed belief that you would have no knowledge of the manufacture of lead crystal. And I was correct.'

His lips thinned. 'Where is your brother, Miss Markham? When do you expect him home?'

She bit her lip.

'I do not know.'

Her stomach clenched into a tight, hard ball of fear. Unable to sit still, she rose to her feet and crossed the room to the desk. Daniel's desk. But there were no clues there. She had searched it thoroughly and there was no hint of where he had gone or what had happened to him. She fingered a contract that lay on the top of a pile of papers awaiting attention, that same all-pervading sense of dread crawling through her veins. This contract was important to Stour Crystal.

Would Daniel really just…go? Would he really be so negligent?

Of the business? Of her? Of their parents?

'I do not know,' she repeated.

Chapter Two

Lord Vernon Beauchamp eyed Miss Markham. Lines of strain bracketed her mouth and worry lurked in those huge hazel eyes—eyes that had sparked such fire at him only moments ago. In fact, all her fire had fizzled out… This was not merely a case of her brother not being at home this afternoon, of that he was certain. But alongside the worry in her eyes lurked caution. Maybe attempting to flirt his way into gaining her good opinion… her *trust*…had been a mistake.

He rose to his feet and approached the desk. She tracked his every movement, her wariness plain.

'Do not be alarmed,' Vernon said. 'Will you not sit down and tell me what has happened? There truly is no need to be suspicious of my intentions towards your brother. If it helps to reassure you, you should know that I have never before met Daniel and I know nothing more than he wrote in this letter.'

He reached into his pocket and produced the letter that Daniel Markham had penned, the letter that had prompted Vernon's journey into Worcestershire. Miss Markham subsided into the desk chair and took the letter, unfolding it to read. Vernon hitched one hip on the far corner of the desk. After a few seconds, she raised her gaze to his.

'The Duke of Cheriton? This letter is not addressed to you…is it?'

Vernon laughed. 'No, I am not a duke. Cheriton is my brother. He had every intention of writing to your Daniel with an invitation to call upon him to discuss his concerns, but I formed a sudden desire to visit Worcestershire and so I offered to travel up here to meet your brother myself.'

Leo—Vernon's brother—had recently married again and the bride's maternal aunt, Lady Slough, had set her sights on Vernon as a suitable catch for her daughter. Not that Vernon had anything against the chit, but Lady Slough sported all the finesse of a wild boar and he had decided that putting some distance between himself and the lady in question would be best for all concerned. He would not put it past Lady Slough to attempt a spot of entrapment.

Vernon had no inclination to enter the parson's mousetrap. Not for a very long time, if ever. Leo already had his heir and spare—plus a daughter—from his first marriage, thus securing the future of the dukedom, so there was no absolutely no need for Vernon to wed. And why would he choose to give up his charmed life of a popular, wealthy bachelor? He wanted for nothing.

Except purpose.

He thrust aside that mocking voice, even though he was unable to deny that restlessness had also played its part in persuading him to travel up here to Worcestershire.

Miss Markham had continued to read her brother's letter, a frown knitting her forehead.

'Henry Mannington? Who is Henry Mannington?' Her voice was unusually deep for a woman and slightly gruff—quite at odds with her petite figure and luxuriant curls.

'You have never heard of him?'

She shook her head and two of those springy, copper-coloured curls of hers bounced over her forehead. She pushed at them absentmindedly, her gaze still fixed on the letter.

'No. Never.'

'He is not a friend of your brother's? A customer? A rival?'

'No. None of those. I *told* you,' she said, with a hint of sarcasm, 'I have never heard of him.' She paused, white teeth nibbling at her lower lip. Then she narrowed her eyes. 'But *you* know who he is. Or you would not have come all the way up here to speak to Daniel.'

Impressed by her quick uptake, Vernon decided there was nothing to be gained in concealing the little knowledge he did possess.

'Henry Mannington is a distant cousin of the Beauchamp family, but none of us has seen him or heard of him for several years. He is a classics scholar with a passion for exploring ancient sites and even as a young man he had no interest in socialising in our circle.'

'The upper ranks of society, you mean?'

There it was again. That hint of disdain in her tone, but recognisable for all that. Miss Markham clearly did not approve of the aristocracy.

'Yes.' He would neither apologise for who and what he was, nor feel guilty for it. Her prejudices were her problem. 'He is my age and we were at university together. Our paths have not crossed since then.'

Miss Markham thrust the letter back at Vernon. 'I cannot see how this will help me find Daniel.' She crossed her arms.

'*Find* him?'

Her cheeks reddened, clashing with her bright hair. Her lips compressed.

'How long is it since you have seen Daniel?'

For the first time her composure wavered, her nostrils flared and her hazel eyes, fringed with thick, dark lashes, sheened.

'Come.' Vernon gentled his voice. 'You are upset. Tell me what has happened. I might be able to help.'

'I do not need help.'

'How long?'

'F-five days.'

Vernon checked the letter. 'Three days after this was written.' He re-read the missive. 'By its wording, Daniel had suspicions about Henry Mannington, but what manner of suspicions? It must be more than Henry claiming kinship with Cheriton, for that much is the truth and easily verified. And Henry is a decent chap, not the sort to become embroiled in matters dastardly enough to drive your brother to beg help from a peer with whom he has no acquaintance.'

Miss Markham stood up and resolutely smoothed down the skirt of the peach-coloured gown that skimmed her petite frame. The colour should have clashed with her hair, which was the colour of an autumn leaf, but the combination put Vernon in mind of the brilliant sunset of the evening before and he felt a smile tug at the corner of his mouth. She glared at him as he also rose to his feet. She really was a tiny little thing, barely reaching his shoulder. She put him in mind of a cornered kitten, fur fluffed up and claws out, ready for a fight.

'There is no need to stand every time I do,' she said, placing her fists on the desk and leaning on them. 'I am not one of your fine ladies, ready to take affront at imagined slights.'

'Maybe you are not,' Vernon said, quashing down the laugh that tickled his throat. That really *would* infuriate her. 'But *I*, you see, *am* a gentleman. And I therefore stand when a lady does.

Whether *she* considers herself a lady or no. And...'
he added, tweaking his neckcloth and smoothing
the wrinkles from his sleeves, merely to irritate
her and to see those remarkably fine eyes flash
fire again '...as for taking affront, I quite see that
particular emotion is alien to your sunny nature.'

He smiled at her scowl and her muttered impre-
cation. Fortunately, perhaps, he could not make
out her exact sentiments. She was indeed a little
hothead, hardly surprising with that head of hair.
His own hair had reddish tones, but it was more of
a dark chestnut colour than the fiery hue of Miss
Markham's. He would warrant his temperament
was less fiery than hers, too.

'Have you made enquiries as to your brother's
whereabouts?'

'Yes... That is, I sent the grooms out to search
the countryside around, but I instructed them not
to make enquiries. Not yet. I did not want to raise
a fuss only to find there was a simple explanation
for his absence.' She sucked in a deep breath and
his eyes were drawn to the swell of her breasts.
'They found no trace of Daniel or his horse. And
so I waited. I kept hoping he would return. Or that
he would write to me.'

'In other words, you have done nothing to find
your brother. You shut your eyes to reality and simply hoped for the best.'

She flashed a look of daggers at him. 'I did not

wish to stir up a wasps' nest of trouble for him if there was no need for it.'

'Trouble? Why should you suspect he was in trouble?'

She stared down at the desk, fingering the stack of papers in front of her. Then she subsided into the chair.

'He was preoccupied...*upset*...in the days before he went missing.'

Her voice was low and husky with a hint of vulnerability and it stirred within him a peculiar urge to protect her. To help. She was nibbling at her full lower lip, her tawny brows creased in a frown as she stared past Vernon, into the distance. Vernon tore his gaze from her mouth, disconcerted by the slow but undeniable tightening in his loins.

'I *knew* he was worried,' she said, 'and yet I did not make him tell me what was amiss. I allowed him to fob me off.'

'I doubt you could have compelled him to confide in you.'

Her gaze met his, a glint of humour in her eyes. 'Oh, I think I could, had I tried. I should have *forced* him to tell me where he was going.'

Vernon felt his lips twitch. 'You have piqued my interest, Miss Markham. How, pray, do you imagine you could have *forced* your brother to tell you?'

'I could have threatened to follow him.'

'And he would have believed you?'

'Of course.' She tilted her chin. 'He knows I never make empty threats.'

His lips twitched again, but he held back his grin. 'I shall have to remember that,' he murmured. 'Do I take it you are older than your brother?'

'Yes. By three years.'

'That explains much.'

Her brows snapped together. 'This—' Her lips tightened. 'I am doing it again. Allowing myself to be diverted, because I am scared... I fear...' She bent her head.

Vernon waited.

'You were right... I *have* been waiting. And hoping. But no more.' She pierced him with a fierce gaze. 'You have spurred me into seeing what I must do. I shall go myself and I shall make enquiries. I shall find out where he went, all those days when he was out for hours upon end, returning home to eat and sleep and then leaving again at first light. He must have left a trail. He would have been seen. He had to eat.' She was on her feet again, pacing. 'Oh! Why did I not go out that first day? Immediately? What a fool I have been, waiting at home like a...like a...*ninny*...when Daniel had need of me.'

'And where do you intend to make your enquiries?'

'Oh! I do not know.' She waved her arm as she paced, brushing aside his query as though it were an irritating fly. 'His usual haunts. The Nag's Head, in Stourbridge, for a start. He often went there for a drink in the evening. Someone there might know where he went. And they will know of other places he frequented.'

'The Nag's Head? A public house?'

She slammed to a halt, staring at him. 'Do not—' her voice throbbed with warning '—tell me I cannot go there because I am a woman.'

Vernon felt his eyes narrow. 'That is precisely what I *am* telling you. Such scandalous behaviour is completely unacceptable. Your reputation would be ruined.'

'Scandal! What do I care for scandal? My brother is missing and I must—'

'You *should* care about scandal. Your good name, once lost, will not be easily recovered.'

'We are not in your overprotected and rarefied world now, my lord. As I said before, I am not—'

'Not one of my fine ladies. Yes, you have already made that point.'

Her mouth set in a mulish line and the dogged determination upon her face reminded Vernon of his niece, Olivia, when told she could not do something she had set her heart upon. But Olivia was eighteen years of age. Miss Markham should… *must*, surely…have more sense.

He'd had enough of this, she was not thinking rationally. She must realise how dangerous such places might be and not only to her good name. He changed tack. Demanding her obedience would not work, that much he had already learned.

'Promise me you will not go haring off on such an ill-advised crusade.'

'But I must, for if I do not, who will?'

'Your father?'

She turned her head aside, but not before he recognised her anguish. 'He is not well. He must not be upset.'

'Other male relatives?'

She shook her head, freeing even more of those fascinating curls to bounce around her face. Her hair appeared to have a life of its own, the curls like flaming corkscrews.

'I am not a fool,' she said. 'I would not go alone. I would take a groom. Or even two. For protection. So, you see, there is no need for you to be concerned, or even to stay here any longer.' She tilted her chin. 'You said yourself you do not know Daniel and neither do you know the area. *You* would not know where to begin looking.'

Vernon eyed her with exasperation as he pondered the mystery of Daniel Markham's disappearance and how, if at all, it was connected to Henry. He should, probably, return to town and wait for Markham to make further contact. But…he considered that option. What was there to return to? Leo would be fully occupied with his new bride and, soon, most everyone would be leaving London to spend summer on their estates or in the seaside resorts.

There was little enticement there to lure him home in a hurry.

And here, in Worcestershire…his blood stirred. All kinds of emotions swirled within him and chief amongst them was intrigue. Not only was there a mystery to solve, but he was *needed*, whether Miss Markham admitted it or not. That thought gave way to another as he realised, with a sense of shock, that to be needed was a rare feeling in his life thus far. The Beauchamps were a close family, but he was not *needed*…he was just there.

The spare, of the 'heir and a spare' fame.

He had learned the lesson that he would always play second fiddle to his older brother as a young man on the town for the first time. He had fallen in love—or so he had thought—with the Incomparable of the day, but although Lady Pamela had happily flirted with him and even encouraged his attentions, she had made it perfectly clear she wanted a man with a peerage, not a duke's second son with a mere courtesy title. Had Leo not been married to his first wife at that time, she would doubtless have set her cap at him.

Vernon's heart had not been broken, although it had been bruised. It was his pride that had been battered.

He loved Leo and he loved his nephews and his niece but he had to admit he still found it hard to find his own place in the world. They ran many businesses in partnership—the estates, their horse-breeding enterprises, the mining interests in Cornwall and the coal mines in the north-east—but, with Leo being the older of the two, as well as the Duke, Vernon was outranked for ever.

He did not want to walk away from the mystery of Daniel Markham's disappearance. He wanted to be involved, to take action, to *help*.

'There is still the question of why your brother wrote to mine,' he said. 'You cannot expect me to leave without finding out how my Cousin Henry is involved and it is both senseless and unnecessary for you to risk either your reputation or your safety when I am better able to make the necessary enquiries. So, Miss Markham, I shall be your flagbearer: I shall visit the Nag's Head and make enquiries on your behalf. And—' he raised his voice as she opened her mouth...to argue, no doubt '—I urge you to remember that other men will tell me things they would not say in front of you.'

'What sort of things?'

He wagged his head at her, stifling another grin at her clear frustration. 'You cannot possibly expect me to divulge such secrets, Miss Markham. Suffice it to say that I have a better chance of prising information from them than you.'

The tiniest wobble of her lower lip reminded Vernon that, however brave the face she presented, beneath it, she must be devastated.

'Do not despair, Miss Markham. I shall find Daniel.'

Hope lit her eyes and, having raised it, he was not about to dash it by voicing aloud the thought that followed: *Alive or dead, I shall find him.*

Footsteps clacked along the hall outside, getting nearer, and then the door behind Vernon opened. Miss Markham's expression blanked and she tensed.

'Dorothea.' A woman's voice. 'There you—oh!'

Vernon looked around. A middle-aged woman, her greying hair bundled into a cap, had entered the room.

'I beg your pardon,' she said to Vernon. 'I was not informed we had visitors.' Annoyance lent an edge to her tone and the look she cast Miss Markham—*Dorothea*—was...bitter.

Dorothea, meanwhile, had hurried around the desk, but halted before she got too close to the other woman. To Vernon's eyes, she appeared to stand at attention, her hands clasped at her waist, her fingers twisting together.

'Mama! There was no need to inform you of L... Mr Beauchamp's visit. He called in on a matter of business and is about to leave. I am sorry. Did you have need of me?'

This was her *mother*? Vernon looked from one to the other, wondering at those noticeable cracks in their relationship.

Mrs Markham gave a tight smile, but ignored her daughter's question.

'I trust my daughter was able to satisfactorily

answer your queries, Mr Beauchamp? It is unfortunate my son should happen to be away from home at present. He is on urgent business, but Dorothea is familiar with every aspect of the manufactory.'

'She has proved most satisfactory, ma'am.'

'Good. Good.' He was clearly of little interest to the woman, for she turned her full attention to her daughter. 'Your father feels well enough to sit in his chair today, Dorothea, so I shall stay with him. Have a small repast sent up around noon, if you please. Now—' she flicked a glance at Vernon '—I must return to my husband, Mr Beauchamp. I am sure you will excuse me?'

Vernon bowed again as Dorothea walked with her mother to the door. There was no further exchange of words between mother and daughter. Mrs Markham left and Dorothea shut the door, muffling the tip-tap of her mother's rapidly departing footsteps. She turned to face Vernon.

'Mr Beauchamp?' He raised his brows. 'Might I ask why?'

'I do not want my parents to wonder why a lord is calling upon Daniel. I cannot allow them to be worried; they have enough to cope with. They believe Daniel is in Birmingham on business—that is another reason I asked the grooms not to spread the news that Daniel is missing, for it would be sure to reach the house servants' ears and they would tell my mother.'

'What is wrong with your father?'

'He had a stroke. Six years ago.' Her face twisted: grief, guilt. 'He cannot walk or talk properly. Mama devotes herself to him.'

'He must require a lot of care. Your parents are fortunate to have you here to help.'

'M-Mama says my visits agitate Papa; she d-discourages me from attending him.' For the flash of a second, a bewildered child stared out of those huge hazel orbs. Then it seemed as though a shutter closed and the brisk, efficient Dorothea Markham returned. 'Daniel took over the running of the business when Papa...when it happened. I help as much as I can, but now Daniel is missing and, somehow, your cousin is involved, and I— *Mannington*!'

Her voice suddenly rang with excitement and she captured Vernon's gaze, her eyes sparkling, sending a jolt of heat sizzling through his veins. He could barely concentrate on her words, so taken aback was he by his unexpected physical response.

'I recall... I am sure I have seen...'

She ran past Vernon to the desk, leaving a trail of floral scent wafting in her wake.

Roses. A summer garden. Quintessentially feminine.

She snatched up a handful of papers from the pile he had noticed before and began to leaf through them. After a few minutes she exclaimed in triumph, extracted a sheet of notepaper, and waved it in the air. 'It did not resonate with me at first, but then… I remembered.'

'May I see?' Vernon reached for the sheet of paper.

Her gaze flicked to his outstretched hand, but she made no move to hand it to him. 'I thought it was the name of a place,' she continued. 'It never occurred to me that Mannington was a person. At last, I have a definite clue.'

Vernon did not retract his outstretched hand, merely waited until she capitulated and handed him the paper.

'Thank you.' He scanned the sheet. It took no time at all, for there were only two words, separated by a pair of initials.

Mannington—R.H.—Willingdale?

Vernon frowned. 'What…or where…is Willingdale? And who, do you suppose, is R.H?'

'I have no idea.'

Silence reigned. A glance revealed Dorothea seemingly deep in thought as she leaned back against the edge of the desk, her arms folded as she gazed unseeingly past Vernon, a vertical groove between her brows.

Vernon reread the words written on the paper.

Willingdale… A village? An estate? The name of a person?

He was torn from his thoughts by a muffled whimper.

Chapter Three

Thea tried so hard to hold back her tears, but she simply could not. She dropped her chin into her chest, hand pressed against her lips as her sight blurred. To her horror a single tear plopped on to her bodice, leaving a damp splodge as the fabric absorbed it. Then another tear fell, and another. A large handkerchief was pressed into her hands. She dabbed at her eyes and forced herself to look up. The sympathy in Vernon's green eyes almost set her off again, but she gritted her teeth and cleared her throat.

'I am sorry. I was just thinking…if only I had paid more attention…'

'You must not blame yourself.'

Thea swallowed her bitter laugh. Blame herself? She had done nothing but blame herself for the past six years.

'Where is he?' The words burst from her. 'Why has he not even wr-written?' Her voice choked in her throat, and she buried her head in her hands. 'I fear the worst…' A sob broke free. Then another. 'B-but I must *know*. I c-cannot bear this…this *ignorance*. I f-feel so…so *alone*.'

Two arms wrapped around her and her head was pressed to a strong chest, the thud of his heart steady and reassuring in her ear. He held her, and stroked her hair, and she gave way to the storm of tears she had dammed up ever since the morning she had discovered that Daniel had failed to come home.

Finally the tears slowed, leaving empty shame at having succumbed to such womanly weakness. What must he think of her? Her breath hitched as she battled for control.

'Do not despair, Miss Markham.' Vernon's deep voice rumbled into the ear pressed against his chest, reverberating through her entire body. Words he had spoken before but somehow, this time, of even more comfort. 'You no longer carry this burden alone.'

Thankfulness and hope floated into her heart. Her need to confide, to have somebody on her side, was so strong it almost overwhelmed her innate caution. She felt torn: she wanted so much to believe him…to follow the instincts that told her she could trust him, but…he was a stranger. She could not be certain of what was in his heart.

As she grew calm again a single thought clarified in her mind. She cared not how she managed it but—if Vernon was going to search for Daniel—she was going, too.

'I am sorry,' she said, mopping her eyes again with his handkerchief, as she wriggled free of his arms. She blew her nose. 'I am not normally given to such displays.'

She crossed to the table near the window to finish off her glass of Madeira, then squared her shoulders and turned to face Vernon. It was time to stop moping and take action.

'Shall we discuss strategy?'

'Strategy, Miss Markham?'

The laughter lines at the corner of his eyes deepened although his lips remained perfectly straight. Thea scowled at this spoilt lord who clearly found her an object of fun.

'I have no need of strategy. With this information…' he picked up the discarded note from the desk, folded it and tucked it inside his jacket '…and a quick chat with your grooms, I have everything I need.'

He swung around and strode for the study door and panic swamped Thea.

What have I done?

'Wait!'

She had handed this stranger information that might help him trace Daniel, but could she trust him? What if he meant Daniel harm? This was happening too quickly. He might have decided *he* needed no strategy, but she needed time to think. To plan.

Above all, she needed reassurance that this man was precisely what he appeared to be: a charming, cultured gentleman. She recalled her fanciful notion that she had glimpsed a wolf beneath his surface: a wolf that watched and waited. What if he had a hidden agenda? What if he was like Jasper Connor who, for months on end, had duped Thea and her entire family into thinking he was something he was not?

Vernon had halted at her command and he slowly rotated to face her. He raised a brow, the epitome of aristocratic arrogance. An idea started to form in Thea's brain. If she could but delay his departure a short while...

'You will stay and have luncheon before you set out?'

'I thought time was of the essence?'

'It is. But a few hours will not make much difference. You must eat.'

Doubt—and masculinity—radiated from the man: his booted feet planted a yard apart, his arms folded tight across his chest, his lips compressed.

Inspiration struck. 'You cannot go to the Nag's Head dressed as you are.'

He glowered. 'What is wrong with the way I am dressed?' He unfolded his arms and took a pace towards her. 'I'll have you know this coat is by Weston. It is—'

'It proclaims you for what you are,' Thea said. She stepped closer, and held his gaze. 'A wealthy gentleman. Places such as the Nag's Head are not patronised by members of the aristocracy, but by ordinary men: businessmen, tradesmen, farmers. They will not speak openly to a man of your ilk. A stranger.

'Why don't you go to the stables and speak to the grooms,' she went on, 'and by the time you return to the house there will be food ready for you to eat and, after that, I shall find you something appropriate of Daniel's to wear.' She looked him up and down. 'You are of a similar height and build to him. His clothes will help you to blend in.'

That should buy her time to put her plans into place.

'Very well.' Vernon paused as he was about to leave the study. 'I just wish I could be certain Daniel's disappearance is connected to Henry Manning. If the two things are coincidental, I might end up on a wild goose chase.'

And that proves I am right to be cautious. If the two enquiries lead in different directions, I make no doubt Lord Vernon Beauchamp will go chasing after his cousin and consign poor Daniel to the Devil.

Vernon strode back to the house half an hour later, not much wiser about how he might discover what had happened to Daniel Markham.

The grooms could not tell him who or what was Willingdale and nor did the initials R.H. mean anything. None of them had ever accompanied Daniel on his more recent daily excursions—although they confirmed Dorothea's story that her brother had been troubled—and nor could they offer any reason for this change in Daniel's behaviour. They were frustrated that they had been stopped from making enquiries—and Vernon had learned that was mainly due to Dorothea's concern that any worries about Daniel's welfare would damage confidence in Stour Crystal—and they had scoffed at the notion that Daniel had run up gaming debts.

'Mr Daniel ain't never been a one for gambling, sir,' the head man, Pritchard, had said. 'Not since his papa lost all their money. Both Mr Daniel and Miss Thea have worked too hard to save the business to put it at risk again.'

Mr Markham senior would not be the first man to gamble away a fortune, but Vernon's comment along those lines had resulted in a fierce denial that the money had been lost at the gaming tables. Pritchard had then clammed up, refusing to elaborate further.

Vernon had not pressed Pritchard, but had caught Bickling's eye and given him the nod before returning to the house, confident his trusty groom would winkle out the truth and pass the information on to Vernon later.

Dorothea—Miss Thea, Pritchard had called her,

which was much less of a mouthful—must have been watching for him, because she appeared at a side door and beckoned him inside. He followed her along a passageway, eyeing her neat figure with appreciation, the smell of roses and summer teasing at his senses.

'I have laid out some clothes for you to change into,' she said over her shoulder, 'and there is food for you in here.'

She threw open a door that led into a shabby but homely parlour, the table laid with cold cuts, meat pies, bread, cheese and fruit, reminding Vernon of his hunger. The decor would have been the height of fashion a decade ago—in stark contrast with the ostentatious entrance hall and its grand staircase and even the more subdued but still luxurious furnishings in the study. Vernon recalled his initial scathing assessment of the well-tended surrounds of Stourwell Court as he had driven up the carriageway. The house—relatively newly built, with no passing architectural fashion left unsampled—had screamed *new money* to one familiar with the sprawling ancient Beauchamp family seat of Cheriton Abbey in the County of Devonshire.

Having learned of the family's financial loss and subsequent struggle, Vernon was unsurprised by the tactic he had seen many times in the past: a family on its uppers, putting what money they could spare into the public rooms where visitors were entertained in order to keep up appearances.

'Did you discover anything new?'

Thea came straight to the point as she closed the door behind them. Vernon was unsurprised—she had already impressed him with her directness, as well as her quick understanding.

'Only the names of some of Daniel's friends who drink at the Nag's Head.' He had no intention of revealing that the grooms had spoken of her family's past financial difficulties. 'Pritchard was of the opinion that Daniel had spent much of his time in Birmingham in the days before he went missing. He also reckons your brother called in at the Nag's Head most nights on his way home. So that will definitely be my first port of call.'

'Will you drive your curricle, or ride?'

'I had not thought that far ahead,' Vernon admitted. 'If, as you say, my clothing would excite interest, then no doubt my curricle and pair will as well.'

'A top-of-the-tree rig such as yours? I should say so,' she said, gravely, but with a twinkle in her eye. When she wasn't scowling she was an attractive woman. 'You may take one of Daniel's horses. They are perfectly decent animals, suitable for a gentleman of your standing.'

Vernon grinned. 'I am delighted to hear it. A man of my consequence cannot be too careful.'

He might as well pander to her opinion of him as a spoilt aristocrat.

'We had better eat.' Thea crossed the room to the table and picked up a plate. 'It will be more practical to go on horseback. We can take short-cuts across country—'

'We?' Vernon strode forward, grasped her arm and tugged her round to face him. 'What…? Oh, no. No, no, *no*! Definitely not. You are *not* coming with me.'

Thea's tawny brows snapped together, meeting across the bridge of her freckled nose as she drew herself up to her full height. Which was short.

'You cannot stop me. Daniel is *my* brother. I *want* to come.'

Vernon stared down at her mutinous expression and heaved a silent sigh. He was hungry and he was anxious to set off, now he had a definite idea of where to start with his search. First he must deal with this hissing, spitting kitten.

Thea shrugged out of his hold, replaced her plate on the table with a crack that made Vernon wince and folded her arms.

'You cannot tell me what to do. I am going.'

Vernon squared his shoulders. 'Not with me you are not.'

'You cannot stop me.'

'You are correct. I cannot stop you going anywhere or doing anything you wish. But I tell you here and now…you will *not* do it with me. I shall return to London and you may never discover what has happened to your brother.'

Her eyes widened.

Good. That has shaken her.

'You would not do that.' Her voice lacked conviction.

Vernon lowered his own voice, injecting a silky menace into his tone. 'If you put me to the test, Miss Markham, I think you will find that *I* do not make empty threats either.'

Her lips thinned as she glared at him. 'What about your cousin?'

Vernon shrugged nonchalantly. 'I shall pay an investigator to track him down and report to me in London. What you choose to forget, Miss Markham, is that I have neither desire nor need to remain here in Worcestershire, or to embark upon a search for a man I have never met. I offered my services because it is unsafe for you, as a female, to go into the places on that list. Which, incidentally, is the exact reason you cannot come with me: *it is not safe*. I admit to some curiosity as to my cousin's involvement, but I shall not lose any sleep over it and you will do well to remember that.'

She hung her head, her eyes downcast. Vernon felt like an out-and-out brute, but knew he must not show any weakness for he had no doubt she would quickly seize upon it and, despite what he said, he really *was* curious to find out what had happened to Daniel Markham.

'So, are we agreed? I shall leave after I have eaten and changed my clothing and you, Miss Markham, will wave me goodbye.'

'Very well. I shall not insist on leaving with you.'

Her mouth drooped and he wondered if she were about to cry again. He had been certain that earlier bout was uncharacteristic. He could not abide women who cried at the slightest provocation, using tears as a weapon to get their own way. But, despite that, he still felt sympathy and also a little guilty, knowing how worried she was about her brother. He reached out and nudged one finger beneath her chin, tilting her face to his. Respect for her crept through him: she was dry-eyed and he was relieved at this proof she was prepared to listen to and accept his reasoning.

'Miss Markham, you must also understand that, quite apart from it being unsafe, it would also be entirely improper for you to accompany me. Your reputation would be in tatters.'

A gleam lit those huge hazel orbs and Vernon was disconcerted by the undeniable kick of his pulse and his sudden impulse to kiss her,

His awareness of her as an attractive woman rattled him into speaking more bluntly than he should.

'We have no idea what has happened to Daniel, but I know you are aware he could have met with foul play. It would be wholly irresponsible for me to allow you to be exposed to possible danger.'

She blinked and her cheeks paled, causing the freckles that dusted her nose and cheeks to stand out in contrast. Vernon felt a brute all over again, as though he had kicked a puppy. Or—perhaps more fitting in Thea's case, given his earlier fanciful thoughts—a kitten. He released her chin and clasped her upper arms, bending his knees to look directly into her eyes.

'I apologise. I did not mean to shock you.'

Her throat convulsed as she swallowed. He had upset her, but she was struggling to conceal her emotions and his respect grew at the way she handled herself in such a horrible situation.

'Do not lose hope, Miss Markham.' He gently rubbed her arms, trying to buoy her spirits. 'There could still be a perfectly reasonable explanation for Daniel's disappearance.'

She huffed a disbelieving laugh, shaking her head, her curls bouncing. 'Such as? No, I cannot be hopeful. He would have written to us. He would not stay away without a word.'

Vernon released her and stepped back from the temptation of taking her into his arms again to offer comfort.

'He might be too ill to write,' he said. 'Or he has lost his memory. Or maybe he *has* written and the letter has been lost en route?' He paced the room and then returned to come to a halt in front of her. 'Whatever the reason, I shall discover it, but you must leave this to me. Do you understand?'

'I understand. Now, if you will excuse me, there are matters requiring my attention.'

'You will not join me?'

'I find I no longer have an appetite. Enjoy your luncheon, sir. Ring for George when you have finished eating and he will show you to Daniel's bed-chamber to change your clothing. I shall see you before you leave.' She left him with a brisk step, leaving the scent of roses lingering in her wake.

After Vernon had eaten his fill, he was shown upstairs by George.

'I shall leave as soon as I have changed,' Vernon told the footman. 'Could you inform Miss Markham that I will see her downstairs in, shall we say, fifteen minutes?'

He wondered if Thea would come to see him off, or if she would stay away, sulking. No, he decided. Sulking was not Miss Markham's style.

George bowed and left. Vernon wasted no time in changing into the clothing that would help him to blend in. He donned the fawn-coloured breeches and the respectable linen shirt and neckcloth left on the bed. The boots, however, were too small. He eyed his Hessian boots and their mirror shine with regret as he realised there was nothing for it but to smear them with soil when he went outside, to dull the shine. A moleskin waistcoat and a brown jacket completed Vernon's transformation from a man of fashion into a respectable country squire.

He ducked to peer into the dressing-table mirror and ruffled his fingers through his hair. At least he would not present himself all neatly barbered at the Nag's Head and wherever else his enquiries might lead. His hair had needed a trim before he left London, but he had decided to leave it until his return. It was a touch long and unruly, but the less well-groomed his appearance, the less notice he would attract.

He rotated, studying the room: Daniel's room. Quashing down any guilt—he was trying to help, not snoop—he quickly searched through drawers and cupboards. Nothing. He must hope that someone at the Nag's Head could either throw some light on the reason Daniel had been riding to Birmingham on a regular basis—if, that is, Pritchard was correct that Daniel had been visiting the city—or that they might solve the mystery of what, or who, Willingdale and R.H. were.

A battered saddlebag had been left on the bed. Inside was a clean shirt and neckcloth, reminding Vernon that this mission might take several days. He slung the bag over one shoulder and, with one last look around, he strode from the room.

In the entrance hall, he waited. The scrunch of hooves on the gravel outside told him that his horse had arrived. He went out to find Bickling holding a dependable-looking bay hunter and sent him running back to the stables to retrieve Vernon's shaving kit and other personal necessities from his valise in his curricle. When Bickling returned, Vernon stowed the articles in the saddlebag as his groom filled him in on what he'd discovered about Mr Markham's lost fortune.

'Seems he raised funds against his business and

invested them all in some non-existent scheme through this swindler who befriended the family and then vanished with their money,' he said. 'The stress caused Markham senior's stroke and, although Pritchard clammed up when I tried to get more from him, it seems this fraudster also had something to do with Miss Markham.'

'In what way?'

Bickling shrugged. 'The man's very loyal to Miss Markham. He wouldn't say more than the bastard took Miss Markham in, too, and that she's never forgiven herself. Blames herself for her father's stroke.'

Had he courted her? Had she fallen in love with him? That's what it sounded like to Vernon. 'Thank you, Bickling.'

'Are you sure you don't want me to come along with you, milord?'

'There is no need, I can take care of myself and, besides, you'll be on edge the entire time if you have to leave my blacks in anyone else's care.'

Bickling was even fussier about Vernon's horses than he was, if that were possible. And he knew that Bickling would be forever saying 'milord', and that would mean no chance of staying discreet.

'I could always take one of the men from here, but they appear short-staffed already. I will be fine going alone, do not worry.'

'Very well, milord.' Bickling's glum face said it all.

Vernon glanced at the front door. Still no sign of Thea. He did not want to leave without saying goodbye so he went back inside. Immediately he heard hurried footsteps approaching from the nether regions of the house. Thea soon appeared, slightly breathless.

'Come with me,' she said. 'There is something you need to see.'

Chapter Four

Thea had to give his lordship credit: he followed her without question to the gunroom. Once inside, he turned a full circle, eyeing the rows of shotguns, rifles and muskets that lined the walls. The windowless room was illuminated by the three lanterns Thea had lit on her earlier visit. Somehow, with Vernon inside, the room seemed to have shrunk and Thea wrapped her arms defensively around her torso and stepped away from him, putting a little more distance between them.

Vernon tilted his head as he met Thea's gaze and those penetrating green eyes of his glinted as they caught the light. They felt as though they reached deep into her soul. She just prayed he could not read her thoughts.

'I trust you do not plan to hold me hostage down here, Miss Markham.'

His comment startled a laugh from her. The thought had crossed her mind. Not to hold him hostage, but to force him at gunpoint to take her with him—a crazy thought that she had dismissed the minute her whirling thoughts, desperate to find a way to go with him, had seized upon it. That crazy idea had, though, led to another plan.

Which was why she had ventured down here to the gunroom in the first place.

'Have no fear, my lord,' she said. 'None of these weapons is loaded. You are quite safe.'

'Then why are we here?'

'It occurred to me to wonder if Daniel was armed,' she said.

'Would he normally go out with a gun?'

'He had a blunderbuss that was always buckled to his saddle, in case of an attack,' she said. 'There have been a few robberies on the roads hereabouts, over the past year or so. Daniel said there has been an increase in vagrants wandering the country-side—former soldiers, he reckoned, although others like to blame the gipsies. But a blunderbuss is not a weapon he could carry in his pocket. Look—' she pointed to the table in the centre of the room '—I found that pistol case in the cabinet. It should have two muff pistols inside, plus the flask and balls. Firearms are Daniel's passion. He bought this case and pistols at an auction in Birmingham a few weeks ago.'

She tilted the case to show the single remaining pistol to Vernon. He whistled.

'So…your brother went out *expecting* trouble. Or even danger.'

'It would appear so, although I cannot understand why he would take that particular pistol. It is very small.'

Vernon moved closer as he peered at the contents of the case, his sleeve brushing Thea's arm, sending a tingle of awareness racing through her. She shivered in reaction, fighting the urge to leave the room. Her discomfort was unimportant…she must do this for Daniel.

'Small but deadly,' Vernon said. 'I should imagine he took it precisely because its size means it is easily concealed. I see he has several cases of duelling pistols…' He selected one case at random and opened it. He whistled again, lifting out one of the guns and sighting along the barrel. 'Manton's. A fine piece. But, too big to conceal and…'

'And what?'

He shot her an apologetic look and grimaced. 'Sorry. I was thinking out loud.'

'But, having begun to speak, you must now finish,' Thea said, irritation at her physical reaction to his proximity making her sharp.

She had no wish to be aware of him as an attractive man. Men were not to be trusted.

'I told you before,' she went on, 'I am not one of your fine ladies who needs mollycoddling. I have dealt with hard reality and survived. Please do not patronise me. Do me the courtesy of dealing with me as an intelligent adult, not a child.'

He sighed. 'Very well. I was about to say that a duelling pistol is not as handy at close quarters.'

Her stomach churned at his words, but she tamped down her fear. She had asked him and he had replied. She could not now blame him because she did not like what she heard. Besides, that was an interesting point to remember. She had already selected and primed a duelling pistol, ready to pack in her saddlebag along with her spare clothing. Daniel had other small pistols—she would take one of those along as well.

'I thought you should see this for yourself,' she said to Vernon. 'As you said, it suggests Daniel was expecting trouble when he left.'

Just speaking those words made her throat constrict with unshed tears but Thea forced her emotions to lie low, knowing she must keep a cool head if she was not to hinder the search for her brother.

'It is time to go,' she said, 'but there is also something else I must show you.'

Vernon raised a brow but, again, followed her unquestioningly. Up the stairs this time and along the upper corridor to the long gallery, where the family portraits hung and where Thea and Daniel practised fencing manoeuvres. The physical exercise had helped Thea to exorcise some of her anger and guilt after Jasper Connor had betrayed her and near bankrupted both Stour Crystal and her family.

Vernon headed straight for the portrait of Thea. 'It is a good likeness.'

For a second, admiration glowed in his eyes, but Thea ignored the answering tug deep in her core. She could not help but be aware of Vernon's allure. She'd wager there were ladies galore in the *ton* who regularly swooned at his feet, given one look from those green eyes, or one of his smiles, brimming with charm, but she was not interested. Not in Lord Vernon Beauchamp nor in any man. Being jilted at the altar tended to have that effect.

'That is not why we are here,' she said and led the way to the portrait of Daniel.

Apart from the portraits of Thea and Daniel, and an earlier one of Mama and Papa—painted before Papa had his stroke—there were only landscapes on the walls. Papa had harboured such grand dreams: dreams of building a dynasty, dreams of using his wealth to ensure his grandchildren might be accepted into the ranks of the upper classes, dreams of this gallery being filled with portraits of the generations to come. Now it might all come to naught. Thea would never give him grandchildren and, if Daniel… She choked off that thought, afraid her precarious control would shatter again if she followed her fears to their natural conclusion.

'That is Daniel,' she said, feeling another lump form in her throat as she looked up at his strong, dark features. 'I thought it would help for you to know what he looks like.'

Vernon examined the portrait in silence.

'He has your eyes,' he said, eventually, 'but I see no further resemblance.'

'He gets his colouring from Mama, but he is tall like Papa,' Thea said. They headed for the door. 'I get my red hair from Papa, but my height—or, rather, my lack of it—from Mama.'

Back in the entrance hall, Vernon picked up the saddlebag by the front door.

'I shall have to hope,' he remarked, regarding his reflection in a mirror with a grimace, 'that I do not meet anyone with whom I am acquainted. They will think I have run quite mad, dressed like this.'

Thea bit back her scathing retort.

'I shall write to let you know what I find out about your brother and how my cousin is connected to him.' A frown creased his forehead. 'I still find it hard to believe Henry has anything to do with your brother's disappearance. I have every hope of discovering the two things are unconnected.'

Which, again, proved Thea was right to follow him as she planned. If Henry Mannington was found to have no connection with Daniel's disappearance, Vernon would go chasing off after Henry and what chance then would Thea have of finding Daniel?

She followed Vernon down the front steps, where Bickling, his groom, held the reins of Warrior, one of Daniel's favourite hunters. Vernon swung into the saddle, raised his hand in farewell and set off down the carriageway at a brisk trot.

Thea watched until horse and rider disappeared from sight, then spun on her heel and raced up to her bedchamber. There was no time to lose. She had already told her mother she was going to visit a sick friend for a few days and Mama, as usual, showed little interest in Thea's activities; she had never forgiven her daughter for the disaster that had befallen their family.

Thea had also written to Charles Leyton, the manager at Stour Crystal, to warn him he would not be able to contact either her or Daniel for a week or so. She hoped she would not be away as long as that, but it was best to err on the side of caution.

It was a relief to be taking action—she had been near paralysed with indecision until Lord Vernon's visit, afraid of the consequences should Stour Crystal's customers, or—God forbid—their rivals, learn that Daniel was missing. Uncertainty was bad for business. If she was responsible for spreading rumours and Daniel turned up unscathed, he would, rightly, be furious with her. She had caused enough trouble for the business six years ago. She could not bear to be the cause of more.

She had slipped across to the stables earlier, whilst Vernon was eating, and taken Malky—the groom who had taught her and Daniel to ride—into her confidence about her plan. He had not been happy but, in the end, he had agreed to saddle Thea's favourite mare, Star, with a conventional saddle so she could ride astride and to meet Thea, with Star, on the edge of the copse behind the walled kitchen garden, out of sight of both the house and the stables.

She changed hastily into the clothes she had kept from Daniel's boyhood, the ones she wore for their fencing bouts and for riding astride. She wondered whether or not she should take Malky with her. It would be the sensible thing to do, at least until she caught up with Vernon, but it would leave the estate short-handed at a busy time.

She examined her appearance in the mirror. She had bound her breasts to flatten them and had dusted fine ash from the fireplace across her skin, dulling it. She was dressed the same as countless young lads around the country, in jacket, shirt, waistcoat, breeches and boots. Her hair…she leaned closer to her reflection. She could pass muster as a lad during one cross-country ride—with her hair plaited and pinned and bundled into a cap—but would that suffice for a longer masquerade?

She reached for her scissors. It would grow again. She unpinned her hair and gathered it together. She swivelled her head from side to side as she gazed into the mirror, considering. Some lads had hair that grew to the nape of their necks, or even longer. She set her jaw. Time was wasting. She cut, hacking again and again at her thick hair until the bunch came free in her hand. She stared at it, lying limp across her palm, trying and failing to quash her distress.

It cannot be helped.

She pushed the hair under her mattress where it would not be discovered, and turned again to the mirror, biting back a cry at the sight that met her eyes. She pushed her fingers through her hair, fluffing it out—her curls more unruly than ever— then ruthlessly scraped it back and tied it with the length of twine she carried in her jacket pocket for emergencies. Her reins had snapped once, several miles from home, and since then she had always been prepared. Never had she envisioned using it for this purpose, however.

It is just vanity. Who cares what you look like?

Unbidden, Vernon's face arose in her thoughts.

Hmmph. She thrust his image aside. *He is a means to an end: finding Daniel. Nothing more.*

It was time to go. Malky would have Star ready by now. Thea cast a last look around her bedchamber, sucked in a deep breath to quell her nerves and picked up her saddlebag. A quick visit to the gunroom for pistols, powder and shot and then she would be gone. As she crept down the back stairs she prayed none of the servants would see her. Her stomach roiled all the way to the gunroom and for the entire time it took her to load the smaller pistol she had decided to take with her.

She slipped out of the side door and hurried along the path to the kitchen garden, following the outer stone wall around until she reached the far corner. Then she breathed a sigh of relief, knowing she was no longer visible from the house. She stood still, leaning back against the wall, feeling the sun's warmth, stored in the stones, radiating through her twill jacket, and waited for her nerves to settle. They did not. Her stomach continued to churn until she felt sick and she realised, with a jolt, that it was not the adventure to come that frightened her so very much but the thought of Lord Vernon Beauchamp's reaction when he discovered she had followed him. Contrarily, that thought irritated her, which then had the effect of finally grounding those butterflies fluttering around inside her stomach.

It was not *his* place to dictate her movements and it was not incumbent upon her to obey him. She was her own woman. Seven-and-twenty years of age. Intelligent. She had no reputation to sully—it simply was not important to her. She would never marry and she was long past the days when she worried about how many partners she might attract at the assembly room in Bewdley. Come to think of it, she could not remember the last time she had visited the assembly room. Losing everything, including a fiancé and, very nearly, her father had effectively put an end to all such frivolity. They had—both she and Daniel—put their heads down and *worked*, with no thought other than to pull the family back from the precipice of bankruptcy. They had teetered upon the brink of that chilling state for a very long time.

Those years… That lump ached once more in Thea's throat. She and Daniel had worked in partnership and they had not given up until the manufactory was safe. They had worked with Charles Leyton and the other men to develop new products that were now eagerly sought after by customers keen to decorate their homes and to display their wealth.

And now, when it seemed they could finally begin to breathe again, Daniel had vanished.

Thea pushed away from the wall. She could see Malky waiting, with Star and another horse, at the top of the opposite bank of the stream, on the edge of the trees. Gratefulness hummed through her. Malky clearly intended to accompany her and she saw now that was the best solution, at least until she caught up with Vernon. Her guise as a lad would protect her a little on the ride between Stourwell Court and Stourbridge, but not completely—a solitary youth might prove fair game for any manner of rogues on the road. She would believe that was what had befallen Daniel, but for the fact his horse had not returned: Bullet would always return to Stourwell Court. He had been foaled here.

She ran down the bank, jumped the narrow channel of water and hurried up the slope to Malky.

'Afore you say aught, miss, I'm coming with you and there's an end to it.'

Malky…he had taught her to ride. Solid. Dependable. Unflappable.

'Thank you, Malky.' Thea turned to Star, put her foot in the stirrup and was soon settled astride the spirited black mare. 'Just until we catch up with his lordship, mind.' Or, actually, before. Or his lordship would merely order her to return home with Malky. That would not suit her purpose at all. 'Let's go.'

They rode across country, taking the shortest route to Stourbridge, and Thea began to breathe a little easier at the knowledge they had made up time. Finally, they arrived at the outskirts of the town and they halted.

'I will be safe enough now,' she said to Malky. 'You should return home. No!' She held up one hand as Malky started to protest. 'You cannot come further. You are needed at Stourwell Court. I shall be quite safe… I intend to let myself be known to his lordship before nightfall. It will be too late by then for him to send me home.'

'And what do you intend to do while his lordship is inside the Nag's Head?'

'I shall go inside, too. It is a respectable enough inn. It will be an opportunity to find out if my disguise will stand casual scrutiny. You cannot deny it is better I begin here—in full daylight—than enter some low alehouse after dark when it is like to be filled with men in their cups.'

Malky sighed. 'I don't like you going inside such places, Miss Thea.'

'*Theo*, Malky. I told you, I am now Theo. And I must go inside or how shall I discover—?'

'I've bin in and out of such places all me life, mi—' He clamped his lips together with a scowl. 'You told me you were going to *follow* his lordship. You never said you'd be risking your reputation and worse besides by going inside such places.'

She touched his arm. 'You cannot stop me, Malky. You know me. You know how stubborn I can be.'

'Never a truer word,' he muttered.

'Must I order you home, Malky? You and I cannot ride into town together, or someone will recognise you and wonder who I am. Trust me… I will stay safe. I shall follow his lordship and, as I said, I shall make myself known to him before nightfall. He is a gentleman. He will protect me.'

'And that's another thing to worry about,' Malky muttered. 'His sort…they think nothing of debauchery and such like and you an innocent and all.'

'I am well able to protect my virtue, Malky,' she said grimly. 'You need have no fear on that score.'

After several more grumbles, Malky finally left her and Thea rode Star up New Street towards High Street and the Nag's Head, her stomach twisting with nerves at what she was about to do and at the thought of Vernon's likely reaction when he discovered she had followed him. But then she thought of Daniel. She was doing this for him. And her nerves steadied as she left Star with an ostler and approached the door of the inn. She hadn't planned much further than simply catching up with Vernon and then tailing him, but she had faith everything would work out all right. She patted her pocket, feeling the reassuring shape of the pistol. She could take care of herself and, whatever might have happened to Daniel, she would make certain she, at least, returned home to her parents.

She followed a man in through the door and turned left, as did he, into a taproom. A sweeping glance took in the dingy walls and ring-marked tables. She watched carefully how the man she had followed in behaved. He slid on to a settle and caught the attention of a serving woman by the simple expedient of raising one finger. The girl brought him a tankard, presumably of ale or porter.

Thea took a seat in an empty corner, where she could take in the whole room and see the door at the same time. As the woman turned from the other customer, Thea raised her hand. The woman acknowledged her and soon delivered a tankard, setting it on the table with a bang that sloshed its contents over the rim. She scooped up the coins Thea had tossed on to the table with a brief grin that made Thea suspect her tip had been overly generous. Nevertheless, she breathed a little easier. The woman had barely looked at her and neither had the other customers.

She sipped her ale—wrinkling her nose at the

bitter taste—and allowed her gaze to slide around the room, examining each occupant in turn. The taproom was not full, with around eight customers, including Thea and the other newcomer, and a man behind the bar whom she assumed was Perrins, the publican—she knew his name from occasional comments Daniel had made about the place. But there was no sign of Vernon.

Where is he?

On the heels of that thought, the door opened and in strolled Lord Vernon Beauchamp.

Chapter Five

There was a lull in the conversation as the men in the taproom eyed up this newcomer. There had been no such reaction when the other man and Thea had entered and she took heart that the other customers had taken her appearance at face value. One single glance confirmed the newcomer was Vernon, but his appearance, far from offering relief, wound Thea's tension a notch tighter as she kept her head bent and her attention on her drink. In her head, as she had planned her first venture into this alien world, she had entered the taproom and Vernon was already seated. She had not reckoned on him following her in. What if he sat at her table?

From the corner of her eye, she watched as he paused inside the door and swept the room, his gaze lingering on each man in turn before moving on to the next. She clenched her teeth as he scrutinised her, wrapping her fingers tightly around her tankard as she fought the urge to check that her hair was still tucked up inside her cap. The colour, surely, would give her away in an instant. After what seemed an age, Vernon's gaze moved on and Thea released her held breath as he sauntered deeper into the room, and selected a seat at a table with three other men. He looked every inch the gentleman he was, despite Daniel's clothing, and Thea sensed the sudden unease of the men he had joined. Even Perrins watched Vernon with suspicion.

'Good afternoon,' Vernon said.

His voice, well-modulated and…well…superior, carried around the room, prompting another pause in the various conversations. Now the immediate danger of him recognising her had passed, Thea began to enjoy herself. Vernon might be a lord, and the brother of a high and mighty duke, but he was out of his depth in this world. She fully expected the three men he had joined to finish up their ale and to leave, but they did not. Vernon reached into his pocket and extracted a pack of cards, looking around the table with his brows lifted in invitation. The men exchanged glances and nodded, and Vernon dealt the cards.

Perrins called across the bar, 'Mind you keep them stakes low, gents. I don't want no trouble in here.'

Vernon laughed. 'I have no choice but to keep them low, landlord. My luck has been out for too long, I fear. But I harbour hopes it is about to change.'

His smile encompassed his three companions, who appeared to perk up, exchanging eager looks.

They played cards for nigh on an hour, while Thea nursed her drink in the corner, growing steadily more indignant. She could hear their banter. Not once had Vernon mentioned Daniel. Or Henry Mannington. Instead, he fed them scraps of information about himself—none of it true, from what Thea knew of him—as he steadily lost, hand after hand. Then, he won a hand and, jubilant, he ordered a bottle of gin and four glasses. Thea could not fathom his strategy. Time was wasting. They needed clues. Why did he not just get on with it instead of throwing his money around? If *he* had experienced the dread of ending up in debtors' prison, he would not be so careless of his money.

Then, with the gin bottle half-empty—the level in Vernon's glass, she noted, had barely dropped—he said, 'That's it. I'm done, lads. You've cleaned me out. Landlord…what time do you have?'

'Half-past four,' Perrins called in reply.

'Half-past *four*, you say!'

His words slurred a little, but Thea did not believe he was in the slightest bit foxed. Vernon swore an oath that made Thea blush, then pushed himself unsteadily to his feet.

'Have I the wrong place, I wonder? I made sure he said to meet here at four.'

'Who're you meeting, then? Anyone we know?'

'Friend of mine. Daniel Markham. Business matter, don't y'know?'

He tapped one long forefinger against the side of his nose and winked at his companions, who promptly vied with each other to suggest other places Vernon might conceivably have arranged to meet Daniel. Thea found herself revising her opinion of his lordship and a grudging respect crept through her. Even the customers who had not played cards proffered suggestions. It seemed they all knew Daniel, but none of them appeared aware he was missing.

'No, no,' Vernon said, in response to each suggestion. 'They do not sound familiar. I'll know the name when you say it, I am sure. Perhaps...' He paused, staring at the table, frowning. He shook his head. Looked around at his companions. 'Maybe it was not in Stourbridge at all? Was it somewhere near Birmingham? Or in Birmingham itself?'

'It could well be,' Perrins said—the first time he had ventured a suggestion. 'He hasn't been in here for the last few nights—I dare say we'm not grand enough for him, now he's consorting with them nobs at the Royal Hotel.'

Royal Hotel! R.H!

Thea gripped the edge of the table to stop herself leaping from her chair, as Vernon pumped Perrins by the hand.

'The Royal! I remember! He *did* speak of the Royal—that must be the place. Now, how could I have got it so wrong? But he definitely spoke of the Nag's Head as well—I must have confused the two.'

'He'll be long gone by the time you get to Birmingham,' one of the other men said. 'You might as well play another hand. He might call in on his way home tonight—it'll save you a long ride.'

'No…how far is it? Ten, twelve miles?'

'Nearer thirteen.'

'We had plans to meet up and spend the evening together. I cannot believe he will give up on me so easily. My horse is fresh. I can cover that in less than two hours. Now, I must make haste… only, before I go, does anyone know a place called Willingdale?'

His question met with shaking heads.

'A man called Henry Mannington?'

As further denials rang around the room, Thea became aware she was now the only customer not taking an active role in the discussion. She stood quietly and, when Vernon's attention was on Perrins, she slipped quickly and quietly from the bar. She did not wish to attract Vernon's curiosity, convinced she would not pass too close a scrutiny from those astute green eyes of his. She retrieved Star from the yard behind the inn, mounted and then waited around a corner for Vernon to emerge. He strolled into the street, still looking every inch the nobleman, surrounded by his customary aura of assurance and entitlement. The ostler must have been watching, for he soon appeared, leading Warrior, and Vernon mounted with a fluid grace that made Thea's mouth go dry. He was so very...*male*. She licked her lips to moisten them, irritated by her involuntary reaction. What was it about this man that touched her in ways no one else had ever done? Even Jasper. The man she had been going to wed, before he had left her standing at the altar.

She tore her thoughts away from that wretch. It had happened long ago. She was older and wiser now, and Jasper was dead—killed in a fire at a wayside inn—and buried. She would never... *never*...put her trust in another man, no matter how handsome his face and no matter what feelings he had aroused as he'd wrapped her in his arms and comforted her, his strong embrace reassuring, his heartbeat steady in her ear.

Thea gave Vernon a head start and then she followed.

By the time dusk began to fall, Thea was beginning to regret her foolhardy decision to follow Vernon. She was bored and she was saddle sore. Vernon appeared in no hurry to reach Birmingham and that irritated Thea beyond measure. Surely the sooner they reached the Royal Hotel the sooner they might discover what had happened to Daniel? She'd made the connection immediately, but had Vernon linked the Royal Hotel with R.H? Certainly he appeared unaffected by the sense of urgency that snapped at Thea's heels—he paused at every wayside inn they passed.

After following him into the second such inn—where, again, he quietly questioned the publican about Daniel, Willingdale and Henry Mannington—Thea realised that unless he was totally oblivious to his surroundings Vernon would soon notice a young lad shadowing his every move. So, of necessity, she'd remained out of sight as he had visited further public houses. She supposed she must be grateful he did not waste as much time as he had at the Nag's Head.

Now, as she rode Star at a discreet distance behind him, she was also hungry and thirsty and—

Thea straightened in the saddle, drawing Star quickly to one side of the lane they rode along. Vernon's form was indistinct in the distance as the light faded, but Thea could just make out two shadows—humped, awkward-looking creatures—moving swiftly parallel with the lane, on the far side of group of bushes from Vernon and his horse. Thea pushed Star into a trot, trusting that her mare's black coat and Thea's own dull clothing would render them invisible to any backward glance. The two—and she could now make out they were men, crouching as they ran—had overtaken Vernon, who appeared not to have noticed he had company.

She recalled all the recent reports of footpads in the area and she realised how reckless she had been in following Vernon in this way. Suppose it had been her they had spotted and now stalked? She had been blind to everything other than finding her brother. The gap between her and Vernon had closed. Without taking her eyes from the two men, she eased Star back to a walk and fumbled with the buckle on her saddlebag. She withdrew the duelling pistol, thanking God she'd thought to prime it in advance. She pulled the hammer to full cock and pointed it skywards. Even though she was a fair shot, she could not risk hitting either Vernon or Warrior.

There was a break in the bushes a few yards ahead of Vernon and the two men paused at that point, still hunched over. Thea could just make out they both held weapons—one short and thick, like a club, the other longer and very slim—and Thea prayed it was not a blade of some sort.

Vernon rode on at an easy walk.

It happened very fast. The two men erupted from the bushes. One grabbed at Warrior's reins as the other, thick club upraised, went for the rider.

Thea dug her heels into Star but, even as she yelled a warning, she saw Vernon's leg jerk sideways. His boot collided with his assailant's head and a scream of pain rent the air as the man staggered back, clutching his face, his club discarded. Vernon shot a swift glance behind him, in Thea's direction, before launching himself from the saddle at the second man, who had come alongside Warrior, still clutching his reins. Vernon cursed viciously as the man jabbed his stick at him. Thea hauled Star to a halt, leapt from the saddle, and ran towards the struggling men, pistol in hand. She stopped a few yards away, pistol still pointing into the air.

Vernon threw a punch, catching his attacker on the jaw with satisfying crack. As the man staggered back, Vernon shot another glance at Thea.

'Don't stand gawping, lad. Guard the other one.'

Thea gulped and pointed the pistol with a shaky hand in the general direction of the first assailant, still moaning on the ground, blood pouring from his nose. Vernon stalked after the second attacker, who was stumbling backwards, his eyes riveted to the menacing figure that followed. He gripped his stick—which Thea could now see had been sharpened at one end—with both hands, pointing it at Vernon. A movement from the man on the ground then secured Thea's attention and she saw no more, but the cries and the curses coming from two men behind her suggested they now grappled and finally, unable to bear the suspense, she glanced round. Vernon, his hand clutched to his side, was bent over, but there was no sign of his assailant.

Vernon's head lifted and she felt the force of his gaze upon her. 'Look out!'

Desperation leant an edge to his shout, but his warning was too late. A solid mass thumped into Thea from behind, knocking her aside. She stumbled, desperately trying to stay on her feet and to keep hold of the pistol, her stomach clenching tight as bile rose to choke her throat.

By the time she steadied herself, the two assailants were disappearing amongst the bushes by the side of the road, one man's arm draped across the other's shoulders as he was dragged along. She aimed her pistol at the bushes, following the rustling sounds, using her left hand to steady her shaking right one.

'Leave it!' That voice brooked no disobedience.

Thea lowered her arm, gulping with relief that she would not have to use the firearm, although she would have fired had she been forced to. What if those ruffians had not run away? What if Vernon had been incapacitated? The enormity of her decision to follow him in this way suddenly hit her. And now…she realised how likely it was Vernon would see through her disguise and her relief seeped away to be replaced by fear at the thought of facing him. He would not be happy. She sucked in a breath.

'Thank you.' Vernon's attention was still on the spot where the two men had disappeared into the bushes. 'I am in your debt.'

In the spot where they stood, where trees overhung the road, the light had all but gone. Thea kept her face averted from Vernon and muttered, 'Glad to help.'

Vernon crossed slowly to Warrior and reached into his saddlebag, keeping a wary eye on the surrounding bushes. All sounds of the men's retreat had faded away, but Thea still breathed a thankful sigh when Vernon withdrew his own pistol. At least they were both now armed and ready for anything.

'How far is Birmingham? I need a bed for the night.'

Thea pointed ahead. 'Two or three miles.'

He grunted. 'I'll stop at the next inn. There must be another between here and the town.

Vernon rubbed his hand across his jaw, the rasp of whiskers against his palm reminding him of the long, weary day behind him. He shoved his foot into the stirrup and hauled himself up to the saddle. He was knackered even before those two had jumped him, but now... He pressed his hand to his side and winced. That bastard had caught him with his stake, but he was sure it hadn't punctured anything vital. When he had first become aware of the two figures lurking in the undergrowth, energy had flooded him, banishing his weariness and helping him to fight them off. But now that unnatural surge had dissipated and all he wished for

was a hot meal and a comfortable bed. He hoped
the next inn would be a decent place. Some of the
places he had stopped at since leaving Stourbridge
had left much to be desired.

Vernon glanced round at the lad, riding a little
behind, out of Vernon's direct line of sight. He was
not the talkative type and that suited Vernon very
well, but he was aware how fortunate it was that the
lad had seen what was happening and come to Vernon's aid. He wondered idly if the boy was local…
that was a very fine mare he was riding. Vernon
frowned, staring at the road ahead as suspicions
stirred. Such a quality, fine-boned animal was an
unusual choice for a country lad. He glanced back
again. The combination of the dim light and the
lad's cap pulled low over his eyes rendered his face
all but invisible.

They had ridden into a village and around a
curve in the road. There before them was a small
inn, the Bell, set between a churchyard and a row
of neat cottages. Vernon could just make out the
church itself, set back from the other buildings,
its square tower silhouetted against the night sky.

'Do you know anything about this place?'

The lad shook his head.

'No matter,' Vernon said. 'Go in and see if it
looks respectable, will you, lad? I'll hold the horses.
Oh, and enquire for the local constable, while
you're there, will you?' Once he left the saddle he
feared it would be more than he could manage to

remount. 'I must report that attack—I was informed earlier there has been a spate of such incidences in the area. I make no doubt the constable will be interested in the information, especially as one of those men looks unlikely to go far.'

The boy merely grunted by way of reply and did as he was bid as Vernon clenched his teeth against the pain in his side and battled the urge to slump in the saddle.

The boy soon emerged, with a couple of men. He nodded at Vernon, who took that to mean the inn was acceptable. He slid to the ground, relieved he need ride no further.

'I'm Joseph Deadly, constable here,' the taller of the two men said. 'What's been a-happening?'

Vernon told Deadly how the two men had jumped him.

'I'll wager it's them gipsies that set up camp by the woods. They often come through this time of year, picking up odd jobs, and we allus seem to get a spate of thievery and such like when they're around.'

Vernon recalled Thea's earlier remark, that Daniel had suspected former soldiers of local attacks rather than the gipsies commonly blamed. His immediate impression of his two attackers meant he was inclined to agree with Daniel.

'I am not sure you are correct, Deadly,' he said. 'Whilst gipsies are not unknown for petty thieving, the ones I've met in the past have not struck me as violent men, unless they perceive themselves under threat. The men who attacked me appeared more like vagrants.'

Deadly shrugged. 'One and the same thing, as far as I can see. You say one of them's injured, sir?'

'He is. I suspect my boot in his face will leave a visible clue to identify the culprit.'

Several men had by now joined them outside the inn, tankards in hand.

'Any volunteers to come with me and pay them gipsies a visit?' Deadly said.

A chorus of enthusiasm met his words and Vernon's heart sank. He hoped he hadn't been the instigator of a lynch mob. Still, that was for the constable to control.

'Never fear, sir,' Deadly added, clapping Vernon on the shoulder and making him wince, 'we'll go to the scene first and scout out from there. But, you mark my words, it'll be them gipsies.'

'Before you go...' Vernon tossed his horse's reins to the lad—who had shrunk back into the shadows—and then took the constable to one side to tell him about Daniel Markham's disappearance. 'Will you make a few enquiries, but discreetly, please? Mr Markham's family do not wish his disappearance to become common knowledge. He was riding a light grey horse. I also need to know if you have any knowledge of Willingdale or of a man called Henry Mannington. You may attend me here in the morning, if you will, to let me know if you have any news for me and to tell me if you've had any luck in tracking down my attackers.'

Deadly touched the brim of his hat. 'Very good, sir.'

Vernon was relieved to call a halt to his enquiries, even though his original intention had been to reach Birmingham and the Royal Hotel that night. He felt in his gut that the Royal Hotel would hold the clue he needed to unravel what had happened to Daniel Markham.

He turned back to Warrior. The lad who had been holding him had gone, leaving the horse's reins weighted with a large stone. Vernon frowned. He had wanted to thank him properly. He looked along the street and there, in the distance, he could just make out the lad riding away on his black mare. His body screamed at him to let the lad go, but his suspicions about the quality of the horse, coupled with the lad's reluctance to look Vernon in the eye and his lack of conversation, set warning bells jangling in Vernon's head. Then he recalled the lad's pistol. How many country lads like him would own a *duelling* pistol?

Is he a runaway?

And those few words decided him. His nephew, Alex—Leo's youngest son—had run away only a few months previously, and Vernon remembered the worry and the grief of the entire family as they had imagined the worst. And then there was

Thea—her anxiety over her brother's disappearance had touched Vernon as he saw how bravely she tried to shield her parents from the knowledge. The thought of another family going through the same horror of not knowing what had become of their loved one made the decision for him: he could not allow the lad to ride off into the night without at least trying to discover his story.

Vernon clenched his teeth and, sweating with the effort, hauled himself into Warrior's saddle. He put his hand to his side again, reaching inside his borrowed moleskin waistcoat, feeling the sticky warmth of blood. He inhaled—he should get it seen to, but then the boy would be long gone and, if he *was* a runaway, Vernon would have lost his only chance to help.

He set Warrior into a trot, biting back a gasp as the gait jolted him and pain scorched across his ribs.

'Damn,' he muttered, beneath his breath. 'Let's get this done,' and he dug his heels in.

Warrior broke into a canter—a smoother pace but still agony to Vernon. He hooked his left hand under the pommel and forced his thoughts away from the pain and on to the lad. As they neared the black mare, the lad glanced back and, for a moment, it seemed as though he would take flight. He did not, however, but reined to a halt and waited, staring fixedly at his horse's mane.

'Why did you leave?' Vernon said as he pulled his horse round in front of the mare.

'Need to get home.'

There was something about that gruff voice… but it hovered just out of Vernon's reach. He watched the boy as he studiously avoided meeting his gaze.

'And where is that?'

A cough took Vernon unaware. Pain forked through him and he sucked an involuntary breath in through his teeth. The boy's head jerked upright and he stared through the darkness at Vernon.

'Are you hurt?'

'Merely a scratch,' he gritted out. 'You left before I could thank you properly.' He fumbled in his pocket, pulled out a half-sovereign. 'Here. I am—'

Vernon bit off his words. The boy had reached out for the coin, muttering *Thanks*, and something about that disgruntled, near-sarcastic tone of voice jogged a memory. He did not stop to think about it…about how unlikely it was…he nudged his horse closer to the dainty black mare and took hold of her reins. The fresh scent of roses assailed his senses.

It cannot—

In one swift movement he snatched the cap from the boy's head. Even though it was too dark to see the colour, there was no mistaking the spring of the curls that tumbled about her forehead, nor the delicate oval of her face, nor the plump softness of the lips that formed a silent *Oh!* of horror. Vernon lifted his gaze to meet a pair of large, startled eyes that he just knew were hazel in colour.

'What the bloody *hell* do you think you are doing?'

Chapter Six

Thea shrank from the utter fury in Vernon's voice, the blood stuttering through her veins. She said nothing. There was nothing she could say. The only sound was of the early stirrings of nocturnal wildlife rustling in the still evening air. She suppressed a shiver. She was unafraid of the dark, but she could not begin to guess how Lord Vernon Beauchamp might now react. She had not trusted him to concentrate on finding Daniel, but had never stopped to wonder about her own safety if…*when*…he discovered her presence.

A growl sounded, muted at first, as though contained deep within him, but it grew and grew until, with a hasty gesture that made Thea flinch, Vernon snatched his hat from his head, thrust his other hand through his hair and then, swinging his right leg over Warrior's neck, he jumped to the ground and strode away. After a dozen paces, he stopped and then hunkered down, his head hanging.

Thea chewed her lip. It was too late to ride away. He knew it was she and therefore she had no choice but to face him. She dismounted and approached the still figure. His breath came in hoarse rasps and, with a flurry of concern, she recalled that fight and his earlier hissed intake of breath.

'Are you injured?' She dropped a timid hand on his shoulder.

'I *said* it is but a scratch.'

He stood and Thea staggered back several paces as he towered over her. He held up his hands, palms facing her, in a gesture of peace.

'It is all right.' There was still a hard edge to his voice, but that raw anger had softened. 'I might be furious, but I have never in my life offered violence to a woman and I am not about to start now, no matter *how* tempted I am to put you over my knee and spank you.'

Thea gasped, but shock soon gave way to her own anger. 'You cannot dictate my movements, Lord Vernon. You are neither my father nor my brother—'

'Thank God for that small mercy.'

'And I do not answer to you.'

'Again, thank God. I can think of nothing worse than being responsible for a little firebrand such as you.' He heaved a sigh. 'Except, of course, I *am* now responsible for you.'

'You are most certainly not responsible for me. I am a woman grown. An adult. And a perfectly capable one at that.' Thea moved closer to him, stretching to her full height and thrusting her face as close to his as she could manage. 'I am responsible for myself. It is nothing to do with you.'

He huffed a laugh of disbelief. 'Then…' he put his hat back on and started back towards the horses '…I shall leave you to it, Miss Markham.' She heard him chuckle as he walked away. 'Dorothea! Dotty is more like it. Yes, that is it.' He spun to face her, continuing to move away, walking backwards. 'Dotty by name, dotty by nature.'

Thea swallowed down an urge to cry. She would not give that brute the satisfaction. She crossed her arms over her chest and turned away, staring fixedly back down the road. She would not turn back until she heard him ride off. *That* would show him how little she cared.

I do not need him. I have money, so I can stay in inns. I have my pistols and I have my wits about me.

Silence reigned. All she could hear, once more, was the sound of night-time creatures moving through the undergrowth. No creak of a saddle as he mounted. No horse's hoofbeats fading into the distance. But she would not look.

'You…' the voice came from directly behind her, making her jump '…are the most wilful woman it has ever been my misfortune to meet.'

Her pulse settled and a warm glow settled deep inside her. For all her bravado, she had dreaded being left alone on a strange road now darkness had fallen.

'What is your plan? Where did you think to spend the night?'

She faced him. She hadn't really planned…at least, not in such detail. She had trusted in her own ingenuity to work out those minor inconveniences when the time came.

'I *planned*…' she stuck her nose in the air '…to stay at inns overnight. That is what they are for, after all.'

'An unaccompanied female, staying in such places?'

'There is no need to sound so very…*scandalised*. I told you before that I am not one of your delicate society misses, fit for nothing other than being dressed in fancy clothes and doing as they are told.'

The man standing in front of her snorted with laughter.

'*What* is so funny?'

'You should meet the females in my family, if that is what you believe. My sister, my new sister-in-law, my niece: they are not women to meekly do as they are bid without question.'

'Then you should be more than comfortable with the notion that *I* am capable of making my own decisions. Besides, it may have escaped your notice, but I would not be staying in inns as an unaccompanied woman, but as a youth. See? Scandal avoided. Not even you recognised me, until now.

Tell me, what gave me away? I shall need to know if I am to escape detection as we continue searching for Daniel.'

'Continue…? Oh, no. You are not coming with me. You are to go home. Right now. You have seen how dangerous it is on the roads. I cannot allow—'

'One: as I said before, it is not your place either to give or to withhold permission. Two: it is now dark and I am not so foolish as to ride all the way home, on my own, at night. Who knows what scoundrels I might meet? Not to mention Mr Deadly and his bloodthirsty band. Three: I cannot wait meekly at home, waiting for news of Daniel. I have had five days of that. Five days of doing nothing other than hoping for the best, as you yourself said. I need to be doing something. *Please*. Allow me to help.'

'But—'

'No one will find out I'm not a youth, I promise.' He was wavering, she could tell. She pressed home her advantage. 'Tell me what gave me away and I'll make sure it does not happen again. Besides…' she stepped closer '…you need someone to watch your back. I proved that, earlier.'

Vernon huffed a sigh.

'What gave me away?'

'Your voice. Specifically…' he tilted her chin up until their eyes met '…the irritatingly hoity tone in which you said your thanks when I gave you that coin.'

Thea bit back a grin. She *had* taken offence at that typically aristocratic gesture towards a lesser mortal who has done them a service. She had not met many as high-ranked as Vernon, but she recognised the type.

'Then I shall ensure I am suitably humble in the days ahead.'

'And,' he continued, 'I have yet to come across a youth who smells quite as…*enticing*…as you.' His voice lowered. 'You smell of flowers—like a garden in midsummer.'

His deep tone did peculiar things to her insides.

'Then I shall neglect to wash myself for a few days,' Thea said. 'We cannot have you too…er… *enticed*, now, can we?'

A muffled snort of laughter gave her encouragement.

'What say you?' she said. 'Are we partners?'

'Partners? Hmmm.' He shook his head. 'I just know I am going to regret this, but…very well.'

'Yes!'

'I insist on one condition, though.'

'Which is?'

'You remain in disguise, every minute of every day. You must think of yourself as a youth—no missish airs and graces, no maidenly protestations and most definitely no tears or swooning. You will be my nephew.' Thea caught a flash of white as he grinned. 'I shall be your Uncle Vernon Boyton.'

'Boyton?'

'One of my brother's minor titles. We use it occasionally when he doesn't want to travel as a duke, with all the pomp that can entail. So, Master Boyton, what name shall we—?'

'Theo,' Thea said, before he could come up with some totally unacceptable name. 'Daniel calls me Thea, so—'

'Not Dotty? I am disappointed.'

'So,' she went on, through gritted teeth, 'Theo will be perfect.'

'I shall endeavour not to forget. Now, I don't know about you, Dot—*Theo*! I *do* beg your pardon—but I am starving. Shall we return to…what was that village? Harborne, that is it…and have something to eat?'

When they reached the Bell they rode around the back to the stable yard where an ostler scurried out of the stables to take the horses. Vernon tossed him a coin in that careless, aristocratic manner that had so irritated Thea earlier. If he had ever known the fear of losing everything, he would not be so unthinking in tossing a coin.

'Take care,' Vernon murmured, as they returned to the front of the inn. 'We must not discuss your brother yet. Wait for when we are alone.'

Those words prompted a flutter deep inside Thea's stomach. *When we are alone…* For a few glorious moments she savoured those words, until common sense intervened. They were taking part in a masquerade. He was of a completely different world to her and, besides, had she not sworn to herself that she would never again look twice at *any* man?

She sneaked a sideways peek at Vernon as they arrived at the front door.

He seems *trustworthy*.

But, then, so had Jasper: handsome and smooth-talking on the outside, concealing deceit and greed and downright cruelty.

The innkeeper greeted them and passed them on to the care of his wife when Vernon requested bedchambers for himself and his nephew.

'I've got joining chambers available, sir, but that'll be no problem for you and the young sir there,' Mrs Topping said as she led them up the stairs.

She showed them into a large room and lit two lamps with a tinderbox from her apron pocket. A huge bed dominated the centre of the room. Mrs Topping held one lamp aloft and ushered Thea to a door in the corner, through which there was a box room with a tiny window and a narrow single bed. There was no outer door, she noted uneasily, just the door into the main chamber.

'These will suit us very well, Mrs Topping,' Vernon said. 'I shall be able to keep close tabs on young Theo here.'

He reached out and, before Thea realised his intention, he tweaked her ear.

'Ouch,' she squealed, rubbing at her ear.

'Oh, dear. That voice of yours will not behave, will it, nevvy?' Vernon said, with a wide grin. 'One minute low, the next squeaking like a girl. You'll be relieved when it's finally broken for good, I dare say. At least then you will *sound* like a man.'

Thea glared at him, still rubbing her ear. He was relishing this, the wretch, and she wondered how many more jokes he would enjoy at her expense.

'Dinner will be ready in half an hour, sirs, if you care to come down to the parlour then,' Mrs Topping said. 'The maid will be up directly with warm water for you.'

After she had gone, Vernon sat on the edge of the double bed in the outer chamber and bounced a couple of times.

'Hmmm, yes, perfectly adequate,' he said, before swinging his legs up and stretching out full length upon the mattress.

Thea averted her eyes and hurried into the smaller room, feeling her cheeks heat as a devilish chuckle followed her.

'Be so good as to send the girl in with the water when she comes,' she snapped, before slamming the connecting door.

She sat on the bed, slumping despondently as she registered quite how sparse and unforgiving the mattress felt under her buttocks. She had not anticipated being at quite such close quarters with Vernon. Neither had she envisaged being stuck in a tiny hole of a bedchamber with the only way out through *his* bed-chamber. She must endure for tonight—to demand better accommodation would only risk revealing her disguise—but if Lord Vernon Beauchamp imagined she would accept such arrangements in any of the nights to come, he might think again.

Tomorrow morning, she would be laying down some rules.

She lay back upon the bed, wriggling to try to get comfortable. Then the murmur of voices and the click of a door closing catapulted her to her feet, to wait for the maid to bring her water through. There was silence from the adjoining room. Thea crept over to the door and put her ear to the wood. There was no sound for the longest time and then…a grunt, followed by a gasp and then the splash of water being poured. She waited, but all she could hear was the slosh of water in a basin and the occasional hiss, as of air being in-haled sharply through gritted teeth.

Impatient to know what was happening and when she, too, might expect some water, Thea tapped on the door. Lifting the latch, she inched it open.

'Are you decent, my lord? Is it safe to come in?'

'Decent *and* safe?' He chuckled, setting her teeth on edge. 'Now there's a question. Yes, you're safe enough, Theo, my lad. My tastes never did run to boys.'

Thea thrust the door wide and stalked into the other room. 'Where is my...*oh*!'

A wide expanse of hair-dusted chest met her gaze. A ripple of...*something*...undulated through her, stealing her breath, and she wrenched her gaze from Vernon, mentally scolding herself. She had seen Daniel's bare chest numerous times, as well as the workers in the fields at harvest time, so why did *his* chest affect her so?

'I wondered what had happened to my water,' she said.

'The maid only brought the one jug. She said she was bringing another *for the young master* straight away. She would think it strange if I allowed you to have the first jugful.'

He was right, but that did not soothe Thea's ruffled feelings. She faked indifference as she scanned the room although all she wanted to do was to feast her eyes once more on Vernon's magnificent torso, with its sculpted muscles, wide shoulders and the tantalising trail of hair that narrowed as it disappeared into his breeches...

Her thoughts stuttered to a halt.

Vernon had dropped his shirt and, as her gaze alighted on it, Thea gasped and swooped on the garment, snatching it from the floor. She shook it out and held it up to the light of the lamp.

'You're bleeding! Why did you not say?'

Vernon—one arm raised above his head as he dabbed at his side with a washcloth—snorted.

'What would've been the point of that? There was nothing could be done about it before and I am dealing with it now. Besides, I did tell you.'

'You *said* it was a scratch.' Thea hurried over to him. 'Let me help.'

She ducked under his raised arm and took the washcloth from his unresisting hand. She wrung it out in the water and turned her attention to the gash across his ribs.

'It *is* a scratch. The knife must have glanced off a rib,' Vernon said. 'Look—'

He indicated one end of the gash, at the front of his torso, about three inches below his left nipple. Thea's mouth went dry at that fascinating flat disc, so different to her own.

'It started here and then glanced away, and around my side. Bit of luck it didn't go in deep.'

He twisted from the waist and Thea saw the long gash became shallower as it followed the curve of his ribcage. Vernon's arm was still raised and, when Thea glanced up, she had to batten down a peculiar compulsion to stroke the soft chestnut-coloured hair that grew underneath. Her heart hammered in her chest as his musky scent surrounded her, but the realisation that Vernon was entirely unmoved by their proximity—concentrating solely on his wound—gave her the strength she needed to ignore her erratic reactions. She began to cleanse the wound, which had stopped bleeding, aware that infection could be a problem.

As if he'd read her mind, Vernon said, 'I asked the maid to bring up a length of bandage and a glass of brandy.'

'Good,' she said. 'It will sting, of course, but that is preferable to an infection of the blood.'

'Sting?' That one word was infused with horror. 'My dear Dotty, the brandy is to drink. I am in dire need of a tonic.'

Thea pursed her lips, aware he was deliberately provoking her by calling her Dotty. She could only hope he would soon tire of the sport if she did not react.

At that moment there was a tap on the door and the maid came in, carrying a jug, a glass containing amber liquid and a strip of cloth. Thea reacted quickly, reaching the maid before Vernon had even turned around.

'Thank you.' She took the glass and bandage from the maid. 'If you could put the jug in the other room, please?'

Vernon had tilted his head and was watching Thea closely, his eyes narrowed. She held his gaze. He needn't think he could intimidate her so very easily. She needed him fit and well if they were to find Daniel, and that meant—like it or not— the brandy was going on his wound. The maid emerged from the inner room.

'Thank you…er…?'

The maid bobbed a curtsy. 'Janey, sir.'

Vernon smiled at her, bringing a rosy blush to her cheeks. 'Thank you, Janey.'

Hmmph. Flirting with the maid in front of me. He's only doing it to annoy me.

Vernon's smile widened as he caught Thea's eye. The maid left the room, closing the door behind her, and Vernon held out one hand.

'I'll have that, thank you,' he said.

Thea wrapped both hands around the glass, holding it tight against her chest, and shook her head. 'You can drink brandy any time. This is needed for medicinal purposes.'

He prowled across the room towards her. Her pulse quickened, and she retreated to the far side of the bed.

'Precisely,' he said. 'And it will fulfil its medicinal function from the inside. In my belly.' He rounded the end of the bed.

'No. Listen…'

She was trapped. There was nowhere to go other than across the bed itself—impossible while holding a glass of brandy. Why hadn't she thought this through before challenging him? He neared her with every step, that bare chest of his filling her vision and turning her insides into a mass of jelly.

'Well?' he queried, silky smooth. 'You asked me to listen.'

'If there is any left, you may drink that,' she said.

'After a cloth has been dipped in and out of it?' He shook his head. 'I think not. Try again.'

He halted in front of her, but made no move to take the glass. Her legs trembled—and not with fear—as she searched her mind desperately for something…*anything*…to say to persuade him. Her gaze, she realised, was still locked on to his chest—so close, so tempting—and she forced herself to look up at his face. Where she caught, and recognised, the roguish glint in his eyes and the twitch of his lips. She frowned.

Vernon threw his head back and laughed uproariously. 'Your expression,' he gasped. 'It was a delight. You did not really believe I would wrestle the glass from you by force?'

He spun round and crossed the room to stand by the lamp. Thea remained still.

'But…' she said. 'You…'

'Come.' He beckoned her. 'Come and do your worst. Of *course* I ordered the brandy to cleanse the gash, foolish girl.'

Fuming silently, Thea walked over to him. Before she could say anything, though, he reached out and cupped her chin, tilting her face to his.

'You are entirely too gullible, my dear Dotty.' He pinched her chin gently before releasing it. 'We are going to have to toughen you up, if you are to pass muster as a youth. Teasing and ribaldry are all part of the disguise.'

He lifted his arm again, and passed Thea a handkerchief. 'Here. Use this. It is clean.'

Thea moistened the handkerchief and dabbed

at the cut, repeating the process until the entire length had been treated. Throughout, Vernon remained silent, only the occasional flinch betraying the sting of the spirit.

'There. It is all done,' Thea said.

She fetched the bandage from the bed, where she had thrown it when Vernon began stalking her. Vernon raised both arms and challenged her silently with a raised brow. Thea narrowed her eyes. He was entirely too cocky. She would not give him the satisfaction of knowing how rattled she was by being here with him half-naked. She moved closer and reached around him to pass the bandage behind his back. Heat scorched her skin as she momentarily pressed her cheek to his chest. She forced herself not to react, but calmly brought the bandage around and tied a half-knot to hold it in place. Then she walked around him several times, wrapping his torso—and those fascinating slabs of muscle that caught her eye every time she passed in front of him—until the gash was covered and she could tie off the bandage.

'There. Now I must go and have a wash and put on some clean clothes, or we shall be late for our supper.'

'Wait.'

A hand grasped her shoulder before she had taken two steps towards the door in the corner. She faced him, raising her brows in enquiry. He reached out and ruffled her hair.

'What *have* you done?'

His soft query, the underlying sadness in his voice, brought a lump to her throat as she recalled her hurried shearing of her locks. She tried to smooth her hair, knowing the attempt was futile.

'It is nothing. It will grow again.'

His lips tightened momentarily. 'It is a mess.'

He then captured her gaze and a teasing glint lit his eyes. 'I refuse to be seen in the company of a youth with such a dreadful haircut,' he said, 'particularly when that youth claims to be a relative of mine.'

He strode to his saddlebag, rummaged around inside, and then turned to reveal a pair of scissors in his hand.

'Oh, no.' Thea backed towards the interconnecting door, shaking her head. 'No, no, no. I refuse to allow you near me with those.'

Vernon followed her, gaining on her. 'I cannot possibly make a worse fist of it than you already have,' he said. 'Joking aside, Dotty…it looks utterly appalling. Come… I shall only tidy up the ends a little. They are so ragged *anybody* could guess you have cut your hair yourself. Do you really want to draw such attention to yourself?'

Put like that, what could she say? With a silent sigh, Thea stalked across to a wooden chair and sat down. She closed her eyes and folded her hands tightly in her lap.

A comb began to tug through her curls, snagging on tangles. She kept her eyes screwed shut as Vernon worked quietly and methodically. Then there was a pause and he lifted one curl, raising a shiver that raced across the surface of her scalp. She clamped her lips together as she heard the metallic snick of the scissors. Each time he fingered another curl her skin grew increasingly sensitised and the heat rose from deep inside her to flush her chest, neck and face as she battled to remain motionless on the chair.

By the time he murmured, 'There. All done', she was a quivering wreck.

She did not look into the mirror. Nor did she pause to look at the hair on the floor. She sped through the door between their bedchambers and closed it softly behind her, leaning back against it as she fought to calm her breathing.

Chapter Seven

'You were in the taproom of the Nag's Head when I came in,' Vernon said.

He waited until their food had been served in the parlour of the Bell before broaching the subject that was on his mind. Ever since they entered the inn, and he had seen Thea properly, by the light of the lamps, he had been plagued with the mystery of where he had seen her before, dressed as a lad.

'You were sitting in the corner, nursing a tankard of ale, and you did not join in the conversation once. When I got up to leave, you had already gone.'

'That should prove I can pass unnoticed.'

Thea, sitting across the table from Vernon, kept her attention on her plate of stew. She had been subdued—withdrawn, even—ever since they had come downstairs: speaking only when spoken to directly, reluctant to hold a decent conversation. And he thought he knew why.

He shifted in his seat as his body reacted to the

memory of that haircut. He'd had no choice but to trim her hair after she had left it such a raggedy mass, but he had not anticipated the...*intimacy*... of doing so: the soft, heavy curls between his fingers, her tightly closed eyes and her full lips—so near, so tempting, so *inviting*—the sound of her breathing, loud in the hush of the bedchamber...

He'd wager Thea had been as affected by the unexpected sensuality of that haircut as he had been. But now...this silence...it was hard to stand. It gave him too much time to think.

He could always tease her again, provoke her until her eyes flashed with fury and her temper flared. But teasing, too, felt perilous... He could not rid his mind of the knowledge that, under that male costume, was a flesh-and-blood woman and teasing between a man and a woman could so easily turn into something...*more*.

He would keep this businesslike. 'Do you not wish to decide our plans for tomorrow? To discuss how we might trace Daniel?'

Her head jerked up, her eyes huge.

'Of *course* I wish to discuss him.'

The pain in that husky voice of hers did strange things to him. It was not pity, although he did feel sympathy for her, but, strangely, following his earlier thoughts, it did not provoke the urge to tease but the opposite. It brought forth the desire to comfort and to protect—a feeling he had only thus far in his life felt in relation to the members of his own family. Why did he feel such responsibility for her? It had been her decision to come along, after he had particularly told her to wait at home for news. It was her decision to dress—quite outrageously—in a youth's clothing and to chop her hair off in that barbarous way. She was, as she had pointed out, an adult capable of making her own decisions.

Was it merely the fact she was a female? He huffed a silent laugh, imagining her fury if he was unwise enough to voice *that* particular thought aloud.

'We should speak to the innkeeper about Daniel and ask whether he can recall him visiting this inn,' Thea went on.

'I have already spoken to him,' Vernon said. 'Whilst you were washing.'

He'd had to get out of his room, after she had blithely informed him she would change into clean clothing for the meal. His imagination had run riot—he could not help but wonder what she had done with her breasts. There was no sign of them, but he distinctly recalled them from earlier that day, in that sunset dress of hers. She must have strapped them down and he had begun to wonder if that hurt, and then he had fantasised about soothing the pain and plumping them up again…and he'd had to remove himself from her vicinity before his rakish tendencies overcame his good sense and he attempted to turn fantasy into reality.

Good God...she's not even my type, yet I was fantasising about her like a sex-starved lad.

'I gave my shirt to Mrs Topping to try to remove the bloodstain and to mend the rip,' he said, 'and I spoke to Topping then.'

She waved a dismissive hand at his explanation. 'What did Topping have to say?'

'Nothing. He cannot remember a man of Daniel's description; he did not know his name and he has never heard of Henry Mannington or of Willingdale.'

'Hmph. Well, at least you obtained the information more speedily this time than you did in the Nag's Head,' she said.

Cheeky little...

Vernon resisted the impulse to reach across the table and cuff Thea's ear. This masquerade was doing strange things to his head. One minute, he found it impossible not to think of the female body hidden beneath those clothes and the next he had almost treated her exactly as he might treat the impertinence of any young lad. He quaffed a quantity of ale, giving his temper time to subside.

'I am not certain what you expected this afternoon,' he said, capturing her gaze as he leaned across the table towards her, 'but—'

'I do not understand why you could not simply ask the questions and leave. You did so at the other inns you stopped at. You did not remain at any of those above ten minutes. We could be at that hotel

in Birmingham by now if you had not been so…
so…intent upon playing a part at the Nag's Head.
This is not a play, my lord. It is real life. There
could be a life at stake…' Her voice choked and
she cleared her throat.

Vernon sat back, frowning. 'If you will allow
me to explain.'

She shot him a smile of apology. 'Now I have
angered you. I apologise. I did not mean to sound
ungrateful.'

'I am not angry. I see why you reached such a
conclusion, but I did not act in the way I did for my
own amusement, but in order that I might learn the
truth and not be fobbed off with shrugged shoulders and denials.

'Those men in the Nag's Head are not stupid.
They knew I was an outsider, so it was of no use
me pretending otherwise. I acted the part of a gentleman down on his luck…my atrocious gambling
habit, don't you know.' He grinned at her and was
rewarded by a faint smile in return. 'Such a man
will always find a welcome in such public houses,
but it takes time to build a rapport and it is necessary to earn a man's trust before asking questions.
Had I gone in and immediately bombarded them
with questions, they would have feigned ignorance
even if Daniel was in the next room. Do not forget,
those men *know* your brother. They would see it
as protecting him. Taking time as I did may have

been frustrating for you, but at least I left the place with some information.

'I did not need to behave with the same circumspection at the other inns because, as far as I am aware, Daniel is not a regular customer there.'

'But why bother to make enquiries at every single inn between Stourbridge and Birmingham? You are wasting time.'

'I disagree. We may now know that R.H. means the Royal Hotel, but that does not mean the answers we seek will fall into our laps the minute we walk through the door. We still need to know what or who Willingdale is and we need to know how Henry Mannington is connected with Daniel's disappearance. What we *do* know is that Daniel made this same journey twice a day for several days in succession. I take the view that, as we are passing, it is worth our while asking the pertinent questions. We do not want to be forced to retrace our steps, do we?'

She bit into her lower lip. Vernon averted his gaze and fixed it on his plate as his pulse kicked. This escapade might prove intolerable if they did not discover the truth about Daniel quickly.

'You are right,' she said. 'I had not thought it through. I am sorry.'

'There is no need to keep apologising.' Vernon indicated her plate. She had barely touched her food. 'Are you not going to eat?'

She pushed the plate from her. 'I find I have little appetite. It has been the same ever since Daniel disappeared.'

The dining room was empty apart from the two of them, the other guests having dined earlier. He reached across the table and covered her hand with his. It felt so tiny. The bones fragile. Again, the urge to protect welled up and he closed his fingers gently around hers.

'It is of no use to tell you not to worry, I know, but I promise we will find the truth. You must not starve yourself, though. Tomorrow will be a long and trying day and you cannot risk falling ill. You will need energy and strength. Even if you have no appetite, try to eat something. I have never known any lad who would not clear that plateful and ask for more so, if you wish to maintain your charade, please try to eat some more.'

Her eyes searched his. They were huge, luminous pools and he felt himself being drawn into their depths. He wrenched his gaze from hers and withdrew his hand.

'We will find out what has happened to Daniel and, God willing, we will find him safe and well,' he said, scraping back his chair. 'In the meantime, I shall go out to the stables and check on our horses and see if the grooms can recall seeing Daniel or his horse.' He smiled at her, adding, 'I never met a groom yet who paid more attention to a rider than his horse.'

He was rewarded with a fleeting smile and the

sight of Thea pulling her plate back in front of her and picking up her spoon. Vernon quashed his guilt at leaving the table whilst Thea still ate. These were exceptional circumstances and, besides, if he did not soon put some distance between them, he did not think he could resist sweeping her into his arms and just holding her. Comforting her. And that he could not risk. He needed a dose of fresh air and some uncomplicated, masculine company, even if that was only the ostlers in a country inn.

Out the back of the inn, all was quiet. Vernon opened the door to the stable to be greeted by the contented sound of horses munching hay. He breathed deep of the soothing, familiar smell of horses, leather, saddle soap and hay. A man holding aloft a lantern emerged from a door at the far end of the row of stalls.

'Is aught amiss, sir?'

'No. I have come to check our horses are settled, that is all.'

They chatted easily about horses for a while, before Vernon said, 'I believe a friend of mine has stopped here several times. He rides a light grey gelding, about sixteen hands high. Name of Bullet.'

The groom smiled around a mouthful of chewing tobacco.

'I remember him, sir. Good strong-boned piece of 'ossflesh. He's called in here a few times—on his way to and from Birmingham.' He leaned closer to Vernon, and lowered his voice, 'One of the wenches here's a bit…you know, sir, a bit generous, shall we say?' He winked knowingly. 'The gent took to calling in to visit with her, if you see what I mean. Janey, she's called, if you've an interest in that direction yerself, sir.'

'Thank you.' Vernon had no such interest in Janey, but he would speak to her for she might hold a vital clue. His pulse quickened. He would find her after he'd finished with the groom. 'Can you remember the last time you saw him?'

The groom cocked his jaw, frowning. 'Lemme see. Last Thursday, it were. Ayuh, that was it. Thursday morning. I remembers, you see, 'cause that's the day the carrier calls in.'

Thursday. That was the day Daniel failed to return home.

'He did not call in on his way home that evening?'

'Not as I recall, sir.'

'Do you know a man called Henry Mannington?'

The groom shook his head.

'Thank you, you've been most helpful.'

Vernon slipped the man a coin. The groom took it and tucked it away with a nod of thanks.

'One last question—does the name Willingdale mean anything to you?'

'No, sir. Never heard of it.'

Vernon crossed the yard to the inn, choosing to enter through the rear door. As luck would have it, as he followed the passage that led to the dining room, Janey was approaching him from the direction of the stairs. Vernon continued towards her and halted just past the closed dining room door. He wondered if Thea was still inside.

'Janey,' he said, as the maid came closer.

She smiled and her hips appeared to take on a life of their own, undulating in a silent *come hither*. She did not halt until her breasts—squeezed by her corset into bulging mounds above her neckline—were a bare inch from his chest.

'Can I offer you anything, sir?' Her tongue played with her top lip.

'Information, if you please.' He kept his tone brisk, careful to offer her no encouragement. He had no wish to wake in the night to find her willing body slipping between his sheets. 'I understand you are…er…acquainted with a friend of mine, Daniel Markham?'

'Danny?' She pouted. 'He promised to bring me a present, but he never came.'

'When was this?'

She didn't hesitate. 'Last Thursday. He was going into Birmingham as usual, and he *promised* to br—'

'To bring you a present. Yes, yes, so you said.'

Vernon reached into his pocket and extracted a coin. A brief glance confirmed it was a crown—more than he intended, but the girl's eyes lit at the sight of it so, with a mental shrug, he pressed it into her palm. If it kept her sweet enough to answer his questions, it was worth it.

Too late, he registered the sound of the door opening behind him. As Janey ostentatiously slid the coin into the deep cleft between her breasts, Thea stalked past with a muttered 'Good night, *Uncle.*'

Vernon suppressed his sigh, knowing what she must think.

'That,' he said to Janey, more harshly than he intended to, 'is for information only. Is that clear?'

Her lips thinned.

Great. Now I have two affronted females to pacify.

He clasped Janey's arm and steered her into the dining room.

'I can't stay,' she said, twisting her arm free from his grip. 'Mrs Topping will be after me and I can't afford to lose my job.'

'Then answer my questions quickly and she will never notice you are gone.'

Damn it! Why did Thea have to come out at that precise moment? With an effort, Vernon tore his thoughts from Thea and back to solving the mystery of Daniel's disappearance.

'Did Daniel tell you why he went into Birmingham every day?'

Janey's eyes narrowed. 'Why do you want to know? Is he in trouble?'

Vernon held out his hand, palm up. 'You took my

money—you answer my questions. If you won't, you can return it now.'

A flush coloured her cheeks. 'I only know he was searching for someone.'

'Who?'

'Are you him?' Her eyes widened. 'Are you this Henry he was so angry with?'

'No.'

'Promise?' Her voice trembled. 'I don't want nothing to do with him. Promise you're not him?'

'I promise. I am a friend of Daniel's and of his family. I want to find him to help him. Now, think, Janey, did Daniel say why he was angry with Henry?'

'It were about money, that's all I know. He saw him at a sale and he followed him, but he lost him. He were fumin' when he called in on his way home. *Fumin'.*'

'You knew Daniel before that day? How long have you known him?'

She shrugged. 'Couple of years. He took to calling in when he went into town, maybe three or four times a year. Until that day. He went up to Birmingham every day after that, looking for this Henry, asking questions about him.'

'Did he tell you what he found out?'

'Some,' she said. ''e found out where Henry stayed when he went to town—some hotel.'

The Royal Hotel! I'd bet my life on it!

'So he said he would go back every day until

either he saw Henry again or until he found out where he lived and that when he tracked him down he was going to kill him.'

'*Kill* him?'

Janey nodded. 'He shook with anger when he talked about him. Said he couldn't talk 'bout it to no one but me. *That's* why he was going to bring me a present, 'cause I'm a good listener, I am.' She sniffed, her eyes welling with tears. 'But he never came back. Five days it's been.'

Vernon patted her shoulder. 'Thank you for your help, Janey. Off you go now, or Mrs Topping will be after you.'

'Thank you, sir.' Janey reached for the door handle, then hesitated. 'I hope you find him, sir. I hope he's not hurt. I was angry at him, thinking he'd lied to me, but now… I just hope he's all right.'

'I hope so, too,' Vernon said as he followed the maid from the room.

Janey disappeared towards the rear of the inn and Vernon stood irresolute in the passageway, eyeing the staircase leading to the floor above. He felt drained. His ribs were sore and his temper felt as though it balanced on a knife's edge.

And up there was Thea. In the adjoining room. Smelling of roses. And…annoyed with him all over again.

He could not face attempting to explain how what she had seen transpire between himself and Janey was entirely innocent. With a huff of impatience, he spun on his heel and headed for the tap-room. It was too early for bed, anyway. He needed time to sift through all he had learned.

And he needed a drink.

Chapter Eight

Vernon woke the next morning with a thundering headache.

He'd spent a restless night and when he finally slept it was to dream fitfully of men lurking in the shadows who, as they emerged into the light, metamorphosed into women, who rubbed around him as he stood frozen to the spot, only for their fingers to sprout claws that raked him, time and time again. He startled awake more than once, sweating, his heart racing.

A little quiet reflection as the dawn light fingered through a gap between the curtains did nothing to ease his troubled mind for, even if what had awoken him *was* only a dream, the underlying worry that plagued him was very real: he was responsible for Dorothea Markham and for her safety. And he had no way of knowing what dangers might lurk ahead of them.

He finally awoke with the conviction that, somehow, he must persuade Thea to return to her parents and to leave him to search on alone for her brother. She would not be easily persuaded. Never had he come across a more stubborn female. Even the women in his family—always ready to challenge a man's authority—were not as tricky to handle. Further consideration, however, set him wondering if that was because they were primarily Leo's responsibility, as head of the family. Vernon had always—their whole lives—been second in command. It was the lot of younger brothers.

As for females who were not members of the Beauchamp family, neither could he recall any of them being so…contrary. Although—and this seemed to be a morning for self-doubt—his renown as a ladies' man could simply be due to his position. Many ladies were eager to impress a wealthy, titled gentleman who was considered a great catch.

He snorted at that last thought. He could never accuse Thea of trying to impress him…she appeared oblivious to his charms. Although, and a slow smile curved his lips at the memory, she was certainly not impervious to his chest. Or to his touch as he trimmed her hair.

The trouble was—he was not impervious either.

He thrust aside the sheet that covered him and swung his legs to the floor. All this thinking was getting him nowhere. He was not second in command now…it was time to get on with finding Daniel Markham.

He washed in the warm water in a jug on his washstand—water he could not remember being delivered to his room and, after dressing, he knocked on the door to the inner chamber. There was no answer and he popped his head into the room to find Thea gone. Unable to quash the terror that jolted him—an after-effect of the night's dreams, his rational mind insisted—he hurried downstairs and there she was, bright-eyed and glowing, clad in her boy's clothes, waiting impatiently for him to appear and eager to continue their journey.

She was altogether too chirpy for Vernon's aching head.

'You are too accustomed to town hours,' she said, teasingly. 'You were sound asleep when I came through your room.'

And the thought of her seeing him sleeping in his bed set his senses all a-jangling, discordant and sharp. And now…he watched Thea from under lowered brows and through bleary eyes as she tucked into another round of buttered toast and sipped from her cup of chocolate.

Nothing wrong with her appetite this morning.

And another thought followed on its heels: he'd expected her to still be annoyed about seeing him with Janey, but it clearly wasn't bothering her in the slightest.

Which was good. Was it not?

'How is your che…your injury this morning,'

Thea asked. 'You look as though it is causing you pain.'

'My chest?'

The light blush that painted her cheeks cheered him somewhat, proving she wasn't totally indifferent to him. Not that he was interested in her, of course.

'It is not my chest that pains me, but my head.'

And the minute he uttered those words he knew his error. The tinge of sympathy he had recognised in those hazel orbs vanished and she immediately became more businesslike.

'Did you discover anything new last night?'

Vernon swallowed his mouthful of eggs and then told her what he had learned from the groom and from Janey. Thea's eyes widened when he told her what Janey had said. As soon as he finished, Thea jumped to her feet, the scrape of her chair setting Vernon's teeth on edge.

'What are we waiting for? Come…' she was already halfway to the door. The woman really was like a lick of flame, darting around so a man could barely keep track of her '…we must make haste.'

'Stop!'

Vernon winced at the loudness of his own voice as it echoed through his head. How much had he drunk last night? He hadn't thought he was over-imbibing, but maybe the local ale was stronger than his customary brew. Thea paused with her hand on the door handle, her tawny brows raised.

'I need to speak to the constable first, to find out if they caught those two ruffians from last night.'

Thea waved a dismissive hand. 'They are not important. We must—'

'Of course they are important. You heard the constable, there have been other attacks. Who knows, they might even have attacked Daniel and left him lying somewhere, or knocked him on the head so he has forgotten his own identity. They might have important information. We need to know one way or the other before we go rushing off to Birmingham.'

'That is true. Let us go.'

The wretched woman was almost bouncing with enthusiasm, those preposterous curls of hers springing around her ears. In these unguarded moments, despite her attire, it was impossible to see her as a youth. She looked young and feminine and…a little adorable. Vernon tore his gaze from her and eyed his plate of congealing eggs. He pushed it away.

'First,' he said, as repressively as he could, his temples still pounding, 'we need to talk.'

She stilled. 'You are going to renege on your promise.'

'Promise? I do not recall promising you anything. You, on the other hand, did promise you would remain at home.'

'I did not.' She dragged out her chair again and sat down. 'I was most careful about my wording. I said, "I shall not insist on leaving with you." And I did not. I *followed* you.' She folded her arms across her chest and her chin jutted forward. 'I will not go home.'

Vernon sighed and pushed his chair back from the table. He leaned back in his chair and stretched his legs out, crossing them at the ankle as he crossed his own arms.

'I have told you what the maid said: Daniel was fuming when he saw Henry and he was determined to track him down. Quite what poor Henry can have done to attract such ire I do not know, but you have to admit this is not a dispute for a woman to become embroiled in.'

'*Poor* Henry? It sounds very much as though I made the right decision to follow you. I can see whose side *you* would be on.'

'Side? Who is talking of sides? All I am interested in is finding the truth. And it will be easier and quicker if I do not have to be constantly worrying about you.'

Thea stuck her nose in the air and averted her face. 'I do not need anyone to worry about me. I shall look after myself. As I did last night and again this morning whilst you were snoring your head off.'

'I do *not* snore.'

'How do you know? You were asleep.'

He closed his eyes and drew in a long, steadying breath. 'The fact still remains that you are at risk.'

'Vernon…'

He felt her breath on his cheek. Smelled the roses. He opened his eyes. Thea was bending over him, her eyes boring into his.

'…I suggest you save your breath for the questions we need to ask,' she said sweetly. 'I am going to Birmingham, to the Royal Hotel. Whether that is by your side or riding three lengths behind is up to you.'

She straightened, her expression one of smug satisfaction.

'And if I do not go to Birmingham? If I return to Stourwell Court for my curricle and pair and then go back to London?'

He knew what her answer would be, but honour dictated he should not concede without some fight.

She arched one brow. 'Then I must go alone.'

Hell and damnation!

He knew when he was beaten. He stood, and gestured to the door. 'In that case there is nothing more I can say. But do not come weeping to me if you get killed.'

She beamed. Positively *beamed* at him. Wretched, *wretched* woman!

The constable called upon them at the Bell just as they were leaving, with bad news.

'We found neither sight nor sound of your attackers, sir,' he told Vernon. 'And you were right. It weren't them gipsies. They'd moved on and Farmer

Whitton, he told us they left yesterday morning, so it couldn't have been them that tried to rob you.'

The constable sounded disappointed. Thea hoped he'd remember this lesson the next time he was quick to point the finger of blame at the gipsies. They were a familiar sight in and around the Stourbridge area. They came and they went, and the men carried out odd jobs and repairs and helped on the farms at harvest times, whilst the women sold pegs and told fortunes for anyone prepared to pay them a penny or two. She did not believe they would attack someone unprovoked.

They set off towards Birmingham in silence, Vernon's scowl an effective barrier to conversation. Eventually, however, his puckered forehead smoothed and his grouchy mood appeared to lift as he showed more interest in the countryside they rode through.

'I feared you had the beginnings of a fever from your wound,' Thea said, after Vernon had commented on the cascading song of a skylark that hovered overhead—a barely visible speck in the deep azure of the sky. 'We do not have the time for you to be laid up in bed.'

He raised a brow. 'You are all heart, Dotty.'

'Well, of course I did not mean I should not care if you became ill,' she said crossly. 'I only meant that…well, as I said—there is no time.'

He laughed, then tipped his head up and breathed in, his chest swelling. 'The fresh air has made all the difference. I woke up with the headache. It is all but gone now.'

Thea had tried hard not to dwell on his likely activities after she had seen him with that maid last night. It had been a shock to see him pressing money on the girl and Thea had climbed the stairs with her heart weighed down with disapproval and…yes…disappointment. Now, knowing that he had been paying the maid for information left her feeling in a charitable mood and so she forbore to point out that the pain he suffered—in his head, at least—was self-inflicted and therefore barely deserving of sympathy. She glanced up at the sky…not a cloud in sight and the sun already high and hot. She tugged at her cap, pulling the peak to shade her face.

'It is fortunate the weather has improved,' she said. 'We had thunderstorms three days running last week—the air was so thick and heavy your headache would not have cleared so readily.'

'Fortunate indeed,' he agreed.

She felt his eyes upon her and kept her attention on the road ahead, sensing he had questions on his mind. She did not have long to wait.

'Do you mind me asking…why are you not married?'

Star skittered slightly as Thea tensed. She relaxed her fingers on the reins and the mare settled again. He had taken her by surprise, asking such a very personal question. She shrugged, aiming for nonchalance.

'It takes two to make a marriage. Why are *you* not married? I assume you are not?'

'No. I am not married. I doubt I shall ever marry.'

'How can you be so sure?' Yet, even as that question left her lips she realised it was possible to be sure…*she* was sure, after all.

'I have no need to wed. And I enjoy my life too much to ever get tied down to one woman.'

'Then it sounds as though you have made the right decision,' Thea said.

'You have not really answered my question.'

'I was betrothed. Once.'

'What happened?'

'We decided we would not suit.'

Not for anything would she admit the reality: being left heartbroken at the altar whilst her parents' main concern had been about the money Papa had given to Jasper to invest on his behalf.

'And no one since?'

'Would you ask such questions of a lady from your own world?'

There was a brief silence. 'No,' he said, finally. 'No, I would not. But that does not imply a lack of respect. It is perhaps a result of the unusual circumstances in which we find ourselves.'

'I see. In that case…no, there has been no one since. I am not interested in marrying.'

'We are two of a kind,' he said with a laugh.

She glanced at him, tall and elegant in the saddle, every inch the gentleman despite the less than fashionable cut of his clothes.

'Hardly,' she said, with an answering grin. 'You are the son of a duke. I am the daughter of a glass manufacturer. We are far removed from one another in almost every way you may imagine.'

Lulled by warm weather, by the roll and sway of Star's back and by the rhythmic thud of the horses' hooves on the road, Thea found it easy to relax and chat, without paying much attention to what she was saying and before very long they were riding into Temple Row where the Royal Hotel stood opposite St Philip's Church and churchyard.

Thea's stomach churned as she perused the simple but elegant hotel, four storeys high, with a central portico. Did this building hide the secret of what had happened to her brother? That maid had said Daniel discovered a hotel where Henry Mannington stayed and Thea was certain this was it. And she had no doubt in her mind that Henry Mannington was responsible for Daniel's disappearance.

She and Vernon had already agreed to reserve rooms for that night, to give them time to question the staff about Daniel and about Henry Mannington. They halted next to a side gateway that led to the stable yard behind the hotel, and Thea jumped to the ground as an ostler hurried out to take charge of the horses. Vernon dismounted in a more leisurely fashion, perusing their surroundings: the church in its spacious churchyard in the middle of a large square surrounded by smart town houses and a school on one corner. Taking stock, Thea thought.

'Have our bags taken inside,' Vernon said to the ostler as he led the horses away.

'Yessir.'

'Should we not question him about Bullet?' Thea hissed.

'There is no need. Not yet.'

'Why not?'

'We already know Daniel has been here, so we need no confirmation that Bullet was in the stables. I shall talk to the grooms later, when they are not as busy.'

And with that, Vernon turned on his heel and began to walk away from the hotel, beckoning Thea to follow. She ran to catch up and grabbed his arm.

'Where are you going? We need to speak to the people in the hotel.'

Is he afraid of what we might discover about Henry Mannington? Is he genuinely interested in finding Daniel?

'Now we are here, I wonder if it is too big a risk for us to go inside together,' Vernon said. 'This…' he swept his arm around, including the hotel and the square in his gesture '…is a wealthy area and the hotel guests may very well include someone who will recognise me.'

'But I do not see why that should matter. You have as much right to go inside the hotel as they do.'

'Yes, but do you not see? If they know me, they will know Leo and they will know my *real* nephews, Dominic and Alexander. You, my dear Dotty, look nothing like either one of 'em.'

'I had not thought of that.' She bit her lip, thinking. 'Could you not say I am a friend?'

Vernon halted in the middle of the pavement, staring down at her with an unfathomable expression.

'No, that will not wash either. You look no more than fourteen years old. No one will believe we are friends.'

He means his reputation would suffer, being seen in company with someone like me.

She tamped down the resentment that swelled on the heels of that thought.

Not me...he means someone like Theo... I must not forget this is not me.

Vernon's gaze again swept the surrounding buildings. 'We must find you somewhere safe to wait whilst I make enquiries inside the hotel.'

'But...we agreed to stay here overnight.'

A rueful smile twisted his lips. 'I did not think it through. It will not work. We must stay elsewhere.'

I do not want to go elsewhere.

She *must* take an active part in the search for Daniel. She could not bear to be left to wait silent in a corner somewhere whilst Vernon went inside to speak to people who must have seen her brother on his visits to the hotel. Besides, how could she be sure Vernon would tell her everything he learned? What if he was told something detrimental about his cousin and he decided to hide it from her?

The only way to change Vernon's mind would be to come up with an explanation for her presence. As Vernon gazed around the square as though for inspiration, tapping his crop against his boot, ideas whirled around Thea's head.

'I have an idea,' she said, as her tumbling thoughts blended together to form a plan, 'but you might disapprove.'

Chapter Nine

Thea's cheeks grew hot under Vernon's scrutiny as his brows shot up in response to her statement.

'That will make a most welcome change, my dearest Dotty,' he murmured. 'It is, after all, so uncharacteristic of you to come up with an idea of which I might disapprove.'

Thea gritted her teeth against a caustic rejoinder, knowing any reaction would only encourage him to tease her further with that accursed nickname.

She caught the twitch of his lips.

And now he is laughing at me!

Silence stretched over several minutes as their gazes clashed. Thea pressed her lips tight, determined not to elaborate until he was ready to listen to her in a serious manner.

'Pray continue,' Vernon said, finally, with a sigh.

'Our story *could* be that you…or rather, that *I*…well…that Theo is your…' Thea lowered her voice to a whisper although there was nobody near enough to hear what she said '…your bastard.' Mortifyingly, her cheeks now scorched and she knew they must be an unbecoming shade of red. She fixed her gaze on a point beyond his right ear. She inhaled and allowed the remainder of her words to tumble out, finding it easier to refer to herself as Theo.

'I… *Theo*…knows you are his father, but he does not know your true identity, but you support him and when you come to visit him and to take him out, you dress less fashionably so you do not draw attention and so that Theo does not guess you are really a duke's brother.'

'That…' Vernon said.

Thea looked up hopefully, her eyes searching his.

'…is an excellent idea.'

She beamed, relief flooding through her as she recalled her earlier suspicions. Surely, if he *were* untrustworthy, he would have raised objections to her plan.

'And,' Vernon added, 'it will provide an explanation for you if…when…we catch up with Henry Mannington. For he, too, will know you are not my nephew. However, for the sake of respectability when I reserve our rooms, you shall remain my nephew and I shall remain Mr Boyton. I do not imagine the Royal Hotel will actually approve of my…er…by-blow mingling with their other guests. We shall keep that story as a last resort.'

'By-blow?' Thea enquired innocently as they headed back to the hotel.

'It is slang for…oh!' Vernon broke off when he caught sight of Thea's expression. 'You little tease,' he said and reached out.

She braced herself for the twist as he took her lobe between finger and thumb but, instead, he tugged gently, and she felt an answering tug deep inside her core. Their gazes fused and her heart lurched as she saw the amusement fade from his eyes to be replaced by an inner fire as heat flared between them. Then fear reared up to overpower her sudden impulse to step closer and to accept his unspoken invitation.

I must never forget Jasper Connor. Men can't be trusted. And Vernon… Dear God! He's the son of a duke. I could never mean anything to a man like him.

She jerked her ear from his grasp. 'Ow!' She glared at him as she rubbed at her ear, taking refuge in anger.

'Do not pretend that hurt, you minx,' Vernon muttered. 'What are you—?'

'*I* am attempting to keep up the appearance of being your nephew,' Thea snapped. 'We do not know who might be watching.'

'Hmph.'

But a sideways glance showed he had taken her point and Thea breathed a little easier that she had averted that awkward moment.

They had by now arrived back at the hotel and they walked through the door into a large reception hall. A servant took their hats. Vernon nudged Thea and leaned down to whisper in her ear, 'It is fortunate I tidied up that unkempt mop of yours, is it not? At least if I do see an acquaintance you will not now shame me by being seen in company with such a ragamuffin.'

His teasing reinforced her conviction she had been right to quash the desire that had flared between them. He had shrugged her rebuttal away as though it were nothing. And no doubt it *was* nothing to him. He was totally unmoved, whilst *she*... the bindings around her breasts all of a sudden made it hard to breathe. Vernon's mention of that haircut revived the memory of how strangely intimate it had been and Thea suppressed a shiver as she recalled the effort it had taken to sit still whilst he moved around her, his body brushing against hers, his fingers threading through her curls, moving across her scalp. Never had she imagined a simple haircut could be so...so...*unsettling*.

'Fortunate indeed,' she hissed. 'For however would your reputation otherwise survive?'

A man dressed in a tailcoat and satin knee breeches approached, and bowed. 'Good afternoon, sirs. My name is Parkes, the concierge. Whatever your requirements, I shall use my best endeavours to fulfil them.'

'Good afternoon, Parkes,' Vernon said and Thea

marvelled at the change that came over him. *No one* could mistake him for other than a highly born gentleman and yet just a few minutes ago he had been joking like a schoolboy. 'My name is Boyton. I should like two bedchambers, if you please, for my nephew and myself. I trust our bags have been sent in from the stables?'

'Indeed they have, sir.' Parkes clicked his fingers and a footman came running, scooping their saddlebags from behind a desk. 'I shall show you to your rooms myself, Mr Boyton.'

'Thank you, but maybe later? Young Theo and I are in dire need of refreshment after our journey. Have you a coffee room?'

'But of course.' Parkes bowed. 'This way, sirs.' He showed them through a nearby door into an empty room. 'I shall send the maidservant in with coffee.'

'Thank you. Before you go, Parkes…' Vernon selected a table by a window that overlooked the street and sat down, 'I had rather hoped to meet an acquaintance of mine here. Mr Henry Mannington. I believe he often frequents your establishment?'

'Mr Mannington? Yes, he is known to me, sir, but I have received no word of an impending visit.'

'That is a pity, for I have some business I most particularly wish to discuss with him. Do you recall his last visit?'

'It was last week some time, sir. Thursday? Friday? I shall have to consult the hotel register to be certain of the day.'

'If you would be so kind,' Vernon murmured.

As soon as the door closed behind Parkes, Thea said, 'Why do you ask only of your cousin? What of Daniel?'

Green eyes contemplated Thea, bringing heat to her cheeks. She squirmed slightly, then said, 'Well, you cannot blame me for…for…'

'For being suspicious?'

That is exactly what she meant, but put as baldly as that, it sounded…rude. Shame mixed with defiance. She had a right to challenge him, did she not? Otherwise, he would never explain anything of his actions to her and she would be left to trail in his wake in ignorance.

Vernon placed both hands flat on the table and sighed.

'I ask first about Henry because it is his patronage of this hotel that prompted your brother's visits. As I said outside…we already know that Daniel has been here and we know he was searching for Henry. We know that he has disappeared. Henry is our only link to what might have happened. Ergo… our main objective must be to track down Henry and to find out what he knows.' He glanced at the door, then reached across the table and touched cool fingers to Thea's cheek. 'There is no underhand motive, Thea. I promise.'

At a noise from the direction of the door, his

hand slipped from her cheek. A maid carrying a tray set with a coffee pot and two cups entered the room, with Parkes on her heels.

Parkes came straight to the point. 'Mr Mannington was our overnight guest on Thursday of last week, Mr Boyton.'

Thursday! Thea forgot any embarrassment at revealing her suspicions of Vernon. *Daniel must have seen Mannington. Talked to him, possibly.*

She strove to mask her excitement in front of Parkes and the maid, who was preparing to pour their coffee.

'Thursday?' Vernon said. 'Now there is a coincidence. I believe a friend of mine was also a guest on that night. Mr Markham? Daniel Markham?'

Parkes paused, frowning in thought. 'No,' he said eventually. 'I am afraid I do not recall that name, sir.'

Thea's spirits plunged. *If Daniel did not come here, where on earth* did *he go?*

'I must be mistaken,' Vernon said in an unconcerned tone. 'I thought he had visited here frequently in recent weeks. Now, if you will pass on Mannington's direction to me, Parkes, I shall call on him myself. He will not wish to miss this opportunity, that I can tell you.'

Thea's attention was caught by the rattle of china. She looked and the maid's knuckles were white on the handle of the coffee pot as she poured Thea's coffee. Thea leaned back in her chair and caught Vernon's eye, flicking her gaze to the maid. He nodded imperceptibly. So he had noticed her reaction, too. Thea's stomach tightened in anticipation.

'I regret I cannot oblige with Mr Mannington's direction, sir,' Parkes was saying. 'I only know that he lives on the far side of Worcester, towards Great Malvern. He has business interests in Manchester and the Royal Hotel is the perfect place for him to stay when he must travel north.'

'It is an ideal location,' Vernon said. 'Now, I must allow you to return to your duties, Parkes, but before you go, does the name Willingdale mean anything to you?'

The maid, on the verge of leaving the room, gasped audibly and Parkes beckoned her back inside.

'Well?' Parkes said. 'What do you have to say?'

The girl met Vernon's gaze with a boldness that made Thea itch to slap her.

'My name is Willingdale, sir. Alice Willingdale.'

I might have known. Thea did not trust herself to look at the girl, who she was now convinced was no better than she ought to be. Daniel had always been something of a flirt, so she should not be surprised he would target serving wenches to find out information.

Vernon stood up and crossed the room to the door, which he opened. 'Thank you for your assistance, Mr Parkes. I should be most grateful if

you will ensure we are not disturbed. And…ah…'
he reached into his pocket and withdrew a coin
'…please take this in recompense for Alice here
taking a short break from her duties.'

As soon as Parkes left the room, Vernon ushered
Alice back to the table and bade her sit, which she
did, a calculating light in her eye.

'Tell us about Daniel, Alice. When and where
did you meet?'

'I don't know no Daniel.'

Thea leaned forward. 'You are lying. I saw your
reaction when Ver…my uncle…asked Parkes about
him.'

Scornful blue eyes turned on Thea. 'Well, that
just shows what a know-nothing *you* are 'cause I
don't know no Daniel and that's that.'

'Theo.'

The warning in that one word silenced Thea.
She had been about to launch into a scathing put
down, but Vernon's intervention reminded her she
was meant to be a fourteen-year-old lad, not a ma-
ture woman confronted by a saucy servant. She
clenched her jaw tight at the smug smile on Alice's
face. Then Vernon jerked his head, indicating she
should leave him to talk to Alice alone. She narrowed her eyes at him, folding her arms across
her chest as she leaned back in her chair. A single
twitch of his brow revealed Vernon's opinion.

He moved his chair closer to Alice, leaning towards her, capturing her gaze with his.

'But you *do* know Henry Mannington.' He smiled into her face. 'I was watching you. You reacted when I asked Parkes for his direction. Will you not tell me what you know of him?'

Alice blushed, lowering her lashes and peeping coquettishly at Vernon as she returned his smile.

'I don't know much about him, sir. Only the same as Mr Parkes told you. But I do...' She glanced towards Thea, then hunched a shoulder as she shifted around in her chair, turning her back to Thea and fully facing Vernon. She lowered her voice and Thea had to strain to hear her words. 'I do remember another man asking the same questions about Mr Mannington. *He* visited me several days in a row, looking for the gentleman, but he *weren't*...' she shot a look of disdain over her shoulder '...called Daniel. That I can say for certain.'

'I knew you were a smart girl, the minute I set eyes on you,' Vernon murmured.

He reached into his pocket and withdrew yet another coin.

What is it with him and money? He's forever throwing it at folk like it's worth nothing.

'What was his name? Can you remember?'

''Course I can remember.' The coin disappeared into Alice's apron pocket. 'It were Charles Leyton.'

Thea gasped, then clapped her hand across her mouth, worried she might put the girl off. Charles Leyton was the name of their manager at the glass works. She tried to signal to Vernon, miming he should ask Alice what this Leyton looked like.

'Very well done,' Vernon said. 'Can you describe him to me?'

'Why do you want to know?' she demanded, suddenly suspicious.

Vernon leaned closer to her and placed one hand on her arm as he said, 'It really is better you do not know. I should hate to put you in danger. Describe him to me and then forget we ever had this conversation.' He dropped his voice to a whisper. 'That is the only way to stay safe.'

'Oh! Well…he was tall…as tall as you, sir.' Her voice trembled slightly. 'And he was handsome as handsome can be, with lovely dark hair and big brown eyes and a *lovely* smile.' She sighed. 'And he were a proper gentleman, sir, that he was.'

'Did he visit you on horseback, or did he drive?'

'Horseback, sir. He rode a huge grey horse, sir. Oh, he were as dashing as any cavalryman.'

Thea's breath caught as her heart thumped against her ribs. She itched to fire questions at the girl, but knew she was wise to leave her to Vernon. She felt her brows twitch together as she mentally compared Vernon's way with women with her brother's and she barely contained her *hmph* of disgust.

Manipulative reprobates, the pair of them.

Chapter Ten

Vernon risked a quick glance at Thea's face. She was scowling, looking like she was ready to explode. He sensed the effort it cost her to sit still and stay quiet.

'Now, I need you think carefully, Alice. You told me this man, this Charles Leyton, asked questions about Henry Mannington. Did they ever meet, do you know?'

'Not here, sir.'

'Then where?'

She shrank back and he softened his tone. 'I did not mean to alarm you, Alice. Do you know where they met?'

'No. All I know is Charles… Mr Leyton, that is…was really angry. He got here last Thursday only to find Mr Mannington had been and gone. Mr M. were in a carriage and left heading for his home, so Charles…he just leapt on his horse and followed. He was about two hours behind.' She leaned closer to Vernon. 'I never seen him so angry, sir, and I never seen him since, neither, so it's no good you asking me where they met, because I don't know.'

Vernon sat back. 'Thank you, Alice. You have been a great help and I…we…are most grateful. You may return to your duties now. And please ask Mr Parkes to attend me here…we shall not, after all, be staying the night, but we shall need some luncheon before we leave.'

He barely noticed the tinge of disappointment in Alice's eyes. He only had eyes for the huge smile that lit Thea's face at the news they would soon be back on the road, following Daniel's trail. As soon as the door closed behind Alice, Thea bounded from her chair and began to pace the room.

'Do you think we should hire a post-chaise?'

She halted mid-stride and directed a serious look at Vernon, who had steeled himself to remain seated when she stood.

'We could use fresh horses along the way. It would get us there quicker.'

'Get us where?' Vernon followed her with his eyes as she began once more to pace, her agitation clear.

She stopped again. 'Why, to Worcester, of course.' She tipped her head to one side, staring at him, wide-eyed and eager. 'How many miles is it to Worcester? Do you know?'

Behind her, the door had opened to admit Parkes. 'It is twenty-eight miles, Master Boyton,' he said.

Thea whirled to face him. 'Twenty-eight? Why, that is not so far, if we—'

'Let us discuss this later, Theo,' Vernon interrupted. 'I am sure Parkes is busy. Our plans can hold no interest for him, other than the fact that we shall not, after all, require overnight accommodation.

'I shall, of course,' he added, smoothly, responding to the slightest firming of Parkes's lips, 'recompense you for the inconvenience.'

Parkes bowed. 'Very good, sir, I shall ensure your bags are brought back downstairs immediately. Alice said you would like to eat luncheon? I have come to inform you that food is being served in the dining room, if you care to follow me?'

It was gone two by the time they set out once again upon their journey, taking the Worcester road out of Birmingham. Thea sent Star ahead of Vernon on Warrior, her back stiff with her displeasure. Vernon sighed and nudged Warrior into a trot until they came alongside Thea.

'*Why* could we not hire a post-chaise?' She cast him a sidelong, accusatory look. 'You are happy enough to throw your money at every person you have dealings with, yet you baulk at spending on something so beneficial. Why?'

'You believe *that* is why I refused to hire a post-chaise? Because it would cost too much?'

Astounded, Vernon stared at her profile. Why

was she so distrustful? Always ready to assume the worst of his motives? He'd had no opportunity to explain his reasoning to her…the busy dining room at the hotel had been too public for such a discussion.

'It is either that, or that you are reluctant, now it comes to it, to discover your cousin's part in some manner of villainy.'

Vernon reached across and halted Star. 'What is your plan, then, Dotty? What action do *you* say we should take?'

'If we hire a post-chaise we could reach Worcester before nightfall and then we can…'

She hesitated, her lips pursed and her brows bunched under the peak of her cap. Vernon saw the moment she began to doubt her plan.

'Hmph.'

She looked so disgruntled and so adorable he longed to reach out and gather her up and give her a big hug. He forbore to tease her, seeing how annoyed she was with herself.

'Why did I not think of that to start with?' The corners of her mouth drooped.

'Because you are always in such a hurry. You do not think through all the implications of what you want to do. I'll hazard a guess that you are not a good chess player.'

'*Chess*? I cannot abide the game. I always seem to…'

'Lose?'

She pouted, then laughed. 'Daniel always says I haven't the patience to play it well. I dare say I am a little…hasty…at times.'

She met his eyes with a silent apology. Then her frown flickered again.

'It is the same as when you rode from Stourbridge to Harborne,' she said, accusing again. 'You wish to stop and enquire at every inn we pass.'

'We *must* call at every inn if we are to establish what has happened,' Vernon said. 'Do you not see? All we know is that Henry Mannington lives somewhere to the south-west of Worcester, that he left here in his carriage on Thursday morning and that Daniel followed him, on horseback, two hours later. Yes, it will be slower, not only because of the need to stop at every inn, but also because we cannot ride too hard in this weather for the horses' sake, not to mention our own. But we are like to miss something if we bowl past in a fast-moving post-chaise. This way, we shall truly be following in Daniel's footsteps.'

'Or in Bullet's hoof-steps,' Thea said, with a flicker of a smile, 'if there is such a word.'

Vernon laughed, reached out and touched the tip of her nose. 'Are we friends again?'

'Friends,' she said, with a rueful smile.

The sun beat down on them from the afternoon sky as they continued on their way towards Worcester. Time passed quickly and with much laughter as Vernon taught Thea some of the slang words common in the rougher areas of London.

Thea had begun this journey determined to show no interest in the exclusive world to which Vernon belonged, but she couldn't curb her curiosity. She was fascinated by the contrast between the world in which he lived—rich, opulent, indulgent—and his descriptions of some of the poorer areas and the rookeries, where the poorest of the poor—and, from what she could gather, the criminals—scraped an existence.

In return, Thea told him tales of her world and the realities of life not only for manufacturers like her family, but also for the men who worked for them. She also told him of the hardships caused by trade embargoes, not only for manufactories like Stour Crystal, but also for the many ordinary hard-working men and women who lived in the area between Stourbridge and Birmingham and who made nails and chains at workshops in their own back yards. Something like a quarter of their output used to be sent to America, and the growing hostility between the two countries had forced many people to turn to poor relief to survive.

Vernon's fascination with her stories made Thea careless and she only just stopped herself confiding in him about her family's misfortune at the hands of Jasper Connor—she could not bear to be the object of his pity.

They rode on, stopping, as before, at every inn

but no one knew—or would admit to knowing—
Henry Mannington. No one had noticed a man of
Daniel's description riding a light grey horse last
Thursday. As the heat built, they discarded their
jackets, taking full advantage of the filtered shade
cast by roadside trees where possible but, when
they had no choice but to ride in the open, Thea
tilted her cap down until her eyes were almost covered.

At Vernon's questioning glance, she said, 'The
sun brings out my freckles. I try to wear a bonnet
with a large peak in the summer. This cap does
little to protect my skin.'

'I had not thought you a woman to be concerned
about such minor matters as freckles,' Vernon said.
'Besides...' he reached to her chin and turned her
face to his '...your freckles are quite fetching.'

Her skin tingled at his touch, and she looked
away. 'Freckles,' she replied, 'are most unfashion-
able.'

'Fashion? Bah! Fashion is merely a whim, based
on a few persons' opinions.'

Thea laughed at him. '*You* say that? You with
your coat from Weston and your boots from Hoby?
What a plumper.' She frowned. 'Plumper? Is that
the right word?'

It was one of the slang words Vernon had taught
her. She was almost sure a plumper meant a lie.

'It is,' he said, with a grin. Then he sobered. 'But

my usual attire, I shall have you know, is not a matter of fashion, but of dressing respectfully.'

'Respectfully? Respectful to whom?'

'To myself. To my peers. Fashion can be extreme—you should see some of the fops and the affectations of their dress. You would laugh, I promise you, to see them with their garish waistcoats adorned with fobs and seals, and their shirt points so high they cannot turn their heads. And many men—even moderately sensible men—wear padding at the shoulders and at the calves to exaggerate their shape and their muscle.'

Thea slid a sly sideways glance at Vernon's broad shoulders and then dropped her gaze to his calf, encased in his tight-fitting boot.

'Is *that* what it is?' she said. 'Padding?'

Vernon flicked her knee, laughing. 'Brat! I have no need for artificial help! No. Brummell has the right idea—simple and elegant. Unremarkable, even. A man should never aspire to be noticed for his clothing.'

'Do ladies indulge in such excesses as the fops?'

'Amongst the ladies of the *ton*, fashions are not so extreme, but they are fickle and they change every Season, necessitating the purchase of an entire new wardrobe if a lady does not wish to appear a pitiful creature in the eyes of her acquaintance.' He sounded almost mocking.

'Why do you continue to attend such events if you hold them in disdain?'

He shrugged. 'It is not disdain, precisely, it is what one does. To tell you the truth, I haven't thought about it much until now. You—' he flashed a smile in her direction '—have forced me to see my life through your eyes.'

'And your conclusion?'

He shrugged again. 'I have led a privileged life, there is no doubt of it. I will return to it willingly— I may jest about certain aspects of it but, overall, it is a good life and I am aware of my good fortune. But this journey…' He looked around, as though for inspiration. 'This journey and your stories have heightened my awareness of the injustices in society.'

'Do many in your position take on charitable work?'

'Many people take pride in donating to charity. They hold fund-raising events and so forth, but when you have wealth that is no hardship—you attend a ball and pay some money, you enjoy yourself and barely notice the loss of the money. That is not the same as actually *doing* something.'

He fell silent, staring at the road ahead.

'I have a role model within my own family,' he said eventually. 'Leo's eldest son, Dominic, Lord Avon—he is the patron of an orphan asylum and school. He is only two-and-twenty, and I confess he puts me to shame. My own nephew.' He shook himself out of his pensive mood, turned his head and winked at Thea. 'My *real* nephew, of course.'

They continued, riding at an alternating walk and trot, unfailingly enquiring after Daniel and Henry Mannington at each and every inn they passed, to no avail. Dusk began to fall and, as they crested a rise in the road, the welcome sight of a wayside inn appeared.

'We shall stop there for the night,' Vernon said.

He pretended not to hear Thea's soft sigh of relief. He was stiff and exhausted, so God knew how poor Thea must feel. He swung from Warrior's back, wincing at his aching muscles and, after a quick look round to make sure they were unobserved, he helped Thea from the saddle, his hands lingering on her slender waist, as he savoured the slide of her body down his and the tantalising brush of her peachy bottom against his groin. He stepped back, not wanting her to feel his arousal, but he found it a wrench to tear his hands from her waist.

The more time he spent with her, the more he... *liked* her. Not just wanted her, as a woman, but actually liked her and enjoyed her company. And he delighted in just watching her: she fascinated him.

He shook all such thoughts from his head as they led the horses into the stable yard, delivering them into the hands of the ostler, who pointed them to a side door, through which they gained access to the dim interior of the inn. The innkeeper—thin-faced and spindle-legged but with a pot belly—came to greet them, wiping his hands on a grimy towel.

'Welcome, sir, and to you too, young sir.' He

bowed. 'Tom Jackson at your service. It is good to see you on this fine evening. What is your pleasure?'

'Good evening, Jackson. My name is Boyton, this is my nephew Theo. We should like two rooms for the night, if you please.'

'Ah.' Jackson's smile faded. 'Apologies, Mr Boyton, but we only have the three bedchambers here, and two are already taken…unless you do not object to sharing the room?'

Vernon's heart sank as the innkeeper regarded him hopefully. He dared not even glance at Thea. He could not think how they might contrive—any solution he came up with threatened to reveal their masquerade. A man such as Vernon Boyton would hardly allow his young nephew to sleep indoors in comfort whilst he bedded down in the stable and the opposite arrangement was unthinkable. He would not expose Thea to such a risk.

'In which direction are you travelling, sir?'

'Towards Worcester,' Vernon replied. 'How far is the next inn along this road?'

'A good five miles.'

A hand tugged at Vernon's sleeve. 'We can share the bedchamber, Uncle,' Thea said in her husky voice. 'I promise I shall not complain when you snore.'

Chapter Eleven

Vernon glared down at Thea's innocent expression, gritting his teeth at the twinkle in her hazel eyes.

Little minx, baiting a man when there's no chance to reply.

His thoughts charged ahead with the possibilities of her suggestion, colouring in the details in lurid detail: him…and her…together all night long…in a room, with a bed.

Then, quietly, she added, 'I am weary, sir', and he could hear the truth of it in her voice, see it in the slump of her shoulders.

He recalled his own thoughts upon arrival—how tired he was and how much more Thea must be suffering for their long day, yet not a word of complaint had passed her lips. And here he was, a supposed gentleman, imagining her seduction. This would not do. Thea was under his protection, he could not take advantage of her. The innkeeper awaited his decision and Vernon was conscious of Thea watching him, now anxious.

'A single bedchamber will be acceptable, Jackson. Thank you.'

'And dinner, sir?'

Vernon glanced again at Thea. The less they saw of the other guests the better.

'Have you a private parlour we might use? We are both exhausted and we'd appreciate some peace and quiet.'

'Of course, sir. I shall show you to your bedchamber and send the girl up with hot water. Follow me.'

The room was not large, but there was a deep armchair by the fire as well as a large soft bed. Vernon dropped their bags at the foot of the bed.

'I shall be comfortable enough in the chair,' he said, without looking at Thea. He had never in his life felt quite as awkward with a female in a bedchamber. Not even his first time. Every movement felt contrived. 'You may take the bed.' Even his voice sounded strained.

'I thank you. I have to confess, it is all I can do not to flop down upon it now and go straight to sleep.' She crossed the room to him, peering up into his face. 'I can tell this arrangement makes you uncomfortable,' she said. 'But I trust you. If I did not, I should never have suggested it.'

Vernon had to smile at the earnestness in her voice and on her face but he wondered at her poise in this situation. Most of the females he knew would be either throwing themselves at him by now, or shrinking away with maidenly giggles. As far as Thea's reaction went, he might as well be Daniel.

Is that it? Does she view me as a brother?

There were times—a certain look, a particular reaction from her—when he had thought otherwise, but now...? He could not quite fathom her and he was unused to feeling so unsure of himself around a woman. However, he could do no more now than follow her lead, even though he still could not stop one dark corner of his mind from speculating quite how she hid her breasts so effectively. He would follow her lead and remain in the part of teasing uncle. He tweaked one of her curls.

'I beg you will not say as much to anyone else,' he said. 'I have a reputation to uphold.'

Her brows rose. 'A reputation for what, may I enquire? Is that your way of informing me you are considered something of a ladies' man in society?'

She grinned at him, then spun away to gaze out the window as a knock at the door heralded the arrival of their washing water. Vernon waited until the maid had placed the jug on the washstand and left them alone again. He badly needed some space to compose himself.

'I shall leave you in privacy for ten minutes whilst I check the horses. Then you can go downstairs and wait for me to join you in the parlour.'

He did not wait for her reply, but left the room

and ran down the stairs. He quickly checked the horses—both comfortable in their stalls and munching hay—and then he returned to the inn, going into the bar. He had time for a quick beer before going back upstairs. A solitary customer sat in the bar and, upon finding out that Vernon was a fellow guest and traveller, he introduced himself as Wigbert Pooley, a salesman. Vernon did not linger, but soon excused himself and went upstairs to knock on the bedchamber door. It opened, and Thea—dressed as Theo, her red curls framing her face like a devilish halo—appeared.

'I shall leave you to freshen yourself,' she said and walked past him towards the stairs.

Vernon stripped off his shirt and unstrapped the bandage Thea had wrapped around his chest the previous evening. He twisted this way and that, examining it in the looking glass. It looked as though it was healing well, with no sign of swelling or redness, and there was no pain. He had got away lightly.

Ten minutes later, he opened the door into the private parlour and cursed beneath his breath. The room was empty. He pivoted on his heel and strode to the bar, stopping short on the threshold at the sight of Thea—colour high and her small fists clenched by her sides—confronting Wigbert Pooley, who was bent double clutching at his privates.

Rage pumped Vernon's blood as relief replaced

fear on Thea's face at the sight of him. He didn't have to be a mind reader to guess Pooley—a beefy, middle-aged man with pendulous jowls—must have propositioned her in some way to provoke such a reaction. In two strides he crossed the room and hauled the man up by his lapels.

'What the hell are you doing with my nephew, Pooley?' he snarled, thrusting his face close to the other man's.

'Nay, sir.' The man's bulbous blue eyes were watering. ''Twas naught but...' he gasped for breath '...a bit of friendly banter. Ain't that so, m'boy?'

Vernon relaxed a little upon hearing him call Thea a boy. For a moment there, he had feared she had been recognised as a female.

'I bought him a beer 'n' all,' the man went on disjointedly. He groaned, feeling tenderly in the area of his wedding tackle. Vernon moved to shield Thea from the sight. 'Paid for out me own pocket. Man gets lonely on the road. Bit of friendly fun never harmed nobody.'

'Uncle.' Thea's hand was on his sleeve, her voice urgent. 'Leave him. There's no harm done. Our food will be served by now.'

Pooley attempted a chuckle. 'Typical lad, eh. Always thinking of his belly.' He straightened with a groan and then waved a hand at Vernon. 'Go on. No harm done, like the lad says.'

With a growl of disgust, Vernon shoved the man

aside and ushered Thea from the bar and into their private parlour. He shut the door behind them.

'I thought I told you to wait in *here* for me? What the devil persuaded you to go into a public bar?'

'I am capable of making my own decisions,' she said, elevating her nose. 'Jackson told me that man travels all around the Worcester area, taking orders and then returning with the goods. He calls at shops and houses alike. I thought he might know Henry Mannington.'

'You should have waited for me,' Vernon growled. 'Another time you might not be so fortunate.'

Thea grimaced. 'Do you *know*…he did not even realise I was female? And, even though he thought me a boy, still he said such things—'

Her mouth snapped shut as the door opened and two maids came in carrying salvers with roast meats and fish, pies and vegetables. Only after they had retreated, and the door had closed behind them, did Thea continue.

'*Disgusting* things.' Her cheeks were pink, but whether with embarrassment or indignation Vernon was unsure. Probably a combination of the two.

'So you kicked him?'

She nodded and his balls tightened in involuntary reflex. He could not be certain, but he thought he caught a smile flicker across her face and he shivered. Another involuntary reaction.

'Where did you learn such a move?'

'Daniel,' she said, shortly. 'He told me if ever I felt threatened, that was the quickest way to discourage a man.'

'Quick and extremely effective. Remind me to show you some further defensive moves as well. You never know when they might come in handy. Now, let us eat. I am ravenous.'

Vernon pulled out a chair for Thea, who hesitated and then sat, murmuring, 'Thank you.'

As soon as Vernon moved away to sit opposite her, Thea said, 'You must take care. If you show me such courtesies in private it will not be long before you forget yourself in public.'

Vernon sighed. 'You are right. I must pay more attention.'

They helped themselves to food and began to eat. Thea kept her attention firmly upon her plate, but Vernon could not prevent his gaze from straying in her direction, time after time. It was driving him wild, watching her slowly chew her food, the tip of her pink tongue darting out from time to time to lick a drop of gravy from her lips. What would he not give for a chance to kiss her…an opportunity to taste and explore her luscious mouth?

He tried to divert his thoughts to different subjects. He could do without feeding this craving—the night to come was already playing havoc with his senses. His brain kept insisting he was a gentleman, but his libido had other ideas. It was fortunate that Thea appeared to have put aside any awareness of him as a man or who knew what might happen? She chatted to him as easily and unaffectedly as though he were a brother. Or, even more lowering, a favourite uncle.

He came to a sense of his surroundings with a start. His mind had wandered and he had been eating mindlessly, ignoring his dining companion. She did not appear offended by his lack of manners, however—she had almost finished eating, her attention on her plate, her brow creased in a frown. Vernon reminded himself of their earlier conversation.

'Did you have an opportunity to question Pooley about Mannington?' he asked Thea.

'I did.' Her upper lip curled. 'He claimed to know the Worcester area well, but he has never heard of Henry Mannington. It was an utter waste of time. I should never have bothered with him.'

'Well, I hope you have learned your lesson.'

Thea glowered at Vernon. 'Learned my *lesson*? What lesson might that be?'

'The lesson, my dear Dotty, is that although you may be *less* vulnerable as a youth than a woman, you are still not *in*vulnerable.'

'I dealt with him, did I not? I did not wait for you to rescue me. I am not some lily-livered society lady to swoon at the slightest provocation.'

And there it was again. A challenge, and a hint of scorn, as though every member of the aristocracy was capable of nothing more than a life of idle pleasure. He would not rise to it, suspecting she said such things to cover a deep-rooted feeling of inferiority, to convince him—and herself—that she and people like her had value. And yet he no longer needed convincing of that. The stories she had told him about her world and that of the people who lived around her…he could not help but contrast the toughness of their lives with the ease of his and for the first time in his life he felt an urge to get involved in politics and to try to make a difference in the world.

'Put your claws away, Thea, I am aware you have courage, but you still cannot face every challenge head on. And nor should you, when you have me by your side.' Her expression remained stormy. 'Come, you know it makes sense.' He covered her hand with his. It twitched, but she did not pull away. 'If I am constantly worried about what you are up to, I shall not be able to concentrate on finding Daniel. And that is our main concern, is it not?'

She bit her lower lip, her brows still bunched. 'Is that *your* main concern, Vernon? Or are you more interested in finding your cousin? What will you do after we have tracked him down?'

He sat back, removing his hand from hers. 'Is that what you believe? That I will abandon the search for Daniel if I find Henry?'

'No. Yes. I do not know. If I am honest…' she captured his gaze, searching '…I have wondered more than once about your motivations. You owe me nothing and you do not even know Daniel, so it is natural to question why you have put yourself out to help us.'

Vernon drummed his fingers on the table, thinking how to explain.

'In a strange way, I am enjoying it. And that is thanks to you.'

'Me?'

The intimacy of dining *à deux* made him speak more honestly than he might otherwise.

'Yes. You. You have not complained…not once…about your discomfort. You have borne the rigours of this journey with a smile and you have helped to ensure the time has passed more quickly.' He captured her gaze. 'I have enjoyed your company, Thea.'

She stilled, her eyes searching his. Then she dropped her gaze and stood up.

'I am weary. I wish to retire.'

Vernon rose to his feet. 'I shall allow you to get settled before I join you.'

An unfortunate choice of words and wholly inappropriate given their circumstances—words that stirred his imagination and fired his pulse. A flush of pink coloured Thea's cheeks, suggesting she, too, found his phrasing embarrassing.

'Goodnight.'

She avoided eye contact and slipped from the room, leaving Vernon to kick himself for such unaccustomed gaucheness.

* * *

Thea climbed the stairs, one hand clutching at the banister, the other pressed to her chest in an attempt to steady the erratic thump of her heart. Last night had been difficult enough, knowing Vernon—a stranger…a deliciously *attractive* stranger—had been sleeping in the adjoining bedchamber with only a door between them. Tonight, though… Vernon might no longer be such a stranger, but that fact made her insides quake even more violently. They would be in the same room. All night.

She paused on the top stair, considering the past two days. How swiftly the time had appeared to pass, yet she felt as though she had known Vernon for much, much longer. And, as desperately as she fought it, she could not deny that the more time she spent in his company, the more she liked him…as a friend and, increasingly, as a man. A charming, intelligent, fascinating and kind man who—every time she felt his astute green gaze upon her—aroused the most wonderful and exhilarating swirl of anticipation deep in the pit of her belly.

Anticipation that was unwelcome. It was hard enough to trust Vernon with finding Daniel, but she must fight her growing feelings for him. She must protect her heart.

I can never trust another man. Not after Jasper.

She entered their bedchamber and made haste to

undress, breathing a sigh of relief as she unwound the binding from her breasts, massaging them with her hands to ease them. She crossed to the wash-stand and used a washcloth to bathe the area, sigh-ing with pleasure as the cool water soothed her itchy, sweaty skin, reaching around with difficulty to cleanse her back, too. The heat had increased her discomfort, but she dared not abandon the binding— her breasts might be small but, if someone was to catch sight of her at the wrong angle, her charade would be exposed and...

She shuddered as she pictured the ensuing scan-dal. Since they had left the Royal Hotel, during the lulls in conversation, she had found the time to look back upon her decision to follow Vernon. Her ini-tial certainty that she need fear no repercussions if her escapade was uncovered had soon faded. The truth, she knew, was more complicated than that. It was not so much that she risked censure and being shunned—she did not have much time for pleasure and rarely attended their neighbours' parties, de-spite being invited. But that episode with Pooley had confirmed her worries about what conclusions would be drawn about her morals and her charac-ter if her conduct ever became known. Those con-clusions, she was certain, would lead many men to think her little better than a whore and they would not hesitate to proposition her at every opportunity. She had seen it before with women who acquired a reputation. They became *'fair game'*.

Which led her to wonder about Vernon's true opinion of her. Over the past day or so she had detected a certain gleam in his eyes, a gleam she had recognised as the interest of a man in a woman. Did he, too, now view her as fair game? Had her impulsive action in following him, and her subsequent insistence upon accompanying him, led him to believe she would willingly share his bed? She hoped not. She hoped he would remain the gentleman, but she had nevertheless redoubled her efforts to conceal her growing fascination with him. She aimed to play the part of his nephew so well he would forget she was female.

She completed her ablutions and scrubbed her skin dry before delving into her saddlebag for the shift she wore at night. She donned it and then brushed her hair until it shone, tamping down her regret as she looked at her reflection in the mirror, mourning the loss of her ringlets even though she had cursed them most of her life. She tried to ignore the wash of heat at the memory of Vernon's fingers running through her curls as he tidied up Thea's choppy effort, consoling herself that her short hair was all the better to continue the illusion she was a boy, but her heart still ached at the sight.

As she cleaned her teeth there was a light tap at the door.

'Wait a minute,' she called.

She rushed to the bed and jumped in, pulling the covers up to her chin. 'You may come in.'

Vernon sauntered in—tall, assured and with a wicked gleam in his eye that stole her breath.

'I don't know, nevvy,' he said, with a wink and a grin. 'For a young lad you are surprisingly bashful… worse than a bride on her wedding night.'

Thea relaxed at his teasing. She had feared he might use his charm and attempt to seduce her, but his manner reassured. He was telling her, without words, that she had nothing to fear. Perversely, that provoked a nagging doubt about her desirability and that doubt was followed swiftly by irritation at her own inconsistency. One minute she was fretting he might think her a female of low morals and try to take advantage, the next she was upset that he did not find her attractive enough to seduce.

'Now, I have no wish to make you blush,' Vernon continued as he removed his jacket, 'but I have no intention of sleeping fully clothed tonight so I suggest you look away.' He turned to face Thea, reaching for the knot in his neckcloth. 'Unless, of course, you wish to ogle my chest again?'

Thea's cheeks burned. 'You flatter yourself, my lord,' she growled.

Vernon chuckled, aggravating her more.

'Your chest holds absolutely no interest for me. You forget I have a brother and have lived my life seeing the men working in the fields.'

'My apologies.' Vernon sketched a bow. 'I had not realised you were quite so *au fait* with the male form. I need not worry about offending your sensibilities then.'

He tossed his neckcloth on to a chair and reached for the fastening of his breeches.

Thea tore her gaze from the auburn curls visible in the V-shaped opening at the neck of his shirt. With a loud *hmph*, she threw herself on to her side to face the wall and gritted her teeth against the devilish chuckle from the other side of the room. She screwed her eyes tight shut, but her imagination supplied plenty of delicious images to accompany the sounds she heard—the swish of cloth, footsteps and then the splash of water. Unable to help herself, she opened her eyes and peeped over her shoulder.

Vernon stood at the washstand, shirtless, his back to her as he bent over the bowl. The candlelight danced across unblemished skin and she watched, fascinated by the play of muscles across his shoulders and back as he continued his ablutions. Her hands itched to touch, to stroke, to discover if his skin was as smooth as it looked. His breeches stretched tight, outlining taut buttocks— thrust temptingly in her direction—and long, lean thighs and her mouth dried as her skin heated. A thrilling sense of anticipation swirled in her belly, then slowed, arrowing in to the juncture of her thighs, provoking a strange restlessness.

An insistent need.

Thea resisted the urge to move, to turn on to

her back, to push aside the covers, to extend her arms and invite him to hold her. How would it feel to throw aside morals and caution and pride, and follow that craving? She lay motionless, still watching as Vernon hummed a tune she did not recognise under his breath, seemingly perfectly relaxed.

Desire.

She recognised it instinctively although she had never before experienced it. Not even with Jasper. *Particularly* not with Jasper. The thought of her former betrothed, her vicious betrayer, had the same effect as though Vernon had snatched up that basin of water and dashed it into her face. She faced the wall again, bending her neck so her face was buried in the covers and only the top of her head would be visible should he glance her way.

She counted inside her head, willing him to hurry, to snuff the candles and to settle down in the chair, upon which Thea had spread one of the blankets from the bed. There were several minutes of silence.

What is he doing? Is he looking at me?

The thought made her feel all…*fluttery* inside. She would not look. If she looked…if their eyes should meet…

The bed dipped and her pulse raced even as her body froze. Her hair stirred and then his hand was upon her head.

'Are you asleep, Thea?'

Thea! Not Dotty! Her heart quailed. She *needed* him to be teasing and provocative. Not kind.

'No.' She kept her face buried in the bedclothes. His hand moved to her shoulder and gently squeezed.

'You have nothing to fear. I shall not take advantage. You are perfectly safe.'

The bed moved again and she heard him move around the room and then the creak of the chair as he sat. A grunt. A bump. Another grunt and another bump. 'Sorry for the noise,' he said. 'Just removing my boots.'

'I made no objection,' she replied, her voice muffled under the bedcovers.

God, she was so hot, stifling, with her head under the covers, breathing in warm, stale air, almost gasping for the cool relief of fresh air.

She heard him shifting around in the chair, probably trying to get comfortable, and felt sympathy. They had both complained of aching muscles from spending so long in the saddle. A night in an armchair would provide little relief for poor Vernon.

'Goodnight. Sweet dreams.' His voice, deep and comforting, wrapped around her.

Thea straightened her neck, taking her face from under the covers, grateful to breathe the relatively cooler air of the bedchamber. The candles had been snuffed out; the room was dark. And intimate. Thea suppressed a shiver.

'Goodnight. I hope you sleep well.'

How strange it felt to say that to someone whilst she lay in bed.

It was a very long time before she slept.

Chapter Twelve

The following morning, Thea remained huddled under the bedclothes, feigning sleep, until Vernon left the room. Breathing a sigh of relief, she turned on her back and thrust the covers down. Vernon had stirred early and she wondered if he, too, had found sleep elusive.

Doubtless he did, but *his* discomfort would be as a result of sleeping in the chair. Unlike Thea, whose mind simply would not allow her to rest.

The maid had brought fresh water not long after Vernon had begun to move about. Looking at the chair, there was no way to tell that anyone had slept there—the blanket was folded neatly at the foot of the bed and, turning, Thea saw he had even dented the pillow next to hers, to make it look as though they had shared the bed. She arose, and crossed the floor to peer through the window, glazed with leaded, diamond-shaped panes. Vernon was just emerging from the stables—their room overlooked the yard at the rear of the inn—and he happened to glance up as Thea watched. His stride faltered and he smiled—a glorious smile that made her breath catch—as he waved. She returned his greeting even as her heart quailed at the effort she must henceforth make to conceal her growing desire to be held in his arms.

She spun away from the window, quashing her nerves. She must concentrate on Daniel, nothing else. She hurried across to the washstand.

Worcester.
At last!

It had been a day of frustrations. Vernon did not know why, but his every attempt at conversation had met with a short reply that effectively ended the exchange. There was none of easy repartee and banter of previous days. He had never known Thea to be so quiet for so long, but she had barely said a word the whole day. Neither would she look at him.

He longed to offer her comfort, but he could not. He could not risk any intimacy building between them, although it would have been so very easy to relax his principles and take her in his arms. But he would not whilst they were flung together in this unnatural charade. And, when they returned to real life, he was certain that his growing obsession with this little spitting kitten, who could also play and have fun and make him smile, would disappear and they would each return to their very different lives and, hopefully, be able look back upon this trip as an adventure.

Whether they would look back with joy or with sorrow depended, of course, on what they might discover about Daniel's fate. And maybe that was what was bothering Thea. They were that much closer to discovering the truth and she must dread the possibility of the worst news.

Vernon stifled a yawn and then circled his neck and rolled his shoulders in an attempt to work the cricks out of them. Never in his life had he spent a more uncomfortable night than last night. It was not only the chair, although that had grown harder and lumpier as the night progressed, but the knowledge that, not ten feet from him, lay a woman who had, almost without him noticing, crept into his heart.

They rode side by side, following the road down and through the city, until they arrived at a stone bridge, spanning a wide river, which was still running high and fast after the recent rains. Downstream, to their left, the huge mass of Worcester Cathedral squatted close to the riverbank, dwarfing the buildings around it. Upstream of the bridge, buildings lined the far bank of the river but downstream, opposite the cathedral, was green pasture land.

'That is the River Severn,' Thea said.

A sideways glance revealed a groove between her brows and tightly pursed lips. She looked like a woman deep in thought—a woman deeply worried, a woman exhausted. Vernon caught hold of Star's rein and steered both horses to the side of the bustling road, bringing them to a standstill.

'We could reserve rooms at that inn we passed in the centre. The Crown.'

'The Crown? Are you sure?'

She nudged her mare closer to Warrior…so close that Thea's leg pressed against Vernon's, sending the blood rushing to his groin. He gritted his teeth and tried to banish the image branded on his brain: Thea, curled on her side in bed, the thin blanket moulded to her frame, draping her narrow waist and accentuating the curve of her hip and the roundness of her bottom.

She leaned towards him. 'You said we should stay at an inn outside the town, where we shall be less likely to run into somebody either of us knows,' she whispered. 'If Mannington does live to the south-west, as Parkes told us, then would we not be better to find an inn over there?' She pointed across the bridge. 'We are more likely to find someone who knows him in that direction.' She heaved a sigh. 'Heaven knows, we haven't learned anything of any use up till now, despite all our enquiries.'

Her face was set, lines of fatigue bracketing her mouth. Vernon hauled in a breath, castigating himself for not standing firm and sending her home at the start. That thought was followed swiftly by the realisation she would not have gone. He had tried. She had been determined to come with him. But he had never known her to be so despondent. He missed his lively, bouncy firebrand.

'Cheer up, Dotty,' he said.

If anything was calculated to pull her free from the doldrums, it was him calling her Dotty. She barely glanced up, her eyes dull as she pulled her cap from her head and swiped her forearm across her glistening brow, in a gesture worthy of any young lad. Her cropped copper curls glinted momentarily in the bright sunshine before she replaced her cap, transforming her once again into Theo. Vernon had thought it would become progressively easier to think of her as the youth she portrayed, but it became harder by the day.

'What reason is there for cheerfulness? This is a foolish quest,' Thea muttered, completely ignoring his use of the nickname she detested.

Where was the fire in her eyes? The passion in her heart? This forlorn Thea was so very different to the woman he had come to know and to admire, with her drive and her verve and her ability to find fun in the everyday.

'Nobody remembered Daniel,' she said. 'And here…' she gestured to the town at their backs '…would anyone notice a stranger? It is so busy, how could anyone remember one man passing through, out of so many?' Then she straightened in her saddle. 'I am sorry. I do not mean to be such a misery. I convinced myself that *someone* would remember Daniel on the road between Birmingham and Worcester, that is all.' She met Vernon's gaze and he could see her fear. 'We cannot know if he ever arrived here—he might have ridden no more than a mile out of Birmingham before... before...' Her voice choked and she turned her head aside.

Vernon cursed himself for not realising how her worst fears must be haunting her. He might be committed to this quest, but he had not the same emotional stake in the outcome. He studied the land on the far side of the bridge.

'I have decided. We shall stay on this side of the bridge after all...who knows how far we would have to go before finding decent accommodation on the road out of town. You, my dear nephew, need some rest. You look exhausted.'

And his heart ached to see her instinctive female response to such a comment as she straightened her back, pinched at her cheeks and tidied her few stray strands of hair under her cap.

'I am fine.' She sounded more like the determined Thea he was used to, but he knew she was putting on a brave front for him. 'Once we've had something to eat and drink, we must begin our enquiries. Even if we find no trace of Daniel, surely *someone* will have knowledge of Mannington and he might hold the key to the mystery.'

She reined Star around and headed back into the town. 'Come along,' she said over her shoulder. 'There is no time to waste.'

Vernon followed, partly relieved to see her regain her former resolve but also worried at how adept she was at concealing her inner pain. He vowed to try again to persuade her to return home and leave him to continue the search alone.

Back outside the Crown, Vernon studied the façade. 'Let us go inside and see what the accommodation is like before we commit to staying. We can have a drink and something to eat, and see if it is suitable. At least we shall be rested.'

Twenty minutes later they were seated in their favoured position in the taproom, at a table in the corner, with Vernon facing out into the room and Thea with her back to it. There were only three other occupants: a man sitting alone, reading a newspaper and two men, their heads together over a table, deep in conversation. A glance reassured Vernon that all three were strangers and he felt he could relax. For now.

Platters of rolls and butter, cheese and cold roast beef, with a dish of pickles and two tankards of ale had been delivered to the table. Thea reached for her tankard and sipped cautiously. She still had not acquired a taste for it. If it was in his power, Vernon would buy her fine wine or champagne, but such a choice would excite too much interest in the youth Theo. The image of Thea, arrayed in a fine gown and jewels and sipping champagne, arose in his increasingly active imagination—an imagination he was helpless to quash, and an imagination that supplied ever more disturbing images of Thea, picturing her as part of his world—in his world and in his life.

Impossible images.

He raised his own tankard and drank long and deep. What the hell was wrong with him? He'd never been a man to indulge in obsessive fantasies, particularly of women.

You've never had to fantasise, that is why, a small voice whispered. *Women have always fallen at your feet. You're only interested in Thea because she is impervious to your charm.*

She is different. She is my friend. She feels a part of me. She is fun, good company and courageous. And sexy, beautiful and desirable.

And what you are starting to think...to hope for...is impossible. She has no interest in you as a man. She treats you as an older brother. Have you no pride? Will you prostrate yourself at her feet?

Vernon bit viciously into his bread roll and chewed, ignoring that infuriating inner voice. It was time for action, not for this idle conjecture. He was thinking like a lovesick youth, not a man of the world in his mid-thirties. He slammed the lid on his daydreams and vowed to focus his full attention on tracing Daniel and on finding out how Henry was involved. And the first step...

'I have been thinking,' he said.

Thea looked up, her brows arched.

'I think it is time you went home and left the rest of this to me.'

'No!'

Heads turned at Thea's loud exclamation and she shot Vernon a look of apology, then leaned across the table.

'I am sorry.' Her husky voice sparked such shivers of desire across his skin he was forced to clench his jaw to hide his reaction. 'I didn't mean to shout, but you *cannot* send me away. We are partners. We are in this together. You cannot expect me to go home when we are finally close to the truth.'

'It could be dangerous. I am a fool. I should never have brought you this far.'

'Dangerous? How so? You told me your Cousin Henry is a gentle soul.'

'He is. Was. It is many years since we have met. He went to live in Italy to feed his passion for the art and architecture, and he also longed to visit Greece and Egypt to view their antiquities. I cannot reconcile the Henry I knew with the man who made your brother so angry he shook with fury, as Janey told us. I have accepted I know nothing about this man and he could very well pose a danger. I should have sent you home on that very first day.'

'And if I point out it is not your place to dictate my movements? Vernon…' his name on her lips sent longing cascading through him '…look…you know I am sensible. If I promise to remain in the background, *please* allow me to stay.'

Vernon smiled at her and shook his head. 'You are inconsistent, my dear Dotty. You have just informed me I cannot dictate your movements and now you beg me to allow you to stay.'

Her lips firmed. 'I am not inconsistent. You can send me away, but I will not go. I am asking you to allow me to stay with *you*.' Her words ignited a fire in his belly. If only they were spoken in different circumstances. 'Otherwise…' she drew back, squaring her shoulders '…I shall simply stay at another establishment and conduct my own enquiries.'

She had taken the decision from him and he was, secretly, glad. He *wanted* her to stay, no matter how unwise.

'You leave me little choice,' he grumbled, determined not to reveal his relief. 'But, you must remain in the background. That idea you came up with, in Birmingham, about being my by-blow… we will keep that in mind. It will provide a good excuse for you not to accompany me when we find my cousin…it would be entirely reasonable for me to keep you away from any member of my family.'

Thea gave him a saucy smile. 'I am glad that is all settled. Might I suggest you go and reserve rooms for us?'

'Your wish is my command.'

Thea had finished eating and had pushed her

plate aside when Vernon returned, but he resumed his seat and began to eat once more. All this fresh air and exercise was giving him an appetite.

'I have paid for two rooms,' he said. 'For three nights to start with.'

'I shall repay you, as soon as we go home.'

Again, the words she chose…*'as soon as we go home'*…sparked a need and a longing in Vernon that he did not care to examine too closely.

'There is no need to repay a single penny. I am happy to fund this little adventure of ours. I was going to say I have enjoyed it…but that is not entirely true, given the nature of our quest and the fact we have yet to find Daniel.'

Vernon resumed eating. The two customers who had been in such deep conversation now stood up and walked towards the door, passing close behind Thea, who was absently crumbling a roll between her fingers. Vernon watched them idly. The first man, finely dressed, fair-haired and sharp-featured, appeared to be of a similar age to Vernon. The second man was older and heavy-set, with a ruddy face and bulging waistcoat. They paused at the door and he clapped the younger man on the shoulder.

'Now, Mannington…' Vernon's heart jolted in his chest as his eyes fixed on the fair-haired man. *Mannington!* The older man—an American, by his accent—continued to speak. 'Don't be a stranger. As soon as you get back, send me word and come dine with us—I know my Cordelia will be pleased to see you again. And we will hope you are not delayed like last time.'

Vernon looked more closely. This could not, surely, be Cousin Henry? Despite the man before him being similar in height, build and colouring, he could see no resemblance in his features and Henry had never been quite as fair…this man's hair was near white in colour.

'I should not be gone more than a couple of days,' Mannington said. No, definitely not Henry. Wrong voice altogether. 'And I shall be delighted to further my acquaintance with your charming daughter.'

Vernon glanced at Thea to see if she had caught Mannington's name and his heart jerked again, this time in alarm. Thea had frozen. Even her lips had drained of colour and each individual freckle stood stark against the pallor of her skin. Her fingers squeezed tight around the roll, her knuckles white, and her eyes were squeezed tight shut.

Vernon stretched his leg out under the cover of the table to nudge Thea, to try to provoke a reaction. Anything to interrupt that death-like stillness.

The two men left the room, but still Thea didn't move.

'What is it?' Vernon kept his voice to a whisper. He longed to reach across the table, to take her hand, to offer her his strength, his presence. But he could not. Not whilst she was dressed as a boy. 'Thea! Talk to me. Please.'

She looked up at that. Shock and disbelief on her face. Eyes stricken. Her chest moving up and down too fast, too shallow. She licked her lips and her brows drew together in a distressed frown.

'That man.'

Her voice shook. Her hands trembled. Vernon stretched his leg forward again and pressed it against hers, offering his physical support in the only way he could.

'Hush. It is all right. I am here. Do you mean Mannington or the American?'

'M-Mannington. Did he see me?'

'No. Neither of them noticed either one of us. It is safe. You are safe. You know I will look after you. There is nothing to fear.'

'Fear?' Thea laughed. A harsh, low sound. 'Am I not to fear a ghost?'

Chapter Thirteen

❦

A ghost?

A movement outside the window caught Vernon's eye. Mannington and the American stood on the pavement outside, still deep in conversation. Thea followed the direction of his gaze and a distressed mewl reached Vernon's ears. She had paled even further and appeared to shrink, her shoulders hunched and her head bowed.

Vernon shoved his chair back.

'I need to go after Mannington.'

'No!' Thea was on her feet, by his side, blocking his way, frantic fingers clawing his sleeve. 'No! You cannot, not until I…you *must* not.' She captured his gaze with glittering eyes. 'Let him go. He will be back. Mannington!' She all but spat the word. 'It is not his name,' she whispered fiercely. 'Oh, I cannot think…and Daniel…what did he do?'

'Hush,' Vernon whispered urgently as her voice rose in both volume and pitch.

He dropped his hand upon her shoulder. She was trembling violently.

'Come on, lad,' he said, in a loud voice for the benefit of the remaining customer who had abandoned his newspaper and was watching them with curiosity. 'Let us go and inspect our rooms.'

I ought to be following Mannington. Finding out what the devil is going on. But I can't leave Thea, not like this.

Thea nodded. Side by side they walked to the door and out into the lobby, from which an oak staircase rose to the first floor. Thea stumbled slightly as they crossed the lobby and Vernon slung his arm around her shoulders—to an onlooker it would be a friendly gesture but, in reality, his fingers gripped her upper arm and he remained ready to support her if she stumbled. Once they had left the bar, Thea seemed to regain some of her strength and they climbed the stairs to the first of the rooms Vernon had reserved for their use.

He realised precisely how much effort it had taken for Thea to walk from the bar and climb the staircase as soon as they entered the bedchamber. He released his hold upon her to turn and close the door and, when he turned back, she had sunk to the floor. She had not swooned, however. She sat, huddled in a heap, with her face sunk into her hands as she rocked to and fro in absolute silence.

He fell to his knees beside her and gently rubbed her back. He ducked his head to try to see her face, but it was completely covered by hands that visibly shook.

'Thea. Please. Talk to me. You recognised Mannington?'

She nodded, her face still hidden.

'Who is he? What has he done?'

A high-pitched whimper escaped her, quickly stifled. Vernon bit back a curse and gathered her into his arms, then regained his feet and carried her to the bed. He set her down near the head, pulling the pillows behind her to cushion her, and then he clasped her wrists and tugged her hands from her face.

She shook her head violently. 'No! No!'

Vernon settled beside her and held her close. 'There is nothing to fear. I am here. He cannot hurt you.'

His mind whirled with conjecture. What was that man to Thea? What had he done? A black, murderous rage swelled deep in his chest and he swore he would make the bastard suffer. Gradually her quivering stilled and her breathing steadied. She relaxed into Vernon's embrace. He pulled back, to look into her face, putting his hand under her chin to force her to meet his gaze.

'I am going downstairs for a few minutes—'

'No!' Terror lit her eyes and she grabbed frantically at his hand. 'I beg of you. He cannot find out I am here. For Daniel's sake! You must not!'

'Calm yourself. I promise I shall not confront

him—I am going to fetch some brandy. You have had a shock; it will help steady your nerves. I shall return before you know it and then we shall talk. No matter how difficult it is for you to confide in me, you must.'

Had the bastard attacked Thea? Possibly even raped her? That rage—hot as molten lava only moments before—had solidified into a cold hard mass that demanded revenge—a revenge that required a cool, logical approach, not the hot-headed, fists-flying solution he had initially craved.

He stroked her cheek, smoothing her curls away, relieved to see a touch of colour in her face again. 'Do you understand?'

Her eyes searched his and his heart stuttered at the trust that shone from them. She nodded—tiny, rapid movements.

'And you must promise me you will not leave this room until I return.'

She nodded again.

'Let me hear you say it.'

'I promise. And…' She paused for so long he wondered if she had forgotten what she had been going to say. 'Thank you,' she concluded eventually.

He smiled at her and pulled her close into a brief hug. Unable to resist, he dropped a kiss on to her curls, pausing for one second to breathe in her evocative scent before leaving to go downstairs.

Before going to the bar to request a bottle of

brandy and two glasses, he stepped outside the front door, fully prepared to exchange at least a few words with the man who had evoked such an extreme reaction from Thea—not to challenge him… merely to establish a preliminary connection—but both Mannington and the American were gone.

At least we know he is here and he will be returning.

As he crossed the lobby, after ordering brandy to be sent to his room, the innkeeper, Mr Horwell—a spare, dark-haired man of indeterminate age—was descending the staircase. Vernon waited for him to reach the lobby.

'Mr Boyton,' Horwell said, with a nod of his head. 'I trust your rooms are to your satisfaction?'

'Indeed they are.'

'You have a further requirement?'

'I do.' Vernon glanced around the lobby. It was quiet now, but when he had reserved their rooms it had been busy with people coming and going. He did not want to be overheard. 'I should like a word with you, if you will? Do you have somewhere private we may talk?'

Horwell bowed. 'But of course, sir. This way.'

He showed Vernon into a back room clearly used as an office.

'Would you care to sit, Mr Boyton?'

Vernon thought of Thea and declined. He must get back to her as soon as possible, but he could not pass up this chance to question the innkeeper.

'I shall not take up much of your time,' he said. 'I shall come straight to the point. Do you know the name Daniel Markham?'

'No, sir, I do not.'

'What about Charles Leyton?'

Horwell shook his head decisively. 'No, sir.'

'And—' Vernon watched him closely '—what can you tell me about Mr Henry Mannington?'

A subtle change came over Horwell. He straightened—almost imperceptibly—and ran one finger around his neck, easing his neckcloth.

'Not a great deal, sir. He visits the Crown from time to time, but he has never been a paying guest.'

Caution radiated from the man.

'Has he lived in the area a long time?'

Horwell's gaze flicked to Vernon's face and then away. He cleared his throat.

'If it will make this easier, Horwell, you should know that I have never met Mr Mannington, but that I do seek information about him. I saw him here earlier in the company of an American gentleman, which is why I thought to ask you about him.'

A muscle leapt in Horwell's jaw.

'Your discretion does you credit, Horwell. I give you my word as a gentleman that anything you tell me will go no further.'

Other than to Thea.

'There will be no repercussions. And I, in return, will be honest with you. Are you willing to help me?'

Horwell stared at Vernon, then nodded, releasing a pent-up breath.

'I shall aid you to the best of my ability, sir, although I do not know a great deal about the gentleman other than he claims kinship to a duke and he is lying to one of my guests.'

Vernon had been gone an age. Still shivery with shock, Thea clambered under the eiderdown and curled in a ball, tugging the folds around her, trying to warm herself. Her brain appeared to be mired in quicksand—the more she tried to free a thought to follow it through and try to make sense of what she had heard and seen, the more she felt as though she was sinking. Her chest squeezed tight, making breathing a chore, and her limbs felt heavy, anchoring her to the bed. She had not managed to follow even one thought to a conclusion when she heard the door open.

'Put the tray on the nightstand, if you please,' Vernon was saying, in a loud voice. 'As you see, my nephew is unwell.'

Thea kept her head buried as light footsteps neared the bed and then retreated. Finally, the door clicked shut and she fought her way out from the cocooning eiderdown, blinking her eyes against the brightness of the room. Strong hands clasped her upper arms and helped her to sit, propping her once more against the pillows leaning against the headboard. Her hand was taken and her fingers wrapped around a glass.

'Sip at this,' Vernon ordered. Then, 'Steady. Do not gulp', as she tilted the glass to her mouth.

She coughed and spluttered as the liquid scorched its way down her throat. She raised watering eyes to Vernon's.

'What is that?'

'Brandy. I did say I would bring some. Have you never drunk it before?'

She shook her head. This was it. He would expect an explanation…and how could she admit the truth and own up to her culpability in the chain of events that had culminated in the loss of their fortune and had caused Papa's stroke? But she must. If they were to find Daniel…she could not hamper the search because of her own guilt and shame.

She sipped again at the amber spirit and this time it warmed and it soothed as she swallowed. She sucked in a determined breath.

'I scarce know where to start.'

Vernon eyed her approvingly and she realised he had expected more reluctance on her part to reveal her story.

'Try the beginning,' he said, sitting on the bed, then swivelling to face her. 'You recognised the man calling himself Henry Mannington.'

'That man…he is not your cousin?'

'No.'

'I am glad. He is…he is *not* a good man. And, yes, I know…*knew* him.'

She chewed at her lip. There was no dodging this. She must face the truth, incredible as it seemed. Perhaps talking of it would finally allow her to make sense of what she had heard and seen this afternoon. Her stomach still roiled with nerves and disbelief.

'I told you I had been betrothed once, several years ago?'

'You did and that you decided by mutual consent that you would not suit.'

'That was not entirely true,' Thea said. She rubbed her eyes, then her mouth. She bent her legs and clasped her arms around her knees, hugging them close to her chest, and sighed. 'His name was Jasper Connor. We met at the assembly room in Bewdley and he asked me to dance. Over the following few weeks we met several times and he asked permission to call upon me at home. We began courting. I was flattered. He was charming, attentive, handsome…he was possessed of all the attributes to turn a young woman's head.'

'How old were you?'

'Twenty, when we met.' She raised her gaze to his. 'He was most plausible. I have thought about it since then…oh, so many times I have gone over what happened. Should I have known? Were there clues I missed? But I can think of none. It was a leisurely courtship. There was no rush…no chivvying me into accepting a proposal…and when he did offer for me, it felt…oh, I do not know how to explain…it felt *natural*. As though it were the next logical step. Do you understand? How could any of us have known what would happen?'

She dipped her head, resting her forehead on her knees.

'How long after you first met did he offer for you?'

'Five months. To the day.' She laughed mirthlessly. 'He even spoke of it as the anniversary of the day we met and he said he hoped it would not be another five months before we could be wed.'

Vernon stroked her hair. 'Tell me the rest, Thea. None of this reflects badly upon you.'

She raised her head and stared at him, reading nothing but concern on his handsome face. 'Does it not? It was I who introduced him into the lives of my family. I who caused…who caused…'

Vernon took her hand, caressing her palm with his thumb. 'Do not distress yourself. Do not talk of culpability. Tell me the facts. What happened after he proposed? You accepted him…and then…?'

She swallowed past the aching lump that had formed in her throat. 'We set the date for our wedding. Papa…' Her voice hitched and she coughed to clear the rasp. 'Papa and Jasper agreed the marriage settlements…and then, and then…three days before the wedding Jasper came to Stourwell Court in such excitement…he had been given *such* an investment opportunity…it could not fail, he said…he would make a fortune. And he said he had thought of Papa and why should he not also benefit from such a wonderful opportunity? But it had to be quick. If Papa did not commit immediately, he would miss this *chance of a lifetime*…and Papa said, afterwards, that he should have known better…he *did* know better…but he trusted Jasper. We all did. Why should we not? And so they went into Stourbridge together, to Papa's bank, and he withdrew his savings and handed them to Jasper and then he raised more by way of a loan secured against the manufactory and then…then… they went to Jasper's solicitor in Birmingham. He handled all the paperwork…'

Vernon stirred and Thea paused.

'Why did your father not use his own solicitor to validate the paperwork?'

'There was no time, according to Jasper. Papa's solicitor is in Kidderminster, but the deal had to be done in Birmingham and Papa *trusted* Jasper. He was like a son to him. He was part of our family.'

'This Jasper…he absconded with the money?'

Her stomach clenched and then churned again as the events of the past unfolded in her memory. She shook her head. 'That was the *cruellest* part, when I look back. No, he did not. Not immediately. He dined with us, as expected, the following day. He…he acted so *normal*. None of us suspected a thing when he said he would not see me again before the wedding, that there were various business matters he must attend to and that he would see us at the church in two days' time. That was the last we saw of him.'

'So you…you went to the church?'

Thea nodded, tears stinging, throat thick. Every moment of that dreadful day was etched into her soul. Her initial anxiety…had there been an unavoidable delay? An accident? Was Jasper ill? Her hurt and humiliation as the minutes passed and no word arrived from the groom. Her heartache and despair when a messenger sent to Jasper's lodgings returned with the news that he had packed his bags and left the minute he had returned after that final dinner at Stourwell Court.

'He did not come.'

That was all Vernon needed to know. She had no words to describe the aftermath…the utter disbelief and the sheer panic of her father in particular as the implications slowly sank in… Jasper had gone. And the money…as hard as they tried to convince themselves there had been some dreadful mistake…a misunderstanding… Papa had the share certificates. Surely the investment was sound… Deep down inside Thea suspected they had all known the truth.

'The next day…' The day that should have been Thea's first day as a married woman. 'Papa and Daniel went to Birmingham to speak to Jasper's solicitor. His office was locked and bare. They discovered the shares were not worth a single penny. The mining venture Papa had invested in did not exist.'

'I am sorry, but what has Henry Mannington to do—?'

'They returned home,' Thea spoke over Vernon, gabbling slightly in her haste. She must tell him the whole now she had come thus far. 'And, as Papa was telling Mama and me...*confessing* to us...telling us we were ruined...that is when he...he...'

A huge sob gathered in her chest and, try as she might, she could not suppress it. Vernon's arms came around her and she leaned into him, grateful for his strength and his calm presence.

'That is when he had the stroke?'

Thea nodded, sniffing. 'It is all my fault! If I had not allowed myself to be flattered by Jasper, none of it would have happened. It is my fault Papa is bedridden and cannot speak properly—'

'You are not to blame. Jasper Connor bears the blame. Nobody else. What happened next? Did you try to trace him?'

'Daniel did. He spent weeks following leads but then, when he finally tracked him down, it was too late.'

Thea felt her pulse kick and gallop as she recalled the reason why she was telling all this to Vernon. The impossible...the unbelievable...

'Go on.'

A gentle hand smoothed her hair. Comforting. Reassuring. Giving her the courage to say the words out loud.

'Daniel finally caught up with Jasper at his funeral.'

She felt Vernon tense. She pulled away, staring up into his face. 'He had been travelling ever since…*that* day. He had stopped overnight at an inn and there was a fire. Jasper died in that fire. Daniel watched as his coffin was placed in the ground.'

'So…' Vernon's brows had drawn together in puzzlement. 'What has this to do with Henry Mannington?'

'Do you not see? Henry Mannington is Jasper Connor.'

Chapter Fourteen

Vernon had not seen it coming. He had been caught up in Thea's tale, heart sore at the pain she had endured, furious at the dirty trick paid on her and her family. He stood up and paced the room as he sorted through the facts, then he returned to sit on the bed again. No wonder Thea had spoken of ghosts. No wonder she had been in such shock.

'We must ensure he does not see you,' he said.

Thea stiffened. 'Is that all you have to say? Your only concern? That Jasper... Mannington, I mean, might recognise me?'

Vernon swept his hand through his hair. 'No. Of course not. I was thinking aloud. It is one of my concerns...the others...'

He could barely order his thoughts. Every instinct he possessed screamed at him to chase after Mannington. Find him...and put his hands around his neck and squeeze the life from him. He had never known his own self-control so precarious.

He rarely lost his temper. He was not a violent man. But something about this woman stirred some primeval force deep within him, a snarling beast that urged him to take action. To protect. To avenge.

He poured himself a glass of brandy and tossed it down his throat, then proffered the decanter to Thea. Wordlessly she held out her glass.

'We need to discuss this in a calm manner,' Vernon said. 'We must try to work out how and why Jasper is still alive and how that ties in with my cousin and your brother.'

Thea sipped her brandy. He was pleased to see she had more colour in her cheeks now. She shuffled around on the bed until she was sitting facing him, cross-legged. If only she knew what she did to him...her shapely legs outlined by the breeches she wore... Vernon averted his eyes, concentrating on her face. The fact that she was completely unselfconscious about her appearance, and about being here, alone, with him in a bedchamber...never had he felt so overlooked as a man.

He cleared his throat and marshalled his thoughts.

'I gleaned some information from Horwell when I went downstairs to order the brandy,' he said. 'It sounds as though Connor... Mannington, that is... is up to his old tricks. He lives at a place called Crackthorpe Manor, which is about four miles out of town on the road to Great Malvern and he has befriended an American businessman, Mr Samuel Temple—'

'Was that the man we saw him with? I thought he had a strange accent.'

'Yes. He is in Worcester on business and is staying here at the Crown. He is very wealthy and is accompanied by his daughter, Cordelia, who stands to inherit his entire fortune.'

Thea sucked in an audible breath. 'An heiress?' She swivelled around, lowering her feet to the floor. 'We must warn her!'

Vernon grasped her arm, restraining her. 'Steady. According to Horwell, Mannington's plans are not going as smoothly as he would like. Mr Temple is set on snaring a nobleman for his daughter.'

'That, at least, is some protection for her. Mannington cannot conjure a title from nowhere no matter what other lies he tells,' Thea muttered. 'And with no title to turn her head, *she* will not be so foolish as to arrive at a church in the expectation of finding her betrothed waiting at the altar.'

'Hey.' Vernon pinched her chin. 'You were not foolish. He is clearly an accomplished fraudster. Now, we must plan how to approach him when he returns—'

'Returns? Why? Where—?'

'You must have heard what they said…'

Vernon fell silent as Thea turned huge, bruised eyes on him.

'I cannot recall. I did not…could not…'

He brushed the back of his fingers along her cheekbone, aching to take her in his arms again. But he resisted, not certain how she might react now those hurtful memories were in the open.

'I'm a fool,' he said. 'Of course you did not take in what was being said. The gist of their exchange was that Mannington has gone away for a couple of days and Temple was inviting him to dine here with him and his daughter upon his return. So, we have that time to plan how we tackle him. And Thea, trust me…at this moment, there is nothing we can do other than try to make sense of all this.'

Thea was still looking up at him. 'Tell me what else Horwell said.'

'Well, he does not trust Mannington, that is for certain. He overheard him tell Temple that Crack-thorpe Manor is his ancestral family home, but Horwell knows for a fact that he has only been living there a matter of weeks because he took on Horwell's niece as a housemaid when he moved in. So he knows Mannington is lying to the Temples, but he hasn't said anything to them because he does not want his niece to lose her job.'

'But someone must warn this Mr Temple and his poor daughter.'

'And we will.' Vernon bit back a curse. 'God knows how many people he has swindled, black-ening the Beauchamp name into the bargain. Hor-well told me he is still claiming to be a cousin to the Duke of Cheriton and not even a distant cousin at that.'

'But he is not your cousin, is he? It is not that Henry Mannington is his real name and Jasper Connor was false?'

'No. At least…we cannot say for sure that Jasper Connor was not a false name, but I do know without the slightest doubt that he is not my cousin.' Vernon scratched his jaw, frowning. 'The fact that he is openly living as Henry… I hate to even think this, but it suggests, does it not, that he has no fear of being exposed as an imposter by the *real* Henry.'

Thea stirred and took his hand between hers. 'I thought the same,' she said. 'I am sorry.'

She was offering him comfort even though her heart must be breaking. And they had not even touched on what this new revelation might mean about Daniel's disappearance.

Vernon surged to his feet and paced to the window. For all his words to Thea, he did not want to sit idly, talking over problems and formulating plans. He longed to be *out there*…doing…taking action. He was a man…it's what men did.

'So will he be sorry when I get my hands on him,' he growled, clenching his fists and leaning on the sill, gazing unseeingly through the glass. 'Two days! It cannot pass quickly enough for me. I shall take great pleasure in exposing him for the charlatan he is.'

He heard the creak of the bed and the pad of her feet as she crossed the room to stand behind him. A small hand settled against his shoulder blade.

'Let us plan. There are questions that need answering, and we must consider them in a logical fashion. We must not allow our emotions to sway our thinking.' Her hand circled, soothing. Then patted. 'I *told* you we made a good partnership. When one of us veers away on a tangent, the other is there to haul them back on the right road.'

He turned. She was so close, gazing up at him. Trusting. Open. How much courage did it take for her to set aside her emotions in order to comfort him? And *his* anger had been directed at Mannington for besmirching his family name; his distress was for a distant cousin he had not even thought of in years, whereas Thea had been jilted by that bastard and now her brother was missing. He forced a smile, and pushed an errant curl back from her forehead, resisting the urge to cup her cheeks. To lower his head. And to kiss those full, tempting lips.

'You are right. We do make a good partnership.'

He sidestepped around her, but she grabbed at his hand, pulling him round.

'Look!'

Her nose was all but pressed against the window. Vernon leaned forward to peer down at the street below.

'That is him, is it not? Mr Temple?' Thea said.

Then she straightened, drawing back. 'And *that*, I presume, is *Miss* Temple.'

Vernon gave her a sidelong look—distracted by the change in her tone—before studying again the two figures in the street below. Temple it was, with a lady upon his arm. She was certainly young enough to be his daughter, but there was little resemblance between the portly American and this dark, willowy, exotic-looking creature. Vernon just managed to contain his low whistle of appreciation. Miss Cordelia Temple was stunning. Conscious of Thea quietly bristling by his side—and why was it women always seemed to take an instant dislike to beautiful females?—he moved away from the window.

'Yes, that is him,' he said. 'Come, let us sit over here…' he steered her to a small round table and pair of chairs that were set back in the corner '…and we shall plot Mannington's downfall. But first, our priority must be to work out what has happened to Henry and to Daniel. What are those questions you spoke of?'

They sat across the table from one another. Thea held up a finger.

'First: where is the real Henry Mannington?'

Vernon recognised in Thea's expression the same resignation that weighed on his mind.

'I fear that, if it was not Jasper who was buried that day, it must have been my cousin,' he said.

Thea reached for his hand and squeezed. 'I am

sorry but I agree. That is the most rational explanation.'

'Which poses an additional question,' Vernon said. 'Did Jasper simply seize upon an opportunity that presented itself to him, or was he involved in Henry's death? Did he set the fire, perhaps?'

'And that is a question only he can answer,' Thea said. 'Now...next...how did Daniel learn that Jasper was still alive?' Her amber eyes searched his. 'Do we agree that Daniel somehow discovered Jasper was alive and set off to track him down?'

'Agreed.' He thought back to what they had learned in Harborne and Birmingham. 'He must have seen Jasper at the Royal Hotel and learned he was using a false identity. Maybe Jasper... Mannington, I mean...left before Daniel could confront him and so, when he learned Mannington was due to stay there on his return journey, Daniel decided to go to the hotel every day until he saw him again.'

'And, in the meantime, he wrote to your brother.'

'And we know that, when Mannington did stay again overnight, he left very early in the morning...'

'Keen to get back to his heiress,' Thea muttered, her brows lowering.

'And Daniel therefore missed him.'

'And decided to follow him, knowing now that he lived near to Worcester and would be travelling on the Worcester road.'

'I wonder why, once he knew Mannington would

return, your brother did not simply stay at the hotel until Mannington returned?'

'I think I can answer that,' Thea said. 'He would not stay away overnight unless he had no choice. He has taken on the mantle of head of the family. He feels responsible for us: Papa and Mama and me. He would rather ride all that way every day than not come home. And, of course, the cost would be a consideration. Our finances might be improved, but they are still not fully secure.'

Which makes his failure to return now even more troubling.

Vernon saw the effort it cost Thea to contain her worry and her grief and his heart swelled.

'Try not to think the worst,' he said, taking her hands across the table and caressing her knuckles with his thumbs. 'There still could be a good explanation for Daniel's silence.'

Although I cannot think of a single one.

He hated to think how desolate Thea must be feeling at this very moment. He felt it, too: grief for Henry, even though he had not seen him for years, and apprehension about what had happened to Daniel. But he must remain positive for Thea's sake.

'What we need to decide is how we move forward from here,' he said. 'Can you recall the name of the inn that burned down?'

'No, but I do know it was in the village of Yarncott, near Oxford.'

'Oxford? That is too far for us to go to make enquiries, with only two days at our disposal. I need to establish a relationship with the Temples before Mannington returns and, through them, with him.'

'*You* need to? Do you not mean we?' She stared challengingly, then her shoulders slumped and she shook her head, her curls bouncing. 'No. Sorry. Of course I cannot be involved. Mannington will know me in an instant.' Her mouth drooped.

'I promise you, Thea,' Vernon said. 'Mannington *will* pay for the suffering he has caused you and your family.'

She drew back. 'Pay? In what way? Money?' She laughed bitterly. 'Money will not buy Papa his health.'

'But it might give him peace of mind, to know the culprit is brought to justice.'

'How do you intend to lure the Temples into trusting you? You cannot use your real name and you do not look much like a wealthy gentleman, dressed as you are.'

'That is true.' Vernon jumped to his feet. 'First, I need to ensure Mannington has really gone away… we already know he is a consummate liar, do we not? Plus, you have given me an idea, Thea. Now, do not leave your bedchamber, or you might ruin my plans. I shall see you at dinner.'

'What is your idea? Tell—'

But Vernon had gone, closing the door on the remainder of her sentence.

* * *

Thea did not see Vernon again until it was time to dine, when she answered a knock upon her door, her heart bumping in her throat even though it was illogical to think it might be Mannington who knocked. Vernon had raised such doubts in her mind…what if Mannington *had* lied to Mr Temple and he was still skulking around the area?

But it was not Mannington. Vernon, looking very pleased with himself, stood on the landing outside and her pulse leapt with fierce joy.

'Oh. It is you,' she said, struggling to conquer her involuntary reaction to the sight of him.

'Were you expecting somebody else?'

'Of course I was not.'

'Come, then,' he said. 'Enough of your dawdling. I am ravenous. I have reserved a private parlour for us to dine.'

Thea stomped on to the landing and banged the door shut behind her. She cloaked herself in anger. She could not bear it if he guessed the strength of her feelings for him.

Infuriating wretch! Leaving me all alone for hours, *to worry myself silly. And then he reappears when it suits him, all smug and self-satisfied. No doubt he has been 'establishing a relationship' with that woman. Well, I wish him luck with her.*

She would not give him the satisfaction of questioning him about his whereabouts—he obviously could not care less that she'd had been going quietly mad, left alone with her thoughts.

'I hope you have not left your bedchamber since last I saw you, Dotty,' Vernon said, tweaking one of her curls as they walked downstairs together.

She had been oh-so-tempted to defy him. But common sense—and fear that Mannington might indeed still be lurking around—had stopped her. They still needed to find Daniel and blundering about when Vernon was establishing...well, whatever he was establishing...would not help.

'I am not foolish enough to ruin our chances of finding the truth,' Thea said, sticking her nose in the air as she stalked past him into the parlour, 'even if *you* are unfeeling enough to leave me in ignorance all this time. But you need not think that means I shall remain confined to my room day after day whilst you gallivant about *establishing relationships* and searching for clues, because I shall not.'

Vernon regarded her with an arched brow and a smile playing on his mouth. 'Are you miffed with me, Dotty?'

She rounded on him. 'Miffed? Why, pray, should I be miffed?'

He shrugged carelessly. 'Oh, I don't know,' he said. 'Just an impression. I am pleased I am wrong.'

She could see by his expression he knew he was right. And that he thought it amusing. He thought *her* amusing.

'Now, this parlour will do nicely for our meals, do you not agree?' Vernon said. 'The less other guests, or the staff, see of you, my dearest Dotty, the better. Then Mannington's return will not co-incide with the sudden elusiveness of my young nephew. I shall invent a disorder for you, I believe.' His green eyes twinkled. 'What say you to a dis-order of the brain? Shall that suffice to keep you confined to your chamber, do you think?'

'There is no need for me to remain out of sight when Mannington returns, as long as we are not introduced,' she said. 'I am dressed as a boy and, as long as I wear my cap, there is no reason for him to even notice me. And *that*, my dear Lord Vernon, is to our advantage. You need my help. A lad may loiter without exciting comment and a man such as Mannington is less likely to censor his conversa-tion in front of a youth than in front of a full-grown man. It will be an excellent opportunity to find out some of his secrets.'

'Oh, no. Absolutely not.' They were seated at the table by now, opposite one another, and Vernon pierced Thea with a narrowed gaze. 'Do not imag-ine for one minute, Dotty, that I shall permit you to risk your safety by sneaking around and eaves-dropping on that scoundrel. Besides, it is not safe for you to wander about on your own in a town this size. You are entirely too innocent. Do you forget that incident with Pooley? There are any number of things that might happen to an unsophisticated lad...things that would make your hair curl. Or—' his eyes glinted '—perhaps I should say, make your toes curl. Your hair needs no assistance in that department.'

Thea glared at him, raising a hand involuntarily to smooth her hair, a hopeless task as she very well knew. Why could she not have smooth, sleek, shining hair? In the mental images she had formed of the ladies with whom Vernon no doubt consorted in his normal, privileged life not one of them had wild curls that spiralled and bounced. And unsophisticated...well, she could not argue with that description of her, not compared to the females he was accustomed to.

She thrust aside her inadequacies, telling herself there were far more important issues at stake.

'Where have you *been* all afternoon?' *So much for my resolve not to question him.* 'I kept thinking about what you said—that Mannington might not have gone away after all. I kept wondering if you might bump into him unawares.'

And if he did, she just knew Vernon would confront him. The fear had plagued her the entire afternoon, worry eating at her in case Vernon was in danger. How would she know? What would she do if something happened and he failed to return, like Daniel? She could not bear it if he simply vanished too.

Vernon's brows shot skywards. 'Is *that* why you are so scratchy? Were you worried about me?'

He grinned at her and she scowled back, desperate to hide the truth. Yes. She had been worried. Frantic, even. And now he sat there, seemingly without a care in the world, looking suave and gorgeous despite his travel-stained clothes, whilst she looked like a scruffy schoolboy with badly cut hair. Oh, how she wished they were sitting there in different circumstances, with her clad in a pretty gown, with her hair nicely dressed…

She tamped down those wishes; they were nonsense.

A man such as he would never look at a woman like her.

Besides. Men were not to be trusted. She had seen the living proof of that not five hours ago in this very inn.

'Why should I worry about a great oaf like you? I have no doubt you can take care of yourself.'

But she had thought the same about Daniel and now she could only pray he was out there somewhere, safe.

Two maids came in carrying trays and served their food and wine, precluding further conversation. Thea drummed her fingers on the table, waiting for the women to leave the room, her stomach churning. It took her several minutes to work out the cause…it was dread. Pure and simple. Now they seemed close to discovering the truth she realised there was a growing part of her that was simply terrified of what they might learn. At least at the moment she had hope. What if her worst fears were realised? What, then, would she have left?

At last the women left, closing the door behind them.

'Well?' She almost spat the word out, fear making her sharp. 'Will you tell me what you have been doing or am I to be kept in total ignorance?'

Chapter Fifteen

Vernon gave Thea a rueful smile. 'I am sorry. I should not tease. This is a difficult time for you, I know. And I am at times guilty of forgetting quite how much is at stake.'

She stared. 'You almost sound as though you are enjoying yourself.'

Vernon winced. 'Put like that, I sound heartless indeed. But I am not. I care about you and I pray we shall find Daniel safe and well but, to be brutally honest, I *am* enjoying the change. Or, more accurately, the challenge. You have accused me of being an idle aristocrat with too much money and too much time on my hands and, despite my business interests, you are right. My brother and I, we employ people to do the hard work. We only need be involved when and if we wish to be. This is… *different*. I am needed. Indispensable. And it is that feeling I relish, not the actual circumstances.'

Somewhat mollified, Thea sipped at her wine.

'So, I shall enlighten you as to how I have spent this afternoon. I spoke to Horwell, following which I wrote two letters, and then Horwell drove me out to Crackthorpe Manor, ostensibly to visit Annie, his niece, but actually to ascertain that Mannington has indeed gone away for a couple of days as he said. Which Annie confirmed.'

That, at least, is a relief. 'But why did Horwell drive you out to Crackthorpe Manor?'

Vernon frowned. 'I asked to hire a post-chaise, and he offered to take me himself. I did think it a bit odd, but...' He shrugged. 'I told him Mannington had fleeced a friend of mine and that I hope to bring him to book, so perhaps he is just relieved to have an ally against the man.'

'Did you meet the Temples?'

Another thought that had plagued her throughout that long afternoon. Vernon, with that...that... *beauty.*

'No. I have a plan and that does not include making their acquaintance just yet. When Bickling arrives—'

'Bickling?'

'My groom.'

'I know he is your groom, but he is at Stourwell Court.'

'And that is why I sent my letter to Stourwell Court,' he said in an exaggeratedly patient tone. 'I have summoned him to come to Worcester and to bring my curricle and also my own clothing. I—'

'You wrote to Stourwell Court and you did not think to tell me?'

'I am telling you now.'

'But… I could have sent for some of *my* clothes.'

'But that makes no sense, Dotty my dear. You cannot parade around here as Dorothea Markham. Quite apart from the risk of Mannington seeing you, I need to gain the trust of Mr and Miss Temple, not drive them away with outrage and scandal. No, you have no choice but to remain as my nephew, Theo, for the time being. But take heart… at least you may remain as my nephew and not my by-blow,' he added with a chuckle.

Thea gazed gloomily at her plate. 'I suppose you are right.' She tried to shake free of the feeling that events were sweeping past her, leaving her mired in a backwater. 'You were telling me of your plan.'

'I was indeed. The reason I have sent for my curricle and my own clothes is that I, my dear Dotty, am about to become *Viscount* Boyton—no more plain Mister for me. I told Horwell this afternoon—in the strictest of confidence, of course—that my trunk has been delayed and that I've been forced to dress in borrowed clothing until it arrives. He is thrilled that a member of the aristocracy is patronising his inn and I have little doubt that particular tale will spread in no time and will reach the ears of Mr Samuel Temple and his lovely daughter, Cordelia, to whom I shall be *particularly* attentive.'

A sharp pain arrowed through Thea and she battled to keep her expression blank, appalled at the jealousy that erupted in her chest. She knew, logically, there was no reason to be jealous. But emotions were not logical.

'This plan of yours,' she said. 'Would it not be better to target Mannington direct? Why bother with the Temples at all?'

Vernon, chewing a mouthful of food, did not immediately answer, but his eyes were on her and, uncomfortable with his scrutiny, she began to eat her own meal. What if he could read her mind? There were times when she was certain he knew exactly the thoughts that chased around inside her head. She focused on her plate.

'That would take too long. A man such as Mannington learns to be cautious of any new acquaintance. If I successfully charm my way into the lives of Mr Temple and his daughter—and I can be *most* charming when I try, Dotty, even though I say so myself—Henry Mannington will have no choice but to acknowledge my acquaintance. He will— quite wrongly, I do assure you—view me as a rival to the hand of Miss Temple.'

Thea pushed her plate aside, any appetite flown. 'I am in no need of your assurances, sir. I am sure it is none of my concern if you *do* aspire to the hand of Miss Temple.' She stole a look through her lashes to gauge his reaction, then stiffened. 'You laugh at me, but it is scarce five hours since I told you I was jilted at the altar. I envy *no* woman the attentions of *any* man. Of that, *I* assure *you*.'

Vernon shook his head at her. 'Not every man is deceitful in matters of the heart, Thea.'

'Are they not?'

She found her hand captured, engulfed by his much larger one, and her stomach performed a slow somersault.

'They are not,' he said firmly. 'Thea...you are weighed down by the guilt over what happened to your papa and you tell yourself it is your duty to stay at home and help your mother. But what happened...it was not your fault. You must know that. All you did was trust the word of a scoundrel. Your father—older than you and, presumably, a shrewd man—was also taken in. Fraudsters such as Mannington are clever with words. They often have charm in abundance. *No one* would blame you for believing his lies and you should not blame yourself or allow your experience to sour you against all men.'

He lifted her hand and pressed his lips to the back, sending jolts of energy sparking through her veins and setting her pulse racing.

'What is more,' he added in an even softer, infinitely more intimate tone, 'you should not continue to punish yourself.'

Thea snatched her hand from his, heart hammering, cheeks burning. 'I don't know what you mean. I do not punish myself.'

He raised his wine glass and drank, his eyes never leaving her face.

'I do *not*.'

'You have buried yourself at Stourwell Court. You never go anywhere. You have given up on life and you should not. You have too much to offer.'

A lump swelled in her throat. She must change this conversation. She could not bear sympathy. Or kindness. She did not deserve it.

'You said you wrote two letters?'

His eyes narrowed, as though he knew exactly why she had changed the subject.

'Indeed. I also wrote to Leo. My brother.'

Thea still could not become accustomed to hearing Vernon talk about his brother—a *duke*—in such a casual manner and the reminder of the inequality in their positions in society added to the ache in her heart. She had battled so hard not to succumb to him. To protect her heart. She had failed. And that terrified her because, on top of what had happened to Daniel, she must face the agony of losing a man she feared she was falling in love with.

'May I ask why?' Her voice, remarkably, did not quiver.

'I updated him on what has happened and asked him to send his man to Yarncott to make enquiries about that fire and then to come here to help us search for Daniel.'

And where was the role for her in Vernon's

plans? He would be busy building his rapport with the Temples—there would be little place for a young lad in their adult world, even if she could risk coming face to face with Mannington. Still less, she thought ruefully as she looked down at her non-descript clothing, a boy dressed as she happened to be. Thea's involvement from henceforth would be strictly limited. The thought of Vernon leaving her behind whilst he nurtured his acquaintance with Miss Cordelia Temple and her father stirred a cauldron of fervent imaginings in her brain. She already disliked that woman with a quite unreasonable intensity.

She hadn't heard Vernon move and yet, there he was, right beside her, his finger beneath her chin.

'Chin up, Dotty. At least we are making some progress.'

She gazed up at him, their eyes locking, and his hand moved to cradle her cheek, setting her pulse skittering and anticipation swirling deep in her core. Before she could react—either to rebuff or to encourage—he snatched his hand away with a muttered oath and returned to his chair.

'Finish your meal,' he said. 'It is growing late and I suggest we should retire early tonight…the less we are seen until my clothing arrives, the better.'

The following afternoon Thea pressed her nose against the window of her bedchamber, which overlooked the street outside the Crown. Vernon was below, on the street, his chestnut waves gleaming in the sunlight as he spoke to Bickling, who stood at the heads of Vernon's blacks.

Thea propped her elbow on the windowsill and her chin on her hand and brooded. For all her talk about eavesdropping on Mannington upon his return, she knew very well she had not the courage. The thought of being unmasked…she shivered with fear. There was much at stake from Mannington's point of view and who knew what lengths he would be driven to in order to protect himself? For that matter, who knew what lengths he had already gone to? No. Vernon's plan did have the best chance of success but, with the duke's man also coming to assist, where did that leave Thea? What was there left for her to do?

Sit here and brood, that is what.

At least they were safe within the inn. Mr Horwell had acted precisely as Vernon predicted, unable to keep the true identity of his illustrious guest to himself, and now the entire inn knew he was really a lord. Thea—as the Viscount's nephew—had been assumed his heir and was accordingly treated with much respect by the staff.

And now, here was Bickling, and Vernon had not even bothered to tell Thea he had arrived. She felt the gap between the two of them widening already. She flung away from the window and went to the door. She needed fresh air and exercise. Perhaps she could persuade Vernon to accompany her on a ride.

Vernon and Bickling were still deep in conversation when Thea reached the street. Both men looked up on her approach and she hesitated, but Vernon smiled and beckoned her over.

Not by a flicker of an eye did Bickling reveal his surprise.

'Master Theo,' he said, touching his cap.

She smiled and nodded at the groom, then said to Vernon, 'I thought I might go for a ride. It is like being in prison, being cooped up indoors all day and, strangely, I have missed the activity.'

'Have you indeed? Well, there is no accounting for it, I suppose. I thought you might enjoy the rest. Wait there, I shall instruct the groom to saddle the horses and we can leave Bickling to see to these two.'

Vernon strode through the arch to the stable yard. Before Bickling could follow him, Thea said, 'I trust all was well at the Court when you left?'

The groom nodded. 'Well enough,' he said. He lowered his voice. 'Though that man of yours… Malky…he took a might of persuading not to come along with me, 'e's that worried about you.'

'There is no need for him to worry. He knows I am with Lord Vernon.'

'That,' said Bickling, flicking a glance towards the archway through which Vernon had disappeared, 'appears to be what troubles him. Only I told him, I did, 'e's no need to fret on that account 'cause…beggin' your pardon, miss…you'm not to his lordship's usual taste and I told him so, I did.'

His words were no surprise, but she nevertheless felt the blow to her heart. It was quite one thing to tell yourself that you weren't *up to snuff*— another slang term taught to her by Vernon—but quite another to be told the same by someone else.

She raised her chin. 'What you fail to realise, Bickling, is that—even were I to his lordship's *usual taste*, as you so charmingly put it—his lordship would be destined for quite a disappointment for he is most definitely not to *mine*.'

She ground her teeth as she caught Bickling's smirk before he leaned into the curricle and extracted a bag from beneath the seat.

'Malky got one of the maids to pack you some clothes, miss. Dresses, they are. Just in case, he said, though it doesn't look like you'll have need of them. I'll have the bag sent up to your room, shall I?'

Slightly mollified, Thea thanked Bickling and watched as he began to lead the horses through to the rear of the hotel. It was not long before Vernon returned, leading Warrior and Star.

'Do you not wish to change your clothes before we go?' she asked him.

'There is little point, with you still resembling a barrow boy,' Vernon said with a wink. 'Unfortunately, there is little we can do about that. And, besides, there is no time to waste. Are you able to mount without help?' he added, as he checked Star's girth.

'You know that I am,' she responded sharply and pushed her left foot into the stirrup iron, springing up to the saddle. 'You have seen me do so often enough during our journey.'

'True.' Vernon mounted Warrior and then reined him around to ride in the direction of the river. 'But I should like to be able to treat you as I would normally treat a lady. I cannot help but feel guilty about everything you have been forced to endure over the past few days.'

'There is no need,' Thea said as Star ranged alongside Warrior. 'It was my choice to accompany you. And, before you suggest it again, I have no intention of going home.'

'I am glad.'

'You are? I thought you were eager to be rid of me.'

She glanced at his profile, glimpsing his rueful expression even as he kept his attention squarely on the road before them.

'I should not admit to this, but I would miss you if you went.' A muscle twitched in his jaw. 'I have become accustomed to having you around.' He turned to look at her, his green eyes boring into her. 'I have enjoyed being with you.'

Thea's stomach swooped. What did he mean?

Did he have feelings for her? Should she speak words of encouragement? But fear kept her silent. She could not bear the humiliation of misunderstanding him...of him trying to explain what he really meant...

Bickling's words came back to haunt her.

You'm not to his lordship's usual taste.

And who should know his master's predilections better than his groom, who would accompany him almost everywhere he went?

'You will soon forget me, when you go back to London,' she said dismissively.

Vernon reached for her hand. 'I shall not fo—'

Thea knocked his hand aside. 'Stop that,' she hissed. 'What if someone were to see? They would think you no better than that Wigbert Pooley.'

For once it was not Thea's cheeks that reddened, but Vernon's. 'My apologies,' he said, stiffly. 'I was forgetting myself.'

'I am sorry if you think I overreacted,' Thea said, following a pause, needing to soothe, hating that she'd made him uncomfortable. 'I did not mean to snap at you.'

'No. You were right, I was wrong. Look, Thea...' Vernon reined Warrior to a halt and twisted in the saddle to face her '...this...' he gestured between the two of them '...I feel a little as though...' He stared down at his hands, then heaved in a breath. 'I don't know. This is not real... We are in such a strange...'

His voice trailed into silence. They had stopped by the bridge and Vernon now looked over the river. Thea followed his gaze. On the opposite bank she could see a portly gentleman, clad in a black tailcoat and a tall-crowned hat, walking by the river. On his arm was a tall figure Thea had no trouble recognising: Miss Cordelia Temple.

'*There* they are,' Vernon said and sent Warrior forward across the bridge.

Thea followed. 'You sound as though you expected to see them.'

'They are the reason we have come this way. Horwell told me it is their custom to take an afternoon promenade along the river in fine weather. I hoped we might encounter them.'

'But…you said I must stay hidden from them.'

'Another thing I was wrong about. Well, not wrong precisely. Unfair? Yes. Unfair. You were right, you cannot remain hidden away for however many days it takes to uncover the truth about Daniel. You can develop—oh, I don't know, a fever of some description once Mannington returns. Until then, you may consider yourself out of prison.'

He threw her a crooked grin that sent her heart racing. Then she looked again at Miss Cordelia Temple and that surge of excitement drained away as she took in the American girl's elegant figure, draped in a silk gown that matched the blue of the sky. White lace and ribbons adorned both her gown and her matching bonnet, and she twirled a white lace parasol over one shoulder.

'But—'

'Shhh, now. Take care.'

Chapter Sixteen

As they passed by the Temples, Vernon reined Warrior around and raised his hat. 'Good afternoon,' he said with a bow of his head. 'Do I have the pleasure of addressing Mr Temple?'

His voice, unlike the softer, gentler tone he used when conversing with Thea, was clipped and haughty. Aristocratic. His transformation into an entitled nobleman despite his slightly disreputable-looking clothing made Thea stare. This man was far removed from the Vernon she had come to know. Was this how he normally looked and behaved and spoke? Self-confidence appeared to ooze from every pore—as it had, she realised with a start of memory, the day they first met.

Mr Temple and his daughter halted, and Temple frowned as he studied Vernon with something approaching disdain.

'You do,' he said, his accent strange to Thea's ears. 'Forgive my informality in addressing you without an introduction,' Vernon said, 'but we are fellow guests at the Crown and I could not ride past without acknowledgement. Boyton is the name.'

Temple's eyes widened. '*Lord* Boyton?'

'Indeed. I beg you will excuse my appearance. I am afraid our luggage has been waylaid and my nephew and I have been forced to resort to borrowed clothing.'

'I did hear a story of the sort,' Temple said. 'So it is true.'

Vernon inclined his head, whilst Thea lurked in the background, her eyes fixed on Cordelia Temple, taking in her poise, her glowing, golden skin and, glimpsed under that *exquisite* bonnet, her smooth black hair.

I'll bet Miss Cordelia Temple is 'to his lordship's usual taste'.

Jealousy, hot and sour, burned in her throat.

'Might I present my daughter, Cordelia?' Temple said.

Vernon slid from Warrior's back with fluid grace and tossed the reins to Thea. She watched, her heart twisting as Vernon took the heiress's proffered hand and raised it to his lips.

'*Enchanté*, Miss Temple.'

The girl inclined her head gracefully and then raised her gaze to Vernon's, meeting it with self-assurance. Dismay weaved its tentacles through Thea. How could she bear this? She could not even comfort herself that Cordelia was ugly, or coarse.

She soon found herself the object of scrutiny from those dark eyes. Cordelia's lips curved as she raised her beautifully arched brows.

'And your companion, my lord?'

'My nephew, Theo,' Vernon said. 'He is somewhat shy, I fear. That is why we are travelling around England together, in an effort to accustom him to strangers.'

'Then we must help you to help him,' Miss Temple said. 'Pops, we should invite Lord Boyton and Master Theo to join us for dinner. That—' she switched her smile from Thea to Vernon '—is the best way for Theo to engage in conversation.'

Thea smiled a secret smile at Vernon's horrified expression. 'But he is too young to dine with adults.'

'Oh, we do things differently back home and that's a fact,' Mr Temple said. 'Of course the boy is welcome. Not tonight, mind you. I'm dining with a couple of businessmen, making contacts and building relationships for the future.' He winked and tapped his nose with one finger. 'There's trouble ahead for our two nations and Samuel Temple will be one step ahead of the competition, you better believe me. That's the way to make money and that's a fact. Now, how long did you say you are in the area, my lord?'

'A week or so, I should imagine,' Vernon said.

A week? Thea almost gasped out loud in her horror until she realised how much time Vernon would need to get close to Mannington once he returned. A whole week, watching Vernon toadying up to that…that… She realised Miss Temple's gaze was upon her and she blanked her expression.

'How old are you, Theo? Fourteen? Fifteen?'

'Fifteen, miss.'

These past days had been the only time since her childhood that Thea had blessed her naturally deep voice. Before she had always cursed it, hating how unfeminine she sounded and the fact that she could not sing to save her life. Daniel had teased her about it mercilessly. The thought of her brother steadied her. They had to find out what had happened to Daniel. Nobody had seen him since he left Birmingham. It was as though he had vanished into thin air. It did not matter how much she might dislike Miss Temple, Thea must play her part.

'Will you do me the honour of taking my arm, Miss Temple?'

Vernon sketched a bow and crooked his elbow. Cordelia smiled graciously as she tucked her hand in his elbow and they began to stroll along the riverbank. Mr Temple, a wide beam lighting his face, walked on her other side, leaving Thea, riding Star and leading Warrior, to bring up the rear.

'My lord, this will not do.' Cordelia slipped her arm from Vernon's after a few minutes and stepped aside, waiting for Thea and the two horses to draw level. 'You say it is your aim to accustom your nephew to strangers and yet you abandon him to ride alone in our wake.'

The full force of her smile—smooth cherry-red lips and sparkling white, even teeth—was directed at Thea. She felt her cheeks heat and, at that, Cordelia laughed—a low, musical sound—then reached up and patted Thea's hand.

'No need to be embarrassed. Come walk with me…may I call you Theo? And you must call me Cordelia.' She tossed her head in Vernon's direction, then turned her attention back to Thea. 'What do you say? Let the gentlemen walk ahead and talk of business and other tedious matters, and you may tell me about your life and I shall confide in you about mine.' She winked. 'Although you must promise not to reveal my secrets to your uncle,' she added in a whisper.

Thea's spirits plunged. Cordelia was *nice*. She was being kind to a youth who she thought was feeling awkward and unsure of himself. That knowledge made Thea feel worse for her dislike, which was not based upon the woman herself but upon Thea's own irrational jealousy. Given other circumstances, Cordelia Temple might be a friend.

'Miss Temple!' Vernon had halted and turned. He glanced at Thea, an impish gleam in his green eyes, before striking a dramatic pose, one hand pressed to his chest, the other extended to Cordelia. 'You strike a callous blow to my pride and my heart,' he pronounced. 'Will you indeed desert me for so green a youth? Come. Take my arm once more. Do not, I beg you, abandon me.'

Thea stared. This man, again, was nothing like the man she had come to know, but neither was he the haughty aristocrat of earlier. Was this how Vernon flirted with the females of the *ton*? Or was he mimicking those men he had told her of...the ones who made *cakes* of themselves, spouting poetry and prostrating themselves at the feet of a pretty girl, all for the sake of a pair of fine eyes? Those tales had kept Thea entertained during their long days in the saddle.

Miss Temple appeared impressed, however, for she started towards him, hands stretched out, crying, 'My lord! Never! I shall not forsake you so cruelly.'

She caught his hand between hers and somehow their entwined hands were pressed to Vernon's chest. Anger licked deep in Thea's belly.

Mr Temple let forth a guffaw. 'Delia, you are a naughty minx. Let go of his lordship this instant. And as for you, sir,' he added as both Vernon and Cordelia broke apart, laughing, 'I'll thank you not to encourage my daughter in such nonsense.'

'I cannot believe you saw through me so quickly,' Vernon said, grinning. Then he sobered. 'Not that I did not mean every word, of course.'

Cordelia laughed again and slapped his arm. 'Of course.'

'My lord! Tell her that ladies in London must

not laugh uncontrollably nor make fun of gentlemen,' Mr Temple said, his thick grey brows bee-
tling. 'We are going there in the fall, but you will
be shunned if you make such a spectacle of yourself, Delia, and that's a fact.'

Vernon raised his brows as he smiled ruefully.
'I am afraid your father is correct, Miss Temple. I
cannot conceive why, for it has never made sense
to me that ladies are expected to control their emotions at all times, but it is so. You may smile, but it
is frowned upon to laugh. Or to voice your opinion
too forcefully. Or, indeed, to show enthusiasm. It
is the height of fashion to be *ennui*.'

'Well, that does not sound much fun to me,' Cordelia announced. 'I am not sure I wish to go to London
after all, Pops. I can't think of anything worse than
spending my time a-fretting and a-flustering in case
I've broken some unwritten rule.'

Thea, following behind once more, found herself in full agreement.

'Well, well, we shall see,' Mr Temple said.
'There is time yet to change our plans. I must say…'
he tipped his head towards Vernon '…I have wondered if it is wise to take my Cordelia to London. I
didn't expect that news about Perceval. Shocking!
I expect such lawlessness in America—it is very
primitive in parts, with savages and such—but I
never thought to hear of a British Prime Minis-
ter being assassinated and that's a fact. Is London
safe?'

'It is as safe as anywhere, sir. No one can pre-empt a madman, such as the fellow who shot Perceval. It is quite unprecedented. Your daughter will be perfectly safe from gunmen, although I cannot promise the same safety against fortune hunters. I fear London society has its fair share of such men—as does Worcester, no doubt—and you will do well to be on your guard. You can never be too careful.'

Mr Temple slapped Vernon on the back. 'You can be sure I've got my wits about me, my lord. It'll take a real sly critter to put one over on Samuel Temple and that's a fact.'

They reached a point on the bank opposite the cathedral and Temple turned to Vernon and thrust out a large hand.

'Good to meet you, my lord. You too, Theo, m'lad. We get the ferry here, back across to the cathedral.' A white and green boat, the name *Betty* painted on her bow, was moored by a small wooden jetty. 'Shall we say dinner at six tomorrow? It'll only be us and our friend Mr Mannington if he is back in time, so no need for young Theo to get himself in a fuss about it.'

'Mannington?' Vernon flicked a warning glance at Thea and she realised she had gasped out loud. 'Is he from America, too?'

'No. We met in Liverpool the night our ship docked. It was a lucky coincidence…we both have interests in the cotton manufactories in the Man-

chester area, so we travelled there together and
then, blow me down, when we came here it was
only to find he lives not four miles away. He persuaded us to stay here for the summer rather than
go to Brighton as I intended.' He nudged Vernon
with his elbow. 'He's the cousin of a dook, y'know.
One up on a viscount—eh, m'lord?'

Thea bit back a grin as astonishment flitted
across Vernon's expression. No doubt he was unused to such familiarity.

'Oh, indubitably so,' he murmured. 'Although…
much as I hate to correct you…a duke is, in fact,
three up on a viscount.'

'Three up!' Mr Temple emitted a low whistle.
'Well, I'll be.' He nudged Vernon once again. 'I bet
you wish you were related to a dook, eh, my lord?'

'I am perfectly content with my birthright, sir,'
Vernon said.

A smile was by now tugging at the corner of his
mouth. He bowed.

'It was a pleasure to meet you both,' he said,
'and I thank you for the invitation to dine tomorrow, which we gladly accept. I, for one, cannot
wait to make the acquaintance of a real-life cousin
of a duke.'

'Aw, shucks, now you're pulling my leg, my lord.
You'll have to forgive me and my rough-and-ready
ways. So long, young Theo, m'lad.' He waved to
the ferryman, leaning on his oars. 'Come along,
Delia, time we moved along.'

He raised his land in farewell and Cordelia smiled, first at Vernon and then at Thea.

'Goodbye,' she said. 'I shall look forward to seeing you both tomorrow.'

Vernon remounted Warrior and they enjoyed a canter, still following the course of the Severn. As it curved, beyond the city, an encampment came into view and Vernon brought Warrior to a halt.

'A gipsy camp, by the look of it,' he said. 'We shall turn back. It is better not to intrude.'

'I have always found the gipsies to be friendly enough,' Thea said, taking in the colourful wagons, the tents and the cooking fires. 'I had not thought you to be prejudiced against them, not after what you said to the constable in Harborne.'

'I am not prejudiced. They often camp on my land in Devon and work during the harvest or mend bits and pieces. They are friendly to a point, but they do not welcome outsiders and they are protective of their own.'

A tall man with dark, curly hair emerged from the nearest tent. He watched them expressionlessly, his hands relaxed by his sides.

'That camp is their home, albeit temporary,' Vernon continued, turning Warrior. 'I have no wish to stir resentment.'

She smiled at him. 'You are right.' She reined Star around, pointing her head back upstream. 'Come on. I'll race you.'

Vernon followed with a whoop. He seemed to

hold Warrior back at first, but Thea—familiar with both animals—knew Star needed no preferential treatment. Vernon clearly reached the same conclusion and he gave the bay his head. They finished nose to nose, both riders slightly breathless, the horses blowing.

'We must walk them now and let the horses cool,' Thea said, stroking Star's damp neck.

The road back to the Crown was busy with carts and coaches and they were forced to ride in single file, precluding conversation, for which Thea was grateful. When they arrived back, Bickling came out to take charge of the horses.

'You go on up,' Vernon said to Thea. 'I must speak to Bickling. I will see you at dinner.'

That evening, Vernon raised a forkful of pigeon pie to his mouth and chewed, eyeing the woman sitting opposite him at the dining table in their private parlour. He still cringed at the memory of his ridiculous posturing after Cordelia had asked Thea to walk with her. It had been the only way he could think to divert her—he didn't believe Thea's disguise would pass such close scrutiny—and so he had put on an act. Thank goodness neither of the Temples had been fooled into thinking he was serious; he did have some pride.

'Miss Temple seems nice,' Thea remarked after a period of silence.

He had wondered how long it would take her

to bring the conversation around to the American visitors. He still could not fathom her feelings. Was she angry with him? Or—and his heart twitched in hope at the thought—was she perhaps a little jealous at the attention he had paid to Cordelia Temple?

She was so easy to read in so many ways and yet when it came to her feelings for him she was a closed book. He felt…he groped for the right word. Off balance. That was it. An uncomfortable and unaccustomed feeling for him, especially where women were concerned. But then, his uncertainty about what she thought and felt was no greater than his uncertainty about what *he* truly thought and felt.

About her.

He did not deny he liked Thea. He liked her very much indeed. And the more time he spent in her company, the more he liked her. He looked forward to seeing her every day. But did his feelings run deeper than that? Yes, he wanted her physically, but was that desire partly driven by these extraordinary circumstances, and because he was honour bound to safeguard her virtue, even from himself…*especially* from himself? All he did know was it was getting harder to stick to his principles.

He had never before, he realised with a start, been such close friends with a woman he was not related to. And that thought led to another…what if she *were* a member of his family? The thought rattled him. He had no need to wed. His life was fulfilled as it was. Why look for complications?

He swallowed his food, conscious she was waiting for him to respond.

'You did not give the impression that you much cared for her company,' he said.

She pierced him with her hazel eyes, green specks glinting in the candlelight.

'It did not take two of us to act like lovelorn fools,' she snapped.

Vernon pondered that as he continued to eat. *Was* there a hint of jealousy there, or was this simply more of her scathing dismissal of the idle aristocracy? She did not appear to be waiting for his reply, attacking her food with more enthusiasm than he had yet seen.

'*Acting* being the pertinent word here,' he commented finally.

She raised her gaze to his.

'My dear Dotty…'

Her eyes flashed her anger. It did help, somewhat, if she was irritated with him and teasing came naturally…it was easier to tease her than to find himself resorting to charm. God knew where that might lead.

'You forget that I am not a viscount in need of a wife and family to continue my family name and to inherit entailed estates. I am still a bachelor for a reason… I have no need to wed.'

She swallowed her food. 'Very sensible. I should imagine rakish aristocrats do not make comfortable husbands.'

'You look for comfort in a husband?'

'I look for nothing. I look for no husband, as you well know.'

'But if you did look for one?' He couldn't help himself, even though this conversation could become treacherous. '*Comfort* would be your first consideration?'

Their gazes fused, the food forgotten.

'I think an *uncomfortable* husband would result in an unhappy life.'

'But what of passion? Desire? Did you not feel those emotions with…?' His voice trailed into silence.

Her jaw set. 'With Jasper? Mannington, I mean.' She sighed, her shoulders dropping, and used her knife to push her remaining food into a neat heap at the side of her plate. 'I felt… I don't know… happy, flattered, eager to set up home together. I suppose I must have thought myself in love with him, but—looking back—I wonder if I was more in love with the notion of being married and having a family than with the man himself.' A tight, bitter smile stretched her lips. 'I was very soon cured of that nonsense.' She put down her knife with a clatter. 'Quite what my marital intentions have to do with your flirtation with Miss Temple I fail to understand, but I warn you…do not raise false expectations as to your intentions merely because it suits your purpose.'

'She is no fool. I'll wager she knows enough of

the world to understand that not every man who pays her some attention wishes to marry her and she has her father to protect her from rakes and fortune hunters.'

'And yet they are friends with J—Henry Mannington and I notice she hung on every word that left your mouth.'

Vernon shrugged. 'Can I help it if I have that effect on women?'

Thea flushed a deep red. 'Not every woman,' she said in her endearing, gruff little voice. 'You believe yourself to be irresistible, but you are not.'

'Am I not, Thea?'

Vernon stretched across the table and captured her hand, holding just firmly enough to stop her tugging it free. It was tiny and warm and soft, the bones fragile, and his heart swelled with the urge to take her in his arms and kiss her senseless, to show her what real desire and passion was, to demonstrate what she was missing, what she had shut out of her life.

'Vernon…'

She pulled again at her hand, but he tightened his grip. A light blush crept from her neck to wash her cheeks. Without any conscious thought as to his actual intention, he stood up and rounded the table, tugging her to her feet. He reached for her other hand and stroked her knuckles with his thumbs. Her lids lowered to shield her gaze, but he saw the tremble of her lip. Surely he could not be mistaken?

She was not unaffected. She no longer tried to pull free, but her posture was stiff. Tense.

What would I give to know exactly what she is thinking? A king's ransom, that's what.

He released one hand and nudged her chin up so her face tilted to meet his gaze. Her eyes were wide—questioning and, yes, uncertain. Then they darkened as her pupils dilated, her shoulders slumped and he felt the warmth of her breath as it feathered across his cheek and heard her whispered gasp as it escaped her lips. A wave of desire sent the blood powering to his groin and he felt the heavy weight of arousal. He pulled her close to his chest, folding his arms around her. She was so tiny. Fragile. And yet she was strong, too, in her spirit and her resolve. The desire to protect, and to avenge, flowed through him and he breathed a deep sigh before letting her go, dropping his arms to his sides.

He had proved to himself she was not immune to him, but he felt an utter bastard, particularly because he still wasn't sure these feelings she aroused in him were not just as a result of them being thrown together in this unnatural way.

But Thea did not step away when he released her. Instead, she reached up and slipped one hand behind his neck, pressing the length of her body to his. Her eyes asked a different question now, no longer uncertain but assured as she went on tiptoes and her mouth sought his.

Chapter Seventeen

Her lips were warm and sweet and open to his questing tongue. With a deep groan, Vernon gathered Thea to him, his exploring hands registering the strangeness of the rough cloth of her jacket and the peculiar rigidity of her back and sides due to the bindings under her shirt. His hands moved lower and he cupped her softly rounded cheeks, lifting to pull her hard against him. He thrust aside the warnings that screamed through his mind as he kissed her and allowed his hands to roam. Her fingers combed through his hair, caressing his skull. He should stop, but…

He did not want to. He wanted more. He wanted her.

He cradled her face in his hands, her cheeks silky to his touch as he devoured her sweetness. He speared his fingers through her soft curls, scattering butterfly kisses over her cheeks, her brows, her eyelids. He feathered kisses along the angle of her jaw and slid his lips to her ear, sweeping his tongue around the delicate shell, then caught her lobe between his teeth and tugged gently, nibbling. She moaned, pushing her hands beneath his jacket and around his back, caressing as she pressed closer.

Time stood still. Nothing else existed. Only Thea, in his arms, her soft lips open to him and her body nestling into his. His heart felt as though it cracked open, welcoming her in to fill a gap he had not known existed until now, but a gap that had always been there. And it was Thea-shaped. She fitted perfectly. She made him whole.

It was Thea who ended that kiss, who stepped back, bringing her hands between them, resting them on his chest. Reluctantly, he released her, shoving his fingers through his hair.

'Someone might come in.' She pressed her fingers to her mouth, her eyes huge and luminous, her cheeks rosy. She uttered a strangled-sounding laugh. 'That would take a bit of explaining.'

Vernon returned to his chair and stood behind it, watching her closely and, once again, uncertain of which path to take. He was cautious of forging ahead, as he'd like to. After her experience with Mannington, her trust would be slowly gained. It could not be demanded.

'Should I apologise?' he asked.

'No!' Startled. Vehement. 'Why should you apologise? *I* kissed *you*.' She sighed and dropped down on her chair, propping her elbows on the table and dropping her head into her hands. 'Shameful as that must seem to you.'

Vernon gripped the back rail of the chair. 'Shameful? Why should I think it shameful?'

She huffed a bitter laugh. 'I might not be part of your world, Vernon, but I do know that my behaviour would be viewed as scandalous. And in my world, too, come to that.'

She avoided his gaze. 'Whereas your behaviour… you would no doubt receive a pat on the back from your peers and an indulgent shrug of the shoulders from your womenfolk. Men are permitted indulgences such as stealing a kiss when the opportunity presents. A woman behaving in such a way is to be scorned.'

'Then it is fortunate that no one other than you and I were witness to it.' Vernon sat down again, feeling curiously deflated. Did it mean nothing more to her than a stolen kiss? 'After all, what is a kiss between friends?'

Her eyes shuttered. 'Indeed.' Her tone was careless. 'It was merely a…a *trifling experiment* between friends.'

Vernon cursed himself for his clumsiness, knowing he had hurt her feelings. Never had he felt more out of his depth with a woman as he floundered for the right words.

'Thea. I—'

Thea interrupted. 'We need to discuss tomorrow before we go upstairs.'

Did his failure to find the right words matter? Maybe this was for the best—for now. If they spoke now of other matters, it might help dispel the awkward aftermath of that kiss and they might return to their former friendship until they found out what had happened to Daniel. And when they did...after they did...then, perhaps, they might think about what the future might hold.

'I cannot dine with the Temples tomorrow,' Thea said. 'Not if Mannington might be present.'

'I agree. Meeting Mannington in passing on the street is quite different to sitting with him at a dining table. He could not fail to recognise you, especially as you would not be wearing a cap. I shall go alone and tell the Temples you are unwell.' He half-smiled at her, attempting to tease. 'I shall tell them I caught you at the brandy.'

'That,' said Thea, stiffly, as she shoved back her chair and stood up, 'is unnecessary. There is no need to pile lie upon lie. Simply informing them that I am unwell is sufficient.'

Vernon rounded the table. He skimmed her curls back from her face. 'I was teasing, Thea.'

She stared up at him, her eyes searching his. 'I know. And I know you are trying to make this better, to make it easier for me. But...'

'But it is hard for you. Take courage, though. Mannington will be back tomorrow.'

Thea clutched Vernon's sleeve. 'You must promise to tell me *every*thing. Good or bad.' She shook his arm. '*Please*. I need to know you will not try to protect my feelings.'

Vernon cupped her cheek. 'I promise.' It was not enough. He needed to give her the reassurance she craved, to shield her as far as possible from the fear that must gnaw at her day and night. 'I promise I will not conceal *anything* I discover.' He raised his brows slightly and smiled into her eyes. 'We are partners, are we not, you and I? Who else can I discuss strategy with?'

She tipped her head, pressing her cheek into his palm, like a kitten seeking a caress.

'Thank you,' she whispered, and for a moment he was gliding, effortlessly, across the waters that so often in the past few days appeared likely to swamp him.

'I must go,' she whispered. 'Goodnight, Vernon. I hope you sleep well.'

Vernon reached the door before her, preparing to open it. Thea halted, her brows raised pointedly, and he released the handle again and stepped aside.

'I forgot,' he said. 'Again. I keep forgetting, but how I wish...'

He shook his head, knowing that to speak his wishes—that he could treat her as a lady—was not wise. Not now. He gestured for her to open the door.

'Goodnight, Thea,' he whispered as she passed him by. 'Sweet dreams.'

* * *

The following day was an utter waste of time from Thea's perspective. In keeping with the tale that she was ill, she remained in her bedchamber all day, with just her thoughts for company. And if she wasn't fretting about Daniel, she was fretting about that kiss…about how *she* had kissed *him*. She had never before behaved so shamefully.

But he started it.

He'd hauled her from her chair and studied her face with such intent, his green eyes glinting in the candlelight and his lips…his kiss…

He kissed me as though he meant *it.*

She hugged that knowledge close. And—from time to time—she allowed herself to glory in the memory of the most wonderful moment in her life so far. That kiss had lit a slow-burning fuse deep down inside her that, no matter how she tried to douse it, simply refused to be extinguished.

Apart from a couple of brief visits from Vernon— when she strove to act as though that kiss had never happened—she had not seen him. He was, he assured her, pursuing his acquaintance with the Temples and had sent Bickling to tour the numerous public houses in Worcester to enquire after Daniel. He promised to call in on her before he went down to dine and Thea found herself pacing the floor from five o'clock, waiting for his visit.

Finally, there was a tap at the door. She flew

across the floor, hauled the door open and grabbed Vernon's arm, dragging him into the room.

'My dear Dotty,' he drawled, removing her hand from his sleeve and tugging at the cuff to smooth out the wrinkles. 'I beg you will refrain from manhandling my second-best coat in such a very uncouth manner.'

Thea blinked and stepped back, taking in his appearance. He looked…magnificent. Utterly gorgeous. Handsome, sexy and every inch the wealthy aristocrat he was. And all for the benefit of Cordelia Temple…

Bickling had delivered these clothes yesterday, but Vernon had not thought Thea worth dressing up for last night. Her heart sank, remembering his dismissal of that kiss.

'And I have to say,' he went on as he strolled over to the window and peered into the street outside, 'in all my years I cannot recall ever being hauled into a lady's bedchamber in quite such a…shall we say…*enthusiastic* manner.'

She was too dazzled by his appearance to take much notice of his teasing. She had thought him resplendent when he first arrived at Stourwell Court, but *this*…

He wore an olive-green tailcoat over a cream waistcoat glittering with gold embroidery and cream pantaloons and at his throat a stunning emerald pin nestled in his beautifully tied neckcloth. She gulped and turned to fiddle with the comb on her dressing table. This was not the Vernon she knew. This was Lord Vernon Beauchamp and she felt…shy. How should she behave? Should she have curtsied? She certainly should not have dragged him into her room as she did.

Vernon appeared not to notice her turmoil as he continued to watch the street outside.

'I say enthusiastic,' he continued, musingly, 'but it could, I think, even be described as *desperate*.'

He turned to look at her, a mischievous grin on his face, which vanished the instant he caught sight of her. 'Thea?' He was by her side in two strides, lightly cupping her shoulders. 'What is it?'

Thea gulped. Reminded herself this was still Vernon. 'You look…splendid.'

Vernon tipped his head to one side, frowning. 'You sound different. Where is my spiky little kitten?'

Kitten? Is that how he thinks of me? As a ball of fluff to amuse and entertain him? A joke? I bet he wouldn't refer to Cordelia Temple as a kitten.

But then what did that kiss mean?

He is a man, a lord who no doubt has enjoyed mistresses galore. What does a kiss mean to him? Nothing!

'You took me by surprise. Your clothes make you look so different. Almost a stranger.'

Vernon tweaked a curl above her ear. 'I am no stranger, Dotty. I am still me.'

His eyes crinkled…an almost-smile that had

Thea grinding her teeth. Why did she always feel so…so…*fluttery* around him? And how was he *always* so self-assured? She had never been a woman to simper and flirt and yet, with him, she had to constantly control her urge to do exactly that. And, worse, she worried that the search for Daniel was almost being overshadowed by her growing fascination with Vernon.

She must keep her focus on Daniel, even though it was increasingly hard to keep her hopes alive.

She perched on the edge of the bed, thrusting down that tangle of guilt and desire, hope and dread. Emotions could not help; they could only confuse and lead her astray. Weak, female emotions must be controlled…particularly this ridiculous infatuation for Vernon. She could not bear to put her trust in another man only to be let down again. Once more, she heard Bickling's amused declaration that she was not to his lordship's usual taste.

'Tell me about your day,' she said.

Vernon, she noticed, did not sit on the bed, but chose the wooden chair by the dressing table. He swung it around to face her and sat, stretching his long legs out, crossing them at the ankle, and folding his arms across his wide chest—supremely confident, relaxed, in charge. And very…*deliciously*…masculine.

Thea contained her inner *hmph* and averted her gaze.

'Actually, I have little to report. I have made

myself indispensable to Miss Temple by escorting her to the shops this morning, whilst her father attended business meetings, so she and I are fast becoming friends.'

The pain that pierced Thea's heart could be borne. She had no choice.

'This afternoon Bickling and I visited more of the public houses in the city,' Vernon continued, 'but we found no one who recalled either Daniel Markham or Charles Leyton.' He sat up, leaning forward, his elbows on his knees. 'I worry you were right the other day.' All trace of teasing had vanished and Thea could not doubt the genuine concern on his face. 'It is as you said: Birmingham is the last place where Daniel was definitely seen. Even though we stopped and asked at every inn we passed, we have found no one who remembers him.' He leapt to his feet and paced the room. 'He must have gone *somewhere* when he left there. Where did he go? Who did he see? Did he ever meet Mannington face to face?'

Thea rubbed her upper arms as she listened to his questions. Her heart swelled as she watched him pace, not with awe this time but with gratitude. How much she owed this man. Without him, she would never have dared to set out on this mission. Although they had found no trace of Daniel, they were close to uncovering the truth. She could feel it. Mannington—shivers of loathing chased up and down her spine at the mere thought of the man—was the key to finding Daniel, of that she was convinced. And without Vernon she would never know the truth because she would never have the courage to confront the man who had jilted her and defrauded her family.

'I must go.'

Vernon stood and Thea followed suit. Vernon came to her and touched her shoulder, fleetingly. Their gazes fused, and Thea felt a lurching tug deep inside.

'I must not be late.' Again he touched her, this time one finger beneath her chin. Again, it was fleeting. 'I have asked Horwell to send up some food on a tray for you.'

Thea forced a smile, dreading the solitary evening ahead of her.

'Please do not be tempted to leave this room,' he said softly, taking her hand. 'I know you are bored, but it will only be for a few more days.'

He pressed warm lips to the back of her hand, sending delightful tingles chasing across her skin.

'Goodnight, sweet Dotty. I shall tell you all in the morning.'

And he was gone, leaving the scent of his cologne lingering in the air and a dull ache in her heart.

Chapter Eighteen

Vernon straightened his sleeves and smoothed his lapels as he waited in the private parlour rented by the Temples for the duration of their stay in Worcester. It was twice the size of the parlour Vernon and Thea had at their disposal, but Vernon preferred the cosiness and the intimacy of their smaller room. The table, at one end of the room, was set for five—one place at the head and two on either side—and a sofa and two upholstered chairs were arranged around the unlit fireplace at the opposite end of the room.

Vernon thought of Thea, all alone in her bedchamber. He would far rather eat his meal in her company than with the Temples and Mannington, even though the point of this was to gain an introduction to the man. Poor Thea, stuck in her bedchamber all day and still uncomplaining, although she was clearly bored. And still as enigmatic as ever. From their very first meeting that morning she had exhibited not one hint of awkwardness after that kiss last night. It was as though nothing had happened…as though that kiss was truly, as she had claimed, a trifling experiment. His own inconsistency irritated him. Her behaviour was precisely what he had hoped for—for them to return to their former easy camaraderie.

Why, then, did he feel so…*rejected*?

The sound of the door opening jolted him from his thoughts. Cordelia Temple wafted into the room on a cloud of expensive perfume and a swish of silk skirts.

She crossed the room, holding out her hand with a smile.

'Good evening, Lord Boyton. How nice to see you again. I am delighted you could join us.'

Vernon took her hand and bowed over it. As he did so the door opened and Horwell entered.

'Mr Henry Mannington has arrived, Miss Temple.'

He stood aside and Henry Mannington strolled in, then stopped short as he caught sight of Vernon with Cordelia. Vernon deliberately lingered over Cordelia's hand, pressing his lips to it as he gauged Mannington's reaction from under his brows.

He is good.

Other than his abrupt halt, not a hint of anger marred Mannington's expression. Vernon straightened, releasing Cordelia's hand. There was no need

for Mannington to suspect he was purposely nee-
dling him. Subtle and sly, those were to be Vernon's
watchwords. He slammed the lid on his desire to
throttle the man for what he had done to Thea and
her family. If ever there was a time for cool and
calculated detachment, this was it.

'Mr Mannington.' Cordelia turned to the newcomer with a radiant smile. 'Such a delight to see
you again. Was your business trip a success?'

'Good evening, Miss Temple, and indeed it was.
I have every hope this particular deal will prove
a huge success. Better, indeed, than I had origi-
nally hoped.'

He took her hand, as Vernon had done, and he
too bowed over it and pressed his lips firmly to
the back, flicking a sideways glance at Vernon as
he did so.

Vernon recognised the possessiveness of the
gesture and the glance. The man was marking his
territory.

We shall see about that.

A light blush had coloured Cordelia's cheeks,
confirming she was not immune to Mannington.
Vernon would have to work hard to gain her trust
before she might believe any warning he might give
her about him, particularly as her father clearly
trusted him. This task might prove more delicate
than Vernon had anticipated. He must bide his time,
watch the three of them together, and exploit any
chink he could find in their relationship.

'Mr Mannington, may I introduce Lord Boyton?'

Vernon, standing in what he knew was an arrogant pose, thrust out his hand. 'Mannington,' he said.

If he hadn't been watching Mannington very closely, he might not have seen the caution that flashed across his expression, could easily have missed the minute hunch of his shoulders that, in an animal, would be the slink of a lesser male before the leader of the pack. Vernon knew he must be on his guard—such a man, feeling the threat, would think nothing of attacking from behind.

'My lord,' Mannington said. He bowed his head, briefly, and shook Vernon's proffered hand. 'It is always a pleasure to meet newcomers to the area.'

If Vernon had not caught Mannington's first, instinctive reaction, he would have been completely fooled by the man's current open expression, pleasant smile and firm handshake. No wonder Thea's family had been taken in by this scoundrel... He trapped that thought before it could develop further. He must take care not to dwell on such thoughts lest Mannington was watching him as closely as Vernon was studying Mannington. Let him believe that Vernon's only interest in him was as a rival for Cordelia. That was a simple conflict compared to the truth.

'His lordship is a guest here at the Crown, together with his nephew,' Cordelia continued. 'Papa and I made their acquaintance yesterday. Speaking of Theo…' Cordelia tilted her head to one side, smiling at Vernon '…where is he, my lord? I do hope you did not forbid him to attend? Do you know, Mr Mannington, Lord Boyton was quite horrified at the idea of a fifteen-year-old youth joining us to dine?'

'Miss Temple, I protest. You do me a gross disservice. Alas, Theo is unable to join us because he is unwell. He asked me to convey his apologies.'

'What?' Mr Temple had joined them. 'Young Theo not well? Does he need a doctor? Henry, my boy, you must know of a decent man hereabouts. Give me his name and I'll send for him immediately to attend the lad.' A heavy hand landed on Vernon's shoulder. 'Can't be too careful with matters of health, m'lord, and that's a fact.'

Mannington's gaze darted between Temple and Vernon, but the only indicator of his feelings was the slightest twitch of his left eye. 'I am certain his lordship will not hesitate to ask for a recommendation should his nephew require medical attention.'

The weight of Temple's hand was uncomfortable—made him feel trapped…controlled, somehow—and Vernon sidestepped, causing it to slip from his shoulder. Not wishing to offend the man, he then placed his left hand between the American's shoulder blades.

'I am grateful for your concern, sir,' he said, 'but Theo has no need of a physician. Rather…and I trust you will think none the worse of him after this confession, Miss Temple…he is in sore need of a darkened room and bed rest. His ills are entirely self-inflicted.'

Temple guffawed. 'The downfall of many a youth. I trust you will curb any excessive tendency in that direction, m'lord…the demon alcohol can all too easily become a master instead of a servant and that's a fact.'

'It can indeed,' Vernon murmured, biting back a smile as he imagined Thea's reaction were she privy to this conversation.

The door opened to admit a maid carrying a soup tureen.

'The food's here; time we sat,' Temple said, heading for the chair at the head of the table. 'My belly feels like my throat's been cut.'

Vernon pulled out a chair for Cordelia, leaving a vacant seat between her and her father. 'Miss Temple?'

'Thank you, kind sir.'

She sat in the proffered seat and, from the corner of his eye, Vernon saw Mannington stalk behind his back to commandeer that vacant chair. Vernon allowed himself a quiet smirk of satisfaction. The seating arrangements suited him perfectly: sitting opposite the pair of them, on Temple's right-hand side, would mean he could watch all three with ease.

'That's it, sit where you will, gents,' Temple boomed. 'No formality at my table and that's a fact. None of that *only talk to your neighbour* here, no matter how highfalutin' our guests might be.'

Vernon could not hold back his grin at that. He leaned down to murmur into Cordelia's ear.

'Highfaluting?'

On the far side of Cordelia, he could see Mannington straining to hear what he said. Taking the opportunity to stir the other man's temper, he lowered his voice to a whisper.

'I cannot say I have *ever* had the pleasure of being described as highfaluting before. What, precisely, does it mean? Is it *exceedingly* unflattering?'

Cordelia gurgled with laughter. 'It means…well, I guess it is a little unflattering. Pops! You must not insult his lordship with unfamiliar American slang.'

'Rubbish! His lordship won't take offence at some good-natured joshing, will you, m'lord?'

Cordelia smiled over her shoulder at Vernon. 'It kind of means high-flown, grandiose. I do hope you are not offended.'

'Of course I am not.'

He rounded the table and took his own seat.

Dishes were set in the centre of the table and wine poured, and the servants left the room. Mannington's plan became clear—by sitting next to Cordelia he could serve food to her plate and speak quietly in her ear as he did so without risk of censure, for who would call him on his manners were he merely asking her what morsels she might prefer?

The meal progressed. Temple held forth on matters of business and Vernon took little part in the conversation, but was surprised at the extent to which Cordelia joined in. She appeared knowledgeable about all her father's many interests, from their cotton plantation in Georgia to their coal mines in Pennsylvania. It appeared, however, that father and daughter lived much of the time in Washington.

'For that is where the power is, m'lord,' Temple said. 'And that is where I can lobby on matters that will benefit me. It is not like here, where all the power is in the hands of the landowners and very little in the hands of manufacturers who employ the people and make goods to export to bring money into the country. You mark my words…' he waved a fork '…change will come here, too.'

'Wealth will always count,' Vernon said.

'That is true,' Mannington said, his long fingers playing with his wine glass. 'But the balance of wealth—and therefore influence—will gradually shift away from the landed gentry and towards those who, as our host has said, actually produce goods.'

Vernon might suspect he was right, but could not resist challenging him.

'What about food? People will always need to eat.'

'I do not deny it…' Mannington tore his bread roll in half and buttered it '…but the war with France will not go on indefinitely and grain will be imported once more. Where there is competition the price will drop. That is a basic tenet of business.'

Vernon quashed his irritation at the implication that he knew nothing of business. It fitted the part he played to be thought an idle aristocrat by these people, even though he hated Thea to think of him as such. And how did she always creep into his thoughts even when she was not present?

He forced a shrug of nonchalance, peering down his nose at Mannington. 'The ruling classes will always be just that,' he said in his most condescending voice. 'I do not expect such as you to understand quite how society and government work together for the common good.'

The other man's jaw tightened. Both Vernon and Mannington had ceased eating, and Temple's gaze darted from one to the other, consternation writ large upon his face.

'*Henry*,' he said, 'is the cousin of a *dook*, my lord. I'm sure we told you that when we met yesterday.'

'A duke, you say?' Vernon held Mannington's gaze as he sipped his wine.

How Leo would relish slapping down the presumption of this scoundrel. And how I would love to see the two come face to face.

He permitted himself an arrogant smile. 'It must have slipped my mind. And which duke might that be?'

'The Duke of Cheriton.'

Not by a flicker did Mannington reveal the tension he must be feeling. After all, for all he knew, Vernon and the Duke of Cheriton might be the closest of friends.

'Ah, yes.' Vernon sipped again at his wine, his eyes never leaving Mannington's face. 'Cheriton. A cousin, you say? Close, are you?'

The muscles around Mannington's eyes tightened imperceptibly. 'Close enough, although we do not, of course, move in the same circles. I have a living to earn. Leo…his Grace…does not.'

'You do not consider running huge estates and being responsible for vast numbers of employees and tenants to be work?'

'No. Managers, agents and bailiffs take care of most of that,' Mannington said carelessly. 'As is no doubt the same in your case, Boyton.'

Vernon shrugged again. 'As you say. I do not concern myself with the day-to-day running of my estates. However, neither do I pretend to move in such exalted circles as Cheriton. I have little interest in politics, for instance.'

'But you are able to sit in the Lords?' Temple interjected. 'You do hold some influence there?'

Vernon turned his gaze on the American. This remark, together with his earlier comment on living in Washington, in order to be close to the men who ran the country, provided him with the perfect lever to unsettle Mannington and keep Temple—and hence his daughter—on his side. Viscount Boyton, as a peer, would indeed be eligible to sit in the Lords even though Lord Vernon Beauchamp, with merely a courtesy title, could not.

He shrugged. 'Oh, I can wield influence if I choose. I have yet, however, to discover a cause about which I am passionate.' He smiled across the table at Cordelia. 'Becoming too embroiled in worthy causes does tend to distract one from the more…shall we say, *pleasurable* aspects of London life.' He raised a brow. 'And Worcestershire life, come to that.'

Cordelia laughed. 'Would you care to expound on that statement, sir?'

He allowed one corner of his mouth to quirk up. 'Expound in what way, Miss Temple?'

Out of the corner of his eye he was aware of Mannington's displeasure. He had straightened in his seat and his chin jutted, although his expression remained one of polite interest. Temple, on the contrary, looked smug.

'I should be interested to hear what aspects of life in London you find the most enjoyable, sir. As Papa said yesterday, we have the intention of visiting London in September to sample its delights.'

'In that case, you have come to the right man,'

Vernon said. He switched his gaze to Mannington. 'I take it *you* are not familiar with London society, Mannington?'

'I choose not to waste my time on such frivolity,' he replied. 'But I might make an exception in the autumn...the attractions of the capital become more obvious by the day.'

'It will be pleasant to have at least one acquaintance in London this fall,' Cordelia said, 'and, if you should choose to go, too, Mr Mannington, that will be even better. Two acquaintances in the whole of the city, Pops. We shall be spoilt for choice.'

'You may rest assured I shall do all in my power to ensure you enjoy your stay,' Vernon said. 'You may only claim two acquaintances. *I* can lay claim to many more and I shall be honoured to introduce you to anyone you choose.'

'Splendid, splendid.' Temple rubbed his palms together with an unpleasant rasping noise. 'Now, are we all finished? I hope you'll not object to drinking your brandy with Delia present, my lord? I know it isn't customary, but we don't stand on ceremony here.'

Vernon did object, as it happened, but didn't say so. He had been hoping to engage Mannington in a more frank conversation than was possible with Cordelia in the room. But his time would come. He could be patient.

Thea's face floated into his mind, her troubled

eyes and her repressed fears pricking his conscience. But not too patient, he promised himself. They needed to find out what had happened to her brother as soon as possible.

As Temple busied himself at a sideboard with a decanter and glasses, Mannington assisted Cordelia from her chair and proffered his arm, which she accepted with a smile. Mannington led her from the table towards the sofa, leaning in to whisper in her ear as he did so. Vernon could not hear what Mannington said, but the flush at the nape of Cordelia's neck suggested his comment was not one that would have been uttered within her father's hearing.

He watched closely, but Cordelia gave no hint that she did not welcome Mannington's attention, neither drawing away nor slapping him down with words. Vernon prayed she had not already developed a *tendre* for the man. Her behaviour at dinner did not suggest her feelings were engaged, but she clearly enjoyed Mannington's company and her behaviour around him was both relaxed and familiar, although that could be due to her upbringing. Vernon was accustomed to society events where strict formality was observed. Woe betide any lady who behaved familiarly with a man who was not a relative. From what he had observed of Samuel Temple and his daughter, American society seemed very different. Perhaps it stemmed from being in business.

And that thought led inexorably and inevitably back to Thea. What was she doing? No doubt she would be fretting about tonight, wondering what he might discover. He briefly entertained the notion of knocking on her door upon his return…of going into her room…sitting on her bed and telling her about the evening's conversation. Then, savagely, he rejected that image. Even the thought of being in her bedchamber with her again rattled him. If he did go in, could he resist trying to seduce her? She was an innocent, for God's sake, and she had been badly hurt in the past. He could not risk hurting her again, not until he knew for certain what he wanted from her. If it was merely carnal…a false craving due to their unnatural proximity over the past few days…then he must resist his urges.

'My lord?'

He came back to the present with a start. 'I do apologise,' he said, smoothly. 'I was wondering how my nephew fares and whether his head will still be sore in the morning.'

Temple chortled. 'Never you mind about young Theo. He'll learn, same as the rest of us had to as youngsters. Now, m'lord, try this.' He thrust a glass of amber liquid into Vernon's hand. 'That is a top brandy and that's a fact. I'll wager you've not tasted such a fine one in a long, long time.'

Sceptical of the other man's ability to detect a fine brandy, Vernon sipped. His brows rose.

'That, sir, is a wager I shall not accept. It is a very fine brandy indeed. What is its provenance?'

Temple winked. 'Ask me no questions, I shall tell you no lie, m'lord. Suffice it to say Henry here had a hand in supplying it.'

Vernon knew what that meant—his estate was in the county of Devonshire and many people, at all levels of society, turned a blind eye to smuggling.

'Now, Samuel, don't you go revealing all of my secrets,' Mannington said, from his place on the sofa, next to Cordelia.

His tone was jovial, but there was an edge of steel to it. Vernon took his place on a nearby chair and Temple stood by the fireplace, hands clasped behind his back as he rocked to and fro on the balls of his feet, spouting forth once again about his business.

Again, the seating arrangement suited Vernon even though the triumphal glint in Mannington's eye set his teeth on edge. The man was laying claim to Cordelia and, although Vernon had no interest in her in a romantic sense, he knew himself well enough to recognise his metaphorical hackles rising at the other man's challenge—his mind stilling and crouching even as his body remained outwardly relaxed. He would bide his time, however, and work on gaining Cordelia's trust and, in the meantime, he would circle and he would watch.

His time would come.

* * *

Later, after saying goodnight, he trod up the stairs, waging an inner battle with himself. He should not disturb Thea...he should not put himself in the way of more temptation...but...what if she was lying awake...unable to sleep...worrying about Daniel...wondering if Mannington had showed up, and if Vernon had discovered anything.

He hesitated outside her door. Ridiculously, his heart beat a little faster in his chest merely at the thought of seeing her. How had he come to this? A man of such experience, reduced to the behaviour of a lovesick youth by a little curly-headed kitten of a woman who could change into a tiger before his eyes.

His thoughts strayed to Leo and his recent marriage to a woman he had met, quite by chance, on a country lane. A woman not of their world—the daughter of mésalliance between a duke's grand-daughter and a silversmith's son—but a woman who had changed Leo's life beyond recognition and for the better, who had brought joy and laughter into his world of duty and distrust. Leo had sworn never to marry again: he had his heir and his spare and a beautiful daughter. But his vow could not withstand love. His heart—once he had allowed himself to listen to it—had overruled all his rational objections.

Vernon bowed his head, resting his forehead against the wooden door. Is that what was happening? *Was* it love he felt for Thea? It was different to anything he had ever felt for any other woman. More than lust. But love?

He lifted his head. Stared at the knots in the door, traced the grain with his eyes.

How can I know? How can I be sure?

Chapter Nineteen

*A*t last!

Thea would know Vernon's footsteps anywhere. She listened to him walk along the landing and heard him pause outside her door. Her pulse quickened. He had said he would see her in the morning, but she had prayed he would change his mind. Then her heart sank at the unmistakable sound of him walking away. She gave herself no time for second thoughts. She darted to her bedchamber door and wrenched it open.

'Vernon!'

He pivoted on his heel to face her.

'Come in. Tell me what happened.'

His jaw set…he looked anything but pleased to see her and pain speared her heart. She had wrapped a sheet around her shoulders as she had no shawl with her and now she pulled it tight around her, defensively. And why would he be pleased to see her, when he had spent the past few hours in the company of Cordelia Temple, dressed in fancy dresses and wearing fine jewels? Had he fallen under Cordelia's spell? Thea clenched her jaw. Not for the world would she reveal even the tiniest hint of her jealousy, but how she wished she was wearing her gown—the bag Bickling had brought from Stourwell Court had contained her two favourite gowns and her pearl necklace and matching ear drops. She could not take such a risk however. She had stowed the bag beneath her bed, to put temptation out of her sight.

Vernon prowled slowly back along the passage, his gazed travelling from her head—and she knew her hair must be dishevelled after she had speared her fingers through it countless times that evening—to her toes, bare on the wooden floor.

'Get back inside,' he growled as he neared her, his frown thunderous. 'What if anyone was to see you dressed like that? Or should I say, undressed?'

Thea backed inside her bedchamber, tugging the sheet closer still to cover her shift, which barely reached her knees, feeling suddenly vulnerable, the intent in his hooded gaze sending shivers over her skin.

He banged the door behind him, then remained still, glowering at her, the muscles either side of his jaw bunched.

'Are you *trying* to get discovered?'

Thea hunched her shoulder as she turned away.

'Of course I am not. There was no one there to see me.'

She went to sit on the bed and then changed her mind. She did not want him looming above her, not when he was in this sort of mood.

'What did you discover?'

'If you mean about Daniel, nothing.'

'Nothing? But—'

'And what did you expect? Did you imagine I would question Mannington over the soup? *And when was it you last saw Daniel Markham?*'

'No.' Thea shook her head, disappointment flooding her. How foolish. Of course he could not baldly ask Mannington about Daniel. 'I did not think. I am sorry, I was just… I built my hopes up.'

Vernon paced across the room and twitched the curtain aside to peer out into the night.

'I need to gain Cordelia's trust,' he said, his back still to Thea. 'Mannington was unhappy to see me there and he made his prior claim to her very clear.'

'What did he say?'

Vernon faced her, a puzzled smile on his face. 'He did not have to *say* anything, Thea. His behaviour was enough. He is wary of me and that is good. I hope Cordelia—and she is an intelligent woman—will see him with different eyes now I am on the scene. If she does not, however, then I shall have to tell her some of what I know about him.'

'But—'

'Do not worry. I shall not expose you. I shall tell

her in more general terms. Mannington is already talking of a lucrative business deal and casting his lure to entice Temple to invest. And I fear my presence might force his hand over Cordelia. If we do not find some clue about Daniel very soon, I think I shall have to send Bickling to retrace our journey from Birmingham to see if he can discover something we missed.'

He paced into the centre of the room, pausing at the foot of the bed.

'I have arranged to take Cordelia for a drive tomorrow afternoon, whilst her father is out on business. I suspect Mannington will also show up—on horseback, probably. He will be on his way home from somewhere and will insist on accompanying us, out of concern for Cordelia's reputation.' Vernon laughed, but there was little mirth in the sound. 'Although her father appears to suffer no qualms about allowing me to drive her around the countryside unchaperoned.'

Mr Temple might have no qualms, but Thea found herself hoping Mannington *would* show up, as Vernon predicted. Her jealousy battled to break free. Hearing the familiar way in which Vernon called the heiress Cordelia burned in Thea's chest and, before she knew what she was doing, she was standing in front of Vernon, gazing up at him. Would he kiss her again? Give her some sign that she meant more to him than just a funny little kitten to amuse himself with?

His eyes darkened and he swayed towards her. Her lids drifted shut and she tilted her face to his. She heard a groan and peeped through her lashes. His gaze was still fixed upon her face but then, as she watched, every plane of his face hardened and, taking her by the shoulders, he set her aside and strode past her to the door.

'Go to bed,' he said in a harsh voice. 'I shall see you in the morning.'

The following afternoon Cordelia Temple, charmingly dressed, with a white lace parasol over her shoulder, joined Vernon as he waited patiently by his curricle for her to appear.

'Good afternoon, Lord Boyton.'

'Miss Temple.' Vernon bowed. 'How very charming you look today. However…' He glanced at the sky. It was still blue, with fluffy white clouds, but from his bedchamber window he had glimpsed black clouds massing in the west. 'I fear you might have more need of an umbrella than a parasol. We shall be wise not to venture too far today.'

'I am thankful for any opportunity to pass the time whilst my father is occupied, Lord Boyton,' Cordelia said. She lowered her voice. 'Even if I do suspect your main purpose was to rile our mutual friend, Mr Mannington. Who, I must tell you, is now *especially* displeased at being thwarted by Pops.'

The laughter in her eyes belied the censure in

her words. Vernon handed her up into his curricle and—aware that Henry Mannington stood nearby talking to Samuel Temple—he brushed the back of her gloved hand with his lips before releasing it, conscious of Mannington's glare boring into him. He had ridden into Worcester, as Vernon had predicted, in time to accompany them on their drive. Samuel Temple, though, had forestalled him—begging to discuss the 'unmissable' business deal Mannington had spoken of last night.

A slight movement from above caught Vernon's eye. A curtain twitched at an upstairs window and his heart sank as he caught a glimpse of Thea's red curls as she turned away, her hand to her mouth. She had made no secret of her contempt for the game of flirtation he played with Cordelia and, despite his reassurance it *was* merely a game, relations between the two of them had been strained when they met over the breakfast table that morning.

He tried to push Thea from his thoughts. He must concentrate on Cordelia.

'And what about *your* feelings, Miss Temple? Are you sad that your faithful swain will not accompany us?'

'Oh, I shall see plenty of Mr Mannington in the next two days, my lord. He is throwing a house party at Crackthorpe Manor from tomorrow and, not only are Pops and I invited, we are to be guests of honour and are to be introduced to more of his business associates. Pops is thrilled at the opportunity to cultivate more useful contacts over here.'

A bad feeling was forming in Vernon's stomach. He liked the Temples and he did not want to see either of them hurt, but he was not yet in a position to confront Mannington or to confide his distrust of the man in the Temples. He could furnish no proof and he still had no clue what had happened to Daniel. For now all he could do was gain Cordelia's trust in the hope she would believe him when he warned her against Mannington.

He was aware that both Samuel Temple and Mannington were now behind him and within earshot.

'Miss Temple, I am distraught,' he protested, pressing his left hand to his chest. 'How shall I survive without your presence for even one day?'

'No need for you to be left out, m'lord.' Temple slapped Vernon on the back as he spoke. 'I'm sure you can squeeze one more guest in, eh, Mannington?'

Vernon turned and looked directly at Mannington, raising his brow. Again, only the minutest twitch in one eye betrayed the man's ire.

'But of course.' He inclined his head. 'You are most welcome to join us.'

'That is most gracious, Mannington, but I am loath to leave my nephew alone in a public inn overnight.'

Satisfaction gleamed momentarily in Mannington's eyes.

'However,' Vernon continued, 'I shall be delighted to join you for your daytime activities and for dinner, of course.' He smiled. 'I look forward to it with great anticipation.'

It'll be an ideal opportunity to snoop around.

He smiled at Cordelia and bowed again.

'It seems I am not to be deprived of your company after all, Miss Temple. You see before you a happy man.'

'Well, well, that's all sorted. We'll see you later, Delia, m'lord. Come along, Mannington…' Temple slung his arm across Mannington's shoulders and urged him back to the inn '…and tell me again how this investment works.'

Cordelia chuckled, bringing Vernon's attention back to her. 'It is fortunate for you, my lord, that I am not so easily duped by compliments and sweet smiles,' she whispered, 'particularly when the minute we are on our own your manner is more that of an uncle to a favourite niece than a beau.'

They had strolled down to the river and back that morning, and Vernon had deliberately refrained from any behaviour that could be construed as courtship. Instead, their conversation had centred on London society to help Cordelia prepare for her sojourn in the capital in the autumn.

Quite apart from anything else, she was far too young for his taste. Why, she could only be a year or two older than his niece, Olivia. *Far* too young. And besides, he only wanted Thea.

He swallowed. He had lain awake half the night trying to unpick his feelings and then one simple question had given him his answer. How would he feel when the time came to say goodbye? He did not have to puzzle over the answer to that. He *never* wanted to say goodbye.

Vernon rounded the curricle and climbed on board, nodding at Bickling, who was at the horses' heads, to release them. The blacks, eager to get going, pranced on the spot until Bickling hopped on behind and Vernon eased his hold on the reins. They set off, heading towards the bridge over the Severn.

'Well, I *am* old enough to be your uncle and my behaviour is called being a gentleman,' Vernon said. 'You deserve to be treated as a lady and you must remember that when you go to London. I know you are aware you will be a target for fortune hunters, so my advice is: do not be fooled into going *anywhere* alone with a man. There are scoundrels in all walks of life, including the *ton*. If you have doubts, never be afraid to say *No*. A decent man will respect you for it and you need not concern yourself with what the other sorts might think.'

'Yes, Uncle Vernon.' Cordelia nudged him with her elbow, laughing, and he smiled down at her.

'Seriously, though,' she continued, 'I am grateful for your advice about how to behave in London. I am sure without it I should end up breaking all kinds of unwritten rules, there are so many to abide by. You men do not know how lucky you are.'

'That is true,' Vernon said. 'But you are a sensible—'

A fork of lightning lit the sky and, after a tense pause, they heard a grumble of thunder ahead of them. Bruised purple clouds roiled over the horizon, building higher by the minute.

'The storm is a few miles away yet,' Vernon said, 'but we will not go too much further. I understand the river here floods quite readily and it is still high from the heavy rain last week.'

He felt Cordelia shudder and he glanced at her.

'Are you scared of thunder? Do you wish to return now?'

'No, it is not that. I was remembering that poor young man who fell into the river last week. They never did find his body.'

Vernon's heart seized in his chest.

'What young man?'

'Nobody knows who he was.' She bit her lip. 'Pops and I...we saw it happen.'

Another flash of lightning forked from the sky, followed by another crash of thunder. Closer now.

'Tell me.'

'I do not know much more. It had been raining for days and, when it finally stopped, we walked down to the river. It was quite a sight, several people were on the bridge, watching the torrent. Papa said he noticed the man ride across the bridge from the city end. His horse was light grey and it caught his eye because it looked like it had been ridden hard. Then, not long after, people started shouting and screaming and pointing. The sky was still dark with clouds. We could not see clearly…it was all a blur…there was a scuffle on the bank and, next thing, a man was in the water. He was swept away *so* fast. Someone on the other end of the bridge said the other man had stabbed him, before galloping off on a dark-coloured horse. They formed a party to search along the river, but found nothing. It was horrible. Pops reckons they were drunk.'

Sorrow gathered—a solid lump in Vernon's chest—as Thea's face surfaced in his mind's eye.

Cordelia frowned. 'You look troubled.'

'Yes.' He sent the blacks up the road at a brisk trot, looking for a place wide enough to turn. 'I apologise, but I must cut our drive short. I need to return.'

'Of course,' Cordelia replied. 'I am sorry. Did you…do you think you know that man?'

'It is possible.'

Vernon cursed himself. He had deliberately not said Daniel was missing when he had enquired after him around Worcester, worried that word of his search would reach Mannington. If only he had said, someone before now might have mentioned the drowning of a mysterious stranger.

'What happened to his horse?' That had been Thea's hope from the start, that Daniel's horse had not found its way home.

'No one knows. It ran off in all the confusion.'

A crossroads loomed ahead and, although there was not much room, there was enough to effect a turn.

'May I ask a favour of you?' Vernon manoeuvred the curricle and pair into a tight circle.

'Of course.'

'Please do not mention my interest in that man— not to your father, not to *anyone*. I cannot explain more now, but I need to keep my connection to him a secret, just for a short while.'

'It is your business, my lord. I shall say nothing.'

Vernon threw her a grateful smile. She really was a remarkable young lady…so young and yet such a level head on her shoulders. Did that come from growing up in America? Or from the travelling? Or both?

'Bickling,' Vernon spoke over his shoulder, 'that goes for you, too. Not a word. We shall say we turned around because of the storm.'

'Very good, milord.'

They completed the remainder of the journey in silence, Vernon in a fever of impatience. He would seek out the constable and find out more about this drowning and then…reluctance crept through him. Once he had more details, it would fall to him to deliver the bad news to Thea and shatter her world. That lump of sorrow threaded through with dread rose up to fill his throat.

Thea felt better once she'd indulged in a little weep after seeing Vernon kiss Cordelia's hand when he handed her into his curricle. The incident had brought all her insecurities to the fore. She lay on her back, staring at a dark patch on the ceiling above her head, and tried to put her thoughts in order. Vernon had spent most of today with that woman…that *girl*…walking with her that morning and driving her around even though thunder threatened. He *said* he must gain her trust and Thea did believe that…but she also knew he must be bored with only her—a scrap of a woman dressed as a boy—for company. Why wouldn't he prefer the society of an American heiress who made him laugh?

She was younger than Thea: prettier, taller, curvier. And more fun. And much, much more suitable for Vernon than the daughter of a glassware manufacturer who even Bickling could see was not his type.

A flash of light illuminated her room, followed a minute later by an ominous rumble.

I hope they get soaked.

Thea swiped at her tears. It was easy to be fun when your father was rich and indulged your every whim, and when your only brother was not missing. She scrubbed her hands over her face. What did it matter? There was no point in worrying about her complexion, or her red eyes, or the mouth that—these days—had a permanent droop. She could do nothing to improve her appearance even if she wanted to. And Vernon wouldn't notice if she did. He had not kissed her again last night, even when she had blatantly offered her lips, and today he had spent as little time alone with her as possible.

And you do not help by scolding him and nit-picking whenever you are together.

Can I help it if he irritates me? With his teasing ways and his flirting with Cordelia and his, 'Stay out of sight as much as possible, Dotty. We don't want Mannington seeing you.' Hmph! What he really means is: Stay out of sight so I can romance dear, sweet, clever Cordelia.

Another flash, this time followed more quickly by a clap of thunder. The storm was nearing, the air thick and oppressive.

She should be happy for him. They would no doubt suit very well, with each of them in possession of a vast fortune, and Vernon in possession of that all-important title—

She sat up at the rap on the door, that bitter inner conversation stumbling into a silence that echoed frighteningly in her head. No one apart from Vernon ever came to her door at this time of day. Vernon was out. Horwell? She found herself praying it *was* the innkeeper, because the other face that hovered in her imagination was that of Henry Mannington, who she knew was here, somewhere, in this inn.

Rap! Rap!

Lightning flared again.

Thea scrambled from the bed and ran lightly to the door. She waited for the thunder to die away before putting her ear to the wood.

'Who is it?'

'Me. Are you decent? We need to talk.'

Vernon. Why is he back?

Thea fumbled with the latch and pulled the door open, walking backwards so she remained hidden from anyone else outside. If he had brought that Cordelia… She caught sight of his expression and, again, her circling thoughts slammed to a halt. Her temples throbbed. Her heart climbed into her throat, her stomach clenching in fierce dread.

'You have news.'

She stumbled to the bed and, clinging to the corner post at the foot, she pivoted and slumped on to the mattress. Their charade would be over soon, but first she must bear what Vernon had to tell her. She wanted to run away, to ram her fingers into her ears—she already knew the worst without listening to the detail. But she would not. She owed Daniel that much.

'Tell me.' How steady her voice sounded when all she wanted to do was scream and scream and scream and then curl into a ball and never wake up. Never have to deal with the truth.

He came and sat next to her, on the edge of the mattress, his legs wide, elbows on knees, forearms dangling between. His head was bowed.

She found the strength to say, 'The news is not good.' A small part of her marvelled that, even now, she cared about easing his task. 'Tell me the end, then tell me the details. I need to know.'

His back expanded as he sucked in a breath, then he looked her in the eyes. Put his hand to her cheek.

'I am so sorry. It seems Daniel fell into the Severn during an altercation. He drowned.'

She willed herself not to cry. There would be time, soon, for tears. Now, she needed to know. She shuddered and Vernon's arm slipped around her, pulling her close, supporting her with his strength and his vitality. She leaned into him, relishing his warmth.

'Tell me. Please.'

He told her what Cordelia and her father had seen, and that he had spoken to the constable who told him that descriptions of the assailant varied wildly and the only detail all the witnesses agreed upon was that he was dressed as a gentleman and that he'd had a knife. The constable doubted they would ever discover his identity.

'When?'

'The day Daniel went missing.'

'But we cannot know for certain it was Daniel.'

'Mr Temple noticed a young man of Daniel's age ride across the bridge on a light grey horse. He said it was sweat-stained. It had been ridden hard. It was that man who fell in the river.'

'You said during an altercation? Who with? Was it Mannington?'

'Nobody knows. The light was failing and no one was certain exactly what happened.'

'But…' There was a straw of hope and Thea grabbed it. 'Daniel can swim. He—'

'Hush, sweetheart. There had been heavy rain—do you remember? In the early part of last week? The river was brimming full and turbulent. The constable told me that if a man fell into the river in full spate, he would almost certainly drown.'

The sobs began deep down, deeper inside her than she believed possible. Deep, racking sobs that wrenched her stomach, robbed her of air, left her gasping and juddering as they scraped her throat raw. Dimly, she felt herself gathered into a strong, familiar embrace and she pressed her face into Vernon's chest and allowed all her pent-up misery and fear and despair to escape the shackles that had kept them buried ever since Daniel had failed to return home.

Chapter Twenty

Finally, Thea slept. Carefully, inch by inch, Vernon moved to sit with his back propped against the headboard and his legs stretched along the bed, Thea cradled on his lap. At some point, as the day outside grew dim and the noise from the bar downstairs grew louder, there was a tap on the door and Bickling popped his head around. He held a lighted candle that illuminated his expression and Vernon answered the questioning lift of his brow with a nod.

Bickling came in, treading quietly, and drew the curtains across the window before lighting the candles. He mimed eating and Vernon nodded again, blessing the man's forethought and understanding, and his lack of questions or, indeed, of censure. Vernon's behaviour had gone way past censure. Whether she liked it or not, Thea would be his wife. He would not leave her to support her parents on her own, nor to try to keep their manufactory running without her brother's support.

Bickling soon returned with a platter laden with slices of cold game pie, cheese, bread and cold beef and a tankard of ale. Vernon eased Thea from his lap. She frowned and grumbled under her breath as he moved her, but she soon settled again.

'Thank you, Bickling.'

'Shall I bring some wine, m'lord, in case Miss Markham awakens? And maybe fruit?'

'Yes, please.'

When he returned, Vernon said, 'I cannot leave her alone tonight. Tell Horwell Master Theo is ill and that you and you alone are to enter this bed-chamber in case of infection.'

'Yes, milord.' Bickling slipped from the room as quietly as he had arrived.

It was a little before three in the morning before Thea stirred. Vernon, dozing next to her on the bed—his senses alert for any sound from the woman by his side—came fully awake immediately. She moaned as she surfaced from the depths of her sleep and tossed from side to side, her arms flailing. Vernon caught her in his arms and held her tenderly, cradling her skull as he gathered her to him. He knew the instant she remembered, her muscles rigid with shock as she sucked in a sharp breath.

'Shh. I am here.'

'Tell me it was a dream. A nightmare.' Her voice sounded harsh in the hush of the night. A tremor shuddered through her. 'No. It was real,' she muttered almost immediately. 'He is gone. Daniel is gone.' She pushed free of Vernon's arms, sitting bolt upright. 'I need to go home. I have to tell Mama. And P-Papa. Oh! Wh-what will this d-do to them? H-how can I t-tell them?'

'You can do nothing right now, Thea.'

Vernon stroked, tracing the delicate bones of her shoulders through the coarse linen shirt she wore as Theo. So fragile. She would not bear this burden alone. He vowed to stay with her. Protect her. Help her. Avenge her and her brother.

He levered himself off the bed and crossed the room to pour a glass of wine. There was food still on the platter, but it looked unappetising after several hours. He selected a dish of berries to offer her, but she shook her head.

'I couldn't eat a thing,' she said. Her voice quavered. He could see the effort she made to keep her emotions in check. She took the glass from his hand and drank, draining the glass.

She is stronger than I think. It is not all about physical strength, or how could any female bear the sorrows that assailed them?

She had such resilience, a mental strength that he could not but admire—an admiration that had grown throughout their journey together. He would give anything to protect her against this devastating blow but, no matter how he raged against God, it was not in his power to make such a gift.

Thea held out her glass and, wordlessly, Vernon poured more wine. Again, she tipped the glass back.

'Steady on,' he said. 'Getting foxed will not help.'

She stared up at him, her eyes glittering. 'Then what will?'

Vernon turned away, suddenly uneasy at her mood, at the intent in her gaze. 'Time.'

'Hah! Time. I do not want time. I want to forget. Time means nothing—it can be gone in the blink of an eye. Or the flash of a knife...that *bastard* Jasper... I'll...'

She banged her glass on the nightstand and scrambled from the bed.

'Hi! Where—?' Vernon ran after her and stretched his arm above her head, propping his fist against the door to hold it shut.

'Let me out!' She tugged at the door.

'No.'

She leant back, putting all her weight into her effort to open the door but it did not budge. She released the handle and turned to Vernon, stamping her foot.

'I want some fresh air.'

'You do not.'

She stepped very close to him, her body brushing his. 'Do you call me a liar, Lord Vernon Beauchamp?'

Her voice was silky, challenging. Her upturned

face was close—temptingly so. Vernon hauled on the reins of his control, reminding himself why they were there...what this conversation was really about.

'You know I do not, but I shall not let you out. Besides, you have bare feet.'

She looked down, studying first her feet, then his. She lifted one foot and stroked it over his.

'So do you,' she whispered.

Heat spiralled through his body, sending shocks of desire and tingles of need radiating to every cell. Every organ.

She captured his gaze again, placed both hands, very deliberately, on his chest and stroked, then slid her hands to his shoulders. His belly clenched and he grew harder still.

'Thea—'

She lifted her hand to his mouth, pressing her fingers to his lips, silencing him.

He closed his eyes, tilted his face to the celling. He knew where this was going. Knew what she wanted. What she needed. Could he withstand her? That was a question to which he feared there was only one answer.

As if she sensed his weakening resolve, she slid her hand around the back of his neck and went up on tiptoes, fitting her body into his. Her fingers speared through his hair, drawing his head down.

Their lips met in a storm of urgent need. Tongues tangled and quiet moans punctuated the night's silence. Without volition, his arms wrapped around her and she leapt, her legs encircling his hips, her heat driving him wild. He stumbled to the bed, lips locked to hers, and lowered her to the mattress, following her down. She tugged at his shirt and he broke away just long enough to pull it over his head, then gathered her to him again, reclaiming those soft, sweet lips and surrendering to the demands of her tongue.

His hands swept lower and encountered the coarse weave of her shirt, the stiff bindings beneath. A woman such as Thea should be dressed in satins and silks. He lifted his torso from hers and tugged at her shirt, pulling it over her head before taking her lips again. Blindly, he fumbled with the knot that held her bindings in place.

She tore her mouth from his. 'Let me,' she breathed, and in seconds the knot was loose and he unwrapped her, his eyes riveted to the prize as small, perfect, pink-tipped breasts bounced free. Her skin was hot and damp and he blew gently across the slopes of her breasts, watching her nipples tighten as his breath cooled them. He massaged and plumped, as he had done in his fantasies, and then he lowered his head, his tongue sweeping across her tender flesh.

His heart pounded with a primal need as he forced himself to go slowly…to give her the pleasure she deserved.

His hands skimmed lower, following her curves

to the fall of her breeches. In seconds, they were off and he played his thumb around the rim of her navel and then circled her flat belly with his palm, pressing lightly. Her hips lifted helplessly, pushing against his hand, as he licked at her taut nipple then grazed it lightly with his teeth. She moaned, clutching at his hair.

'Hush, my sweet,' he whispered. 'Lie still. Let me pleasure you.'

Her hands came between them then, to his chest, and pushed. He pulled away, disappointment flooding him as he looked down at her.

'Do you want me to stop? You only have to say the word.'

Dazed hazel eyes searched his face. Then she levered herself up on her elbows and looked down, her eyes locking on the erection that strained his breeches.

'No. I want to see you.'

He hadn't thought he could get any more aroused, but he was wrong. He had thought to give her pleasure and to sacrifice his own but...once his breeches were gone...

'Thea—'

'I want *you.*'

'You do not know—'

'I do. Mama told me. The night before my wedding. I know, Vernon. And I know that I want you.'

She sat up fully now. Her hands splayed against the muscles of his chest, then moved lower. Not hesitantly, but sure…determined… She unbuttoned his breeches and then slipped her hand inside and grasped him. He could not contain his groan of pleasure as he seemed to swell even more at her touch. She stroked and he grabbed her wrist and pulled her hand away.

'Not yet, sweetheart, or this will be finished before we start.'

And Thea—and how was he still surprised when she took control like this?—scrambled on to her knees and pressed her mouth to his in a hard, demanding kiss.

'Then let us start,' she said, and lowered her head to nip at his nipple, sending shock waves rippling through him.

He stood and took off his breeches—her wide-eyed stare sending his pulse soaring even higher—and then lay her back on the bed, kissing her lips as his hands again traced the curves and hollows of her body. He followed the trail of his hands with lips and tongue, lower and ever lower, lingering at the sensitive spots where she arched and moaned, seeking her scent—not the floral, summer garden scent she had worn as Thea, but the scent…the essence…of *her*.

The scent that was driving him wild.

Her thighs parted as he stroked the soft cleft hidden between and he slipped a finger inside. He groaned out loud.

So hot. So wet. So ready.

He hauled on the reins of his control and stroked and played, finding the little nub that would help her find her release. Soft, feminine gasps and moans accompanied the arching of her body as she pressed into his touch. He trailed his lips down the silken skin of her stomach and then traced a path with his tongue through crisp auburn curls to her swollen lips. He pushed into the wet folds and licked, teasing her tender flesh and sucking lightly.

Dear God!

Her evocative scent triggered an eruption of hot molten desire within him. He moved, covering her, his leg between hers, and he cradled her face, kissing her open-mouthed, his tongue pushing inside. She moaned, clutching at him, and he shifted, settling between her widespread thighs. He flexed his hips and nudged into her, then pushed steadily into the welcoming heat, stretching her. His jaw clenched with the need to go slow. To take care.

He was taking too long. She wanted…she needed…she tilted her hips as she clutched at his hips.

Come on!

'Please! Vernon?'

She rocked her hips against him once more and, with a loud groan of surrender, he pushed fully into her, stretching her more than she ever thought possible. He lay still then and she could feel her throbbing flesh tighten around him.

Is that it?

There had been no pain, as Mama had warned, just a little discomfort. But…instinctively she knew there was more…just out of her reach. She lifted her knees and wrapped her legs around his hips, rocking her pelvis again. And then, he began to move and those feelings…those wonderful, elusive, exhilarating feelings…surged again. They grew and they swelled, and she reached and she yearned, higher and higher until, with a helpless scream, her entire body went rigid before exploding into a thousand brilliant, white-hot stars—scattering and soaring, up and up and up into a vast nothingness. Pulses of pleasure radiated through her entire body as Vernon drove into her harder and faster than ever. Then he, too, tensed, as he roared his climax. She felt his seed pump into her as she drifted, dreamily, back down to earth.

Vaguely, she was aware of Vernon kissing her and then settling down beside her. She snuggled into his warmth and slept.

Chapter Twenty-One

Thea woke with pain stabbing at her temples and a mouth that tasted like…well, she did not want to think *what* it tasted like. Something nasty. That was as far as her sluggish brain would allow her thoughts to stray. She rolled on to her back and her left shoulder wedged up against something solid. Something *warm* and solid. Her breath seized. She cranked one eyelid open. She knew what she would see before she turned her head. Who else could it be? The huff of quiet breathing reached her straining ears. He still slept. She swallowed and moved her right hand over her own body. She swallowed again, her heart pitter-pattering, as she encountered her naked belly.

Memories—hazy and disjointed—floated, disembodied and surreal, through her thoughts: memories of kisses, caresses, murmured endearments. Her fingers sought the triangle of soft curls at the apex of her thighs and heat flooded her as she remembered the touch of his hand, his…her brain stumbled over the memory…his *mouth*. The memory of him inside her, covering her. The weight of his body on hers. And the memory of pleasure. Intense, glorious pleasure.

Nerves now invaded her stomach. *She* had enticed him. Just as with that kiss. That memory was the sharpest yet. She had needed him so badly: needed his comfort, his reassurance, needed something…*anything*…to ease the pain of losing Daniel. This was no seduction of an innocent, even though she *had* been an innocent. She had known what she was doing.

Thea's fingers again strayed to where her thighs joined and to the soft, secret folds hidden within. She felt a little sore, but she remembered no physical pain from last night, only pleasure. There had been a momentary discomfort as he entered her… stretching her…but that was all. She shuddered in remembered delight.

The bed rocked.

'Good morning.'

She snapped her head to her left, feeling the flush of embarrassment flood her face as she met a pair of smiling green eyes. Vernon had turned to face her, propping himself up on his elbow. She managed a faltering smile in response, battling the urge to allow her gaze to roam that wonderful chest, bared to her eyes as the sheet slipped to his waist.

His hand cradled her cheek. 'How are you? Head sore?' He sobered. 'Heart sore?'

She nodded. He eyed her thoughtfully, then put his arms around her and pulled her into his chest.

'I wish I could protect you from the pain of the next few days, weeks and months, sweetheart, but I cannot.' He stroked her hair back and tilted her face to his. 'Thea…last night… I should not have given in—'

Thea, beginning to relax against him, stiffened and pulled away. 'You do not have to explain. It was my fault. I do not blame—'

A large hand covered her mouth and he laughed, shaking his head at her. 'Thea. *Please* will you allow me to finish? I was about to say I shouldn't have given in to my base desires.'

'Oh,' she said in a small voice.

'You were vulnerable. I took advantage.'

'No. No, you did not. I—I *wanted* you. I do not blame you.'

He smiled, a devastatingly smile full of charm that set her heart racing. 'And I wanted you, my sweet. In fact, I want you again, right now—' he moved his hips and she felt the proof of his desire '—but I shall resist.' He lay back and lifted her across his chest, and he kissed her, slowly and dreamily, his eyes closed as his hands gently caressed her back and bottom. All too soon, he ended the kiss, settling her back on the mattress by his side.

'I must return to my room before the maids are up and about or we shall start the scandal of the century.'

He brushed a kiss to her cheek, then rolled away, pushed the blanket aside and left the bed. Thea's gaze roamed his body—the broad shoulders, slim waist, firm buttocks—and her mouth dried as she realised she wanted him, too. But he was right. It was too risky.

He pulled his shirt over his head and picked up his boots and the rest of his clothing. 'It's still early. Try to sleep. We will talk later.'

And he slipped out of the door, closing it softly behind him.

Sleep was impossible. Thea lay on her back, staring up at the now familiar stain on the ceiling, as she moved the tips of her fingers in circles over her temples. Her spinning thoughts steadied, seeming to mirror the movement of her fingers. She slowed the speed at which she rubbed her temples and the words, images and fragmented thoughts whirling around her brain began to coalesce into comprehensible sentences.

Daniel was dead. Nothing could change that. And it must fall to her to tell her parents. But, first, she would confront Mannington. Jasper Connor. And he would pay for what he had done.

Later, over the breakfast table, Thea buried her awkwardness at facing Vernon again and she told him her intentions as he tucked into a plate of ham and eggs. A single slice of toast, barely nibbled at, lay disregarded on the plate in front of her.

'Will you come with me to face Mannington? Now?'

Vernon frowned. 'We need to discuss this. It will do no good rushing in at half-cock.'

'But he must pay for what he has done.'

'The only way he will pay is for the law to convict him.' He reached to take her hand. 'Thea. Sweetheart. Think! If we *were* to confront him this morning...where is our proof? All we will do is warn him that we are on to him. A man such as he might produce any number of men prepared to attest to his character or to give him an alibi on the night Daniel was attacked.'

'But you can expose him as a fraud. He is not Henry Mannington.'

'He is not Henry Mannington, cousin to the Duke of Cheriton. But I cannot prove he is not called Henry Mannington. We can only expose him as a liar...a man who has claimed an important connection that is not true. That will destroy his credibility, but it will not convict him. He will be free to move elsewhere and to continue with his fraudulent ways.'

'But he cannot deny he stole from Papa...' She stopped. He could. Of course he could. 'We need proof he is really Jasper Connor.'

A brief smile curved Vernon's mouth. His eyes

were sympathetic. Thea sipped at her coffee, quelling her irritation. She did not want sympathy. She wanted justice.

She sucked in a deep breath. 'What do *you* suggest then?'

He raised a brow. 'Do not be cross with me, Thea. I *am* trying to help.'

'I know. I am sorry. I am just…'

Frustrated. Angry. Impatient.

'I am listening.' She mollified her tone. 'Do you have a plan?'

He gave her a twisted smile. 'I am not sure plan is quite the right word. It is four days since I wrote to Leo. I would expect that whomever he sent to Yarncott to enquire into the fire at the inn will get here today. If we can prove my cousin was a guest at that inn the night it burned down, then we will have some proof that Jasper survived and the man buried was Henry Mannington.'

He sighed, thrusting a hand through his hair. 'It will not be easy to make any accusation stick.'

'Then why not let me confront him? If you are with me, he cannot harm me. He might be so shocked he will let something slip.'

'No! Absolutely not. I am letting you nowhere near that villain.' He frowned and she thought she detected a hint of guilt in his eyes. 'Thea…with everything that happened yesterday… I didn't have a chance to tell you this. Mannington is throwing a house party at Crackthorpe Manor, starting this afternoon, with the Temples as guests of honour.'

She swallowed. 'How long for?'

'Two days. Thea… Mannington has some business scheme that he has been dangling under Temple's nose, as a carrot to a donkey. This party…this gathering…is more about business than pleasure. Temple is already keen to invest and I fear it is the same sort of scheme with which he swindled your father.

'I am honour bound to warn Temple—although I worry he will see only the usefulness of Mannington and not realise the danger—but before I warn him I want to use this house party to snoop around Crackthorpe Manor and see if I can find any proof of Mannington's real identity.'

'So…' her voice quivered despite her effort to prevent it '…you will be gone until tomorrow?'

Vernon shoved back his chair and rounded the table to crouch by Thea's side. He put his hand on her thigh and, in spite of her misery, she felt the echo of pleasure throb in her core.

'I shall be back here tonight. The moon is nearly full and it is only four miles away. But…' He leapt to his feet and paced the small parlour, back and forth. 'You know the man, Thea. Would he compromise Cordelia to force a marriage, do you think? I worry my presence will drive him to take desperate measures if he thinks he might lose such a wealthy prize.'

Their eyes met and any disappointment that he would be spending so much time away from her vanished beneath the sick fear she felt on Cordelia's behalf.

'Is he capable of such a thing?'

'I think him capable of almost anything,' Thea said. 'You have to warn her…and her father, too, before you leave the Manor to come back here. They must be on their guard.'

'I shall,' Vernon said grimly.

'What about the other guests? What if you are recognised?'

'I doubt I shall be. I understand most of the guests will be businessmen and their wives. They do not move in the same circles as me.'

Those words reminded Thea of the gulf that still yawned between the two of them, that Vernon, no matter how kind and no matter how much he appeared to desire her…

And does he? Or is it merely that I am the only available female and I threw myself at him last night?

He was an aristocrat. Brother to a duke. And Thea…she belonged in the same circles as those businessmen of whom he spoke.

Her pain at that thought was submerged by the agony of Daniel's death and her concern for the Temples, and it was utterly dwarfed by the thirst for revenge.

'You must warn them but, before you do, *please*

do what you can to find out the truth about Mannington.'

She dropped her gaze to her plate, to hide the tears that had gathered without warning. How could she sit here, calmly discussing Daniel's killer? She was aware that Vernon had regained his feet. He took her hands and urged her, too, to stand.

'I know just what you need. Come.' He grabbed her cap from where she had hooked it on the back of her chair and plonked it on her head, before urging her towards the door. 'Let us go for a ride. I don't know about you, but I find myself in need of a dose of fresh air and the rush of wind in my face. What do you say to a gallop?'

She forced a smile. Staying indoors, sinking into the mire of her grief, would help no one. And the thought of getting away from the inn and spending time with Vernon, whilst she still could, was appealing. 'I say let's go.'

Then she frowned. 'Wait!'

Vernon, halfway to the door, stopped and spun on his heel to face her, his brows raised.

'Tell me again what Cordelia told you about Bullet,' she said.

'He ran off. Many of the people on the bridge who saw what happened raced down to the riverbank. They would have been shouting and screaming—enough to terrify the most placid animal.'

'So why did he not come home?' She clutched

Vernon's hand. 'Do you not see? Daniel…he could have survived. He could have got Bullet and—'

'And what? Thea.' The pity in his green eyes made her heart sink. 'If Daniel did survive, where is he? Why has he not been in contact? Bullet will turn up sooner or later. Come, enough of this. Let us go for that gallop.'

No sooner had Vernon left for Crackthorpe Manor that afternoon than Thea began to pace. She could not settle. She tried to read, but she could not concentrate. Instead, she picked over all that had happened since the day Daniel had left home. Their refreshing morning ride along the river—this time straight past the gipsy encampment—had temporarily assuaged Thea's desperation to take action. Some action. *Any* action. But now she was once again cooped up in this inn whilst Vernon investigated Mannington.

And the knowledge that he would also be with Cordelia Temple—the Temples had set off in Mannington's carriage at noon—did nothing to help. Frustration and insecurity scoured her insides despite the night before. How could Vernon possibly prefer a woman like Thea over one like Cordelia?

I wish I could go there and see for myself what is happening.

Around and around the parlour she paced, like a caged animal. If only she could do something to help.

Then she stopped. Stared at the window, her thoughts whirling.

Bullet! What if...?

Why did I not think of that before? What if Mannington *has him?*

She would recognise him in an instant. To Vernon, he would just be another grey horse. She went to the window. The weather was fine but breezy, the heat not so oppressive since yesterday's thunderstorm had cleared the air. Vernon had pointed out Crackthorpe Manor—its stone walls glowing a warm buttery yellow in the June sunshine—as they had turned away from the bank of the Severn and returned to the road that led from Worcester to Great Malvern.

I am sure I can find it again.

There was no one to stop her as long as she could evade Bickling and his inevitable awkward questions. She rummaged through her saddlebag and extracted the pistol she had packed when she left home to follow after Vernon. It occurred to her that she was doing the same thing—following him once again, against his express orders.

Orders. Pfft. He cannot tell me what to do.

A commotion arose in the street outside and she crossed to peer again from the window. A mud-spattered carriage had drawn up outside the Crown and, as she watched, one of the two men on the box jumped down and ran to let down the steps and open the door. An elegant gentleman with black hair emerged. He settled his hat upon his head then turned, reaching to help someone else from the vehicle.

She leaned forward, wondering if these new-comers might recognise Vernon. A fashionably-dressed lady came into sight, pausing on the top step, and then Horwell appeared on the pavement below, bowing, and Thea spied Bickling hurrying out from the passage that led to the stables. Here was the perfect opportunity for her to leave without awkward questions and opposition. Determined to grab it with both hands, Thea did not stay to watch, but rushed down the stairs and out the rear door. She sped across the yard and into the stables, where she was brought up short by a figure standing in the shadows inside the door.

'Oh! You startled me.'

The man moved into the light. 'Sorry.'

Thea blinked. It was the Gipsy they had seen at the camp, the day they first met the Temples.

What is he doing here?

A groom coming out of the tack room at the rear distracted her, and when she looked again, the Gipsy had vanished.

'Yes, master?'

She shook the puzzle of the Gipsy from her mind. 'Saddle the black, will you?'

It was done in no time. She was up in the saddle and riding away from the Crown within ten min-utes of first thinking of the idea and without being noticed by either Bickling or Horwell, both still occupied with the smart couple and their companion, an elderly, stooped man with white hair.

Thea kicked Star into a trot. She would ride to Crackthorpe Manor. Tether Star somewhere out of sight and then…somehow…she would search Mannington's stables. Without being seen. Her heart faltered.

What if Mannington sees me? Recognises me?

Stop this! He'll be busy with his guests, as will his servants, too busy to notice one extra strange face around the place. She fingered the hard shape of the pistol in her pocket, gaining comfort from it.

She found Crackthorpe Manor with little difficulty. The house and stables were sheltered on three sides by a narrow belt of woodland and Thea approached the buildings through the trees, not bold enough—or foolish enough—to ride up the main carriageway. She tethered Star to a sturdy sycamore in the middle of the belt and continued on foot to where the trees gave way to smooth, verdant lawns. Here, she could see the stable yard set to the side and behind the house, at a distance of a hundred yards or so. All appeared quiet there but, from the far side of the house and over the sounds of leaves rustling in the breeze and the birdsong, she could make out the faint drone of conversation and the occasional guffaw of laughter. The guests had arrived, then, and the party had begun.

She examined the stables again, noticing a track leading behind them and through the trees. Did she dare? She could look around openly and search for Bullet, and where better to hide Star than in plain sight? She ran back to her mare and leapt into the saddle and soon found that track. She pulled the peak of her cap to shade her eyes, and headed Star towards the stables.

As she rode through the stone pillars of the gateway a groom emerged from the barn.

'Afternoon,' she said, deepening still further her already deep voice. 'I've brought a message for my uncle, Lord Boyton. He is a guest here.'

'Boyton? Oh, him. He's the one with that pair of blacks.' A note of envy crept into his voice. ''andsome pair, they are, and no mistake.' The groom took Star as Thea slid to the ground. 'D'you know the way?'

'Yes. Are there many guests? Their horses must keep you busy.'

'There aren't too many: them from Birmingham shared carriages and the guvnor sent our carriage to Worcester to bring some others, so it's not too bad.'

The groom led Star into the barn and into a vacant stall where he tethered her before loosening her girth. Thea followed, trying to penetrate the dim interior with eyes accustomed to bright sunlight, searching for Bullet.

'I'm trying to persuade my uncle to buy me

a grey hunter,' she said. 'Do you have any greys here?'

'Greys? Only the dappled mare down there and she's a pig. Don't like 'em myself…too much hard work to keep 'em clean.'

Disappointment dragged at Thea. This had been a waste of time. She had been foolish to think… the phrase clutching at straws came to mind. She should return to Worcester. But she had told the groom she had brought a message for Vernon. He suspected nothing now, but he would think it odd if she left without seeing Vernon first.

'I had better go and find my uncle,' she said. 'Thank you for taking care of my mare.'

Chapter Twenty-Two

Vernon's bad feeling about this house party—and about Henry Mannington's intentions towards the Temples and, in particular, Cordelia—intensified as he was introduced to his fellow guests. It seemed that Henry Mannington harboured greater ambition than Jasper Connor ever had. Not content with attempting to reel in Samuel Temple, it appeared—from the snippets of conversation Vernon overheard—that all the guests here were eager to invest in this 'opportunity of a lifetime'. Mannington was clever. He had clearly prepared his ground in advance…he had no need to use further powers of persuasion. His guests seemed quite capable of selling his scheme to each other and, simultaneously, themselves. It was depressing there were so many fools in this world. Mayhap they deserved to be fleeced.

Vernon sipped his wine and wandered along the terrace to the corner. Mannington had sent his carriage to convey the Temples to Crackthorpe and they had been here since noon, sharing luncheon with their host before the remaining guests arrived. Cordelia—looking, it had to be said, a little uncomfortable—had been persuaded to step into the role of hostess, as there was no lady of the house. Vernon had not had a chance to speak privately to her; Mannington had kept her occupied and mostly by his side.

He propped his shoulders against the wall and planned how and where to begin his search. On this side of the house four French windows faced on to the terrace, the two furthest from him standing open. They led into a salon, through which Vernon had been shown upon arrival.

Most of the guests were outside, although a couple of the ladies remained in the salon, complaining of the bright sun and the brisk breeze. Altogether there were twenty people in attendance, including himself and Mannington, but only five of them were women. Temple was holding court in the middle of the largest group gathered on the terrace, but... Vernon straightened, every muscle tensing ready for action...there was no sign of either Mannington or Cordelia.

They were here five minutes ago.

He sauntered along the terrace, heading for the open windows, peering again through the other windows he passed to see if they were inside that room—a corner room, furnished as a sitting room, with two further windows that overlooked the rear of the house. There was no sign of either Mannington or Cordelia and Vernon's concern mounted. Then, as he neared the first of the open windows, he released his pent-up breath as Cordelia stepped through, Mannington on her heels.

'Miss Temple.' Vernon bowed. 'I thought you had deserted me.'

He caught her flash of relief before her face relaxed into a smile. 'Lord Boyton, how pleasant to see a familiar face.'

Behind her, Mannington's smile widened but it did not reach his eyes. Vernon proffered his arm.

'Would you care for a stroll in the garden?'

Mannington stepped forward, between Vernon and Cordelia. 'Miss Temple is eager to rejoin her father, Boyton.' He turned to Cordelia. 'If you care to see the garden later, Cordelia, I shall be delighted to escort you. I can tell you anything you wish to know about the flowers growing there.'

'You must be a keen plantsman, to be able to put a name to so many flowers, Mannington,' Vernon drawled. He had caught a glimpse of the abundantly stocked borders on his approach to the house. 'Most impressive in such a short period of time.'

'A short period of time, Lord Boyton?' Cordelia's smile was perplexed. 'How so, when this is Mr Mannington's family home?'

'It is?' Vernon held Mannington's glare. 'I must have misunderstood. My mistake.'

A muscle leapt in the side of Mannington's jaw.

'I suggest you pay more attention to the facts in future, Boyton,' he said silkily, 'or you *might* discover that misinformation can result in all kinds of unfortunate consequences.'

Vernon was conscious that Cordelia had paled as she looked from one man to the other. He laughed and leaned close to put his lips to her ear, drawing a scowl from Mannington.

'It would appear our Mr Mannington does not take kindly to being teased, Miss Temple,' he said, loud enough for Mannington to hear. 'It is, I fear, a serious shortcoming for a man to have no sense of humour.'

'Come, Cordelia.' Mannington cupped her elbow in a proprietary manner and indicated the group that included her father. 'I shall escort you to your father.'

Vernon maintained his polite smile as Cordelia shook her head and pulled her arm from Mannington's grasp. She smiled at him, patted his hand, and said, 'No, you go ahead, sir. I know how eager you are to discuss business, but I shall be of more use entertaining your female guests. Go on, now.' She made a shooing motion with hand.

Reluctance in every line of his body, Mannington stalked off to join his other guests. Vernon recalled Cordelia's look of relief when she had first seen him.

'Has he been bothering you, Miss Temple?'

'Only in as much as he appears to believe there

is an understanding between us, which I have assured him is not the case. It is nothing I cannot handle, however.'

'I trust you are correct. Remember my warnings about fortune hunters and, please, take care.' On the drive over to Crackthorpe, a question had begun to plague Vernon. 'I apologise for resurrecting an unpleasant memory, but I must ask... on the day that man drowned in the Severn, did Mannington call upon you during the day? Or later that evening?'

She stared up at him. 'Why, no. He was due to dine with us, but he did not keep his appointment and then, later, he sent word that he had left Birmingham later than intended and hence arrived home too late to join us.'

Vernon's pulse kicked. At last! Their first proof... The maid at the Royal Hotel had told them Daniel was angry at missing Mannington, who had left Birmingham *early* that day. Not late. And the information settled a discrepancy that had nagged at Vernon: Mannington had been in his carriage; Daniel's assailant had left on horseback. Vernon hadn't been able to reconcile the two. But...what if Mannington had driven straight home, then ridden back to Worcester to dine with the Temples? And what if he had then come face to face with Daniel at the far side of that bridge? Witnesses had spoken of an altercation...the two men running... shouting...raised fists and the slash of a knife. He cast a swift glance at where Mannington stood talking to his guests.

'Cordelia.' He injected a wealth of serious intent in that one word.

She frowned. 'What is it?'

'There is something you need to know about our host. We need to talk in private. Meet me in that room at the far end of the terrace.' He pointed to it. 'You go first. I shall follow in a few minutes.'

'Lord Boyton...you are not intent on compromising me, are you?'

'No. Please trust me on that. But I *am* intent on saving you and your father from a huge mistake.'

Five minutes later, Vernon slipped into the sitting room and closed the door behind him. Cordelia waited by the fireplace, her hands clasped before her. Vernon crossed the room to her and began to talk. He did not mince his words, but told her everything he knew, including how Mannington had jilted Thea. The only secret he kept was that Theo was Dorothea Markham. The colour slowly leached from Cordelia's face as he spoke and, when he finally told her that the man who had drowned was Daniel Markham and that his murderer was Henry Mannington, she swayed, one hand to her mouth, eyes stricken.

'Oh, my goodness,' she whispered. 'I cannot believe...'

Vernon clasped her upper arms, supporting

her, and she leaned into him. He folded his arms around her.

'I am sorry,' he said. 'It is a harsh tale to tell, but I can no longer stand by and see you and your father taken in by such a villain.'

Despite the risk of being seen, Thea could not resist the urge to see for herself what was happening at the house party. She hugged close to the house wall, following the murmur of conversation until she reached the corner. She could see several knots of people gathered on a terrace, glasses in hand as they chatted and laughed. She scanned the people, but could not see Vernon's tall figure and chestnut hair amongst them. Neither, she realised with a jolt of annoyance, could she see Miss Cordelia Temple. The few women present were middle-aged matrons. She risked poking her head around the corner of the house and there he was, with Cordelia as Henry Mannington—and this was the first time she had seen him so clearly since discovering he was still alive—strode from them to join a group of men, including Samuel Temple. Although Henry's—*Jasper's*—expression was agreeable, his stiff gait signalled his displeasure. Either Vernon or Cordelia had angered him and Thea would bet on the former being responsible.

Vernon stood close to Cordelia, their faces serious as they spoke. Then Cordelia disappeared inside the house and Vernon stood, idly contemplating the view from the terrace as he sipped his wine. Thea ducked back behind the corner, seeking Mannington amongst the groups on the terrace. Good, he hadn't noticed her and was still deep in discussion with Samuel Temple and a couple of others. She watched him, noticing as he grew increasingly uneasy, glancing several times back towards the house, to where Vernon stood. Eventually, Thea took a chance and peeped around the corner again. Vernon had disappeared.

Where is he?

He had not crossed the terrace to mingle with the other guests, which meant...

He has followed Cordelia!

She tried to persuade herself that Vernon—as he had said he would—was searching for evidence against Mannington. But then where was Cordelia? And all her old insecurities and distrust reared up to mock her for daring to wonder if Vernon might truly care for her.

She withdrew once more around the corner, her insides in turmoil, and she made her way back along the house wall. At the first window some sixth sense made her hesitate, even though the room had been empty when she passed it earlier. Cautiously, she peered around the edge of the window frame—and bit back a gasp, her heart plummeting, bruised and sore.

Cordelia was in Vernon's arms, her head on his shoulder. Tenderness shone in his expression as he held her. Thea's throat tightened with misery. Only last night, he had made love to her. He had given her pleasure—such intimate pleasure that she blushed to even think of it. And now he was making love to Cordelia.

Had he imagined Cordelia in his arms last night and wished it was her?

Once a fool, always a fool!

Not content with allowing herself to be deceived by Jasper Connor, she had gone and fallen in love with the most unsuitable man she could ever imagine. A rake. An aristocrat who—if he ever chose to wed—would choose either a high-born lady so as not to dilute his blue blood, or a woman with a fortune to add to his wealth and his consequence.

Neither of which I am. How could *I be so stupid?*

Tears smarted in her eyes and stung her nose.

I will not stay here. I cannot face him, ever again. I will go home, devote myself to Mama and Papa and we will mourn Daniel together. I will spend my life atoning for the misery I've brought to my family.

But she remained, despite her avowals, her gaze riveted to the couple in the room, misery coursing through her. Then a movement caught her eye. The door was easing open and Henry Mannington slipped into the room, behind Vernon's back and, before Thea realised his intention, he had crossed the room and grabbed Vernon's shoulder, hauling him away from Cordelia and around to bring them face to face.

His voice was a muffled roar as he drew back his fist. Thea gasped, but then sighed with relief as Vernon blocked his punch with almost leisurely ease.

She could see him reply to Mannington, his hands raised, palms facing his furious host. But if he intended to placate the other man, he failed, for Mannington once again let loose with a wild punch. Vernon, in an almost contemptuous gesture, shoved Mannington aside, then turned to Cordelia, whose eyes were round with shock above her hand-covered mouth. Mannington, however, reached into his sleeve and withdrew a wicked-looking, thin-bladed knife. Cordelia screamed and Vernon spun on his heel to face the threat.

Thea waited no longer. She delved into her pocket as she sped around the corner of the house and on to the terrace, where the first French window also led into that sitting room.

Let it be unlocked.

The gods were on her side and she wrenched it open and charged inside, holding her pistol aloft. She skidded to a halt, six feet away from where Vernon faced Mannington, who was crouched slightly, knife in hand.

Vernon glanced at Thea and sighed. 'Dotty... I do *not* need rescuing.'

'But—'

'Dotty?' Cordelia looked from Thea to Vernon and back again. 'Who…? Are you…? Do you mean…?'

'Thea?'

Holding Mannington's horrified gaze, Thea reached up and pulled her cap from her head. In that same instant Vernon pivoted on the ball of one foot and let loose a well-aimed kick at the knife, which flew from Mannington's grasp. Vernon then grabbed the other man's lapels, pulled him around to face him, drew back his fist and let fly at Mannington's jaw. Mannington spun around with the force of the punch and collapsed on to a side table that held a collection of porcelain figurines, knocking the entire display over as he fell to the floor. There was an almighty crash and Thea allowed herself a moment to savour the sweet taste of revenge before bleak reality shrouded her again.

Daniel was still dead and Cordelia had been in Vernon's arms.

She was vaguely aware of the sound of running footsteps and raised voices from the hall. Then the door crashed wide, wrenching her gaze from the prostrate form of Daniel's killer.

'Thea!'

The roar rocked the room.

The world seemed to tilt on its axis.

Then she realised—dimly and from a distance— that it was she who was tilting as her legs gave way and she crumpled to the floor.

* * *

The man who filled the doorway occupied Vernon's attention for less than a second. He recognised him, vaguely, but his focus was on Thea. Was she all right? He fell to his knees beside her and snatched the pistol from her senseless fingers. He held it out in Cordelia's direction.

'Take it,' he bit out, without looking at her. 'Use it if he—' he indicated the newcomer with a flick of his head '—causes trouble.'

As soon as she took the gun, he turned back to Thea, leaning over her as he checked her over, making sure...

She's breathing. She's only passed out. She—

'Why, you—! Get your filthy hands off my sister!'

Sister?

Slowly, Vernon straightened and turned his head to look properly at the newcomer. From the corner of his eye he could see Cordelia, pistol gripped in both hands, pointing it unwaveringly in the direction of the man. He pictured the portrait Thea had shown him. The portrait of Daniel Markham.

So that is why he's familiar.

Vernon stood up, then bent and scooped Thea into his arms.

'I'm warning you, mister...'

He settled her gently on a sofa before turning to face Daniel and thrusting out his hand.

'Beauchamp,' he said.

Daniel ignored it. '*Beauchamp?* Another one claiming kinship to the Duke?' A sneer twisted his mouth.

'As it happens,' a smooth, familiar voice interposed, 'that particular claim is not without foundation.'

A tall figure—this time *very* familiar—had appeared in the open doorway.

A laugh gathered, deep down, swelling Vernon's chest and filling his throat. Trust Leo. Always there at the opportune moment. His brother, suave and assured as ever, sauntered into the room. He took in the prostrate form of Mannington and then the gently stirring form of Thea. His brows rose and he met Vernon's gaze, a quizzical gleam lighting his silvery-grey eyes, and as swiftly as that bubble of laughter had risen, it subsided.

Vernon held Leo's stare, daring him to take control. Leo's eyes narrowed slightly, then his lips quirked and he wandered over to the window, hitching one hip on to the sill. The slightest of hand gestures confirmed the stage belonged to Vernon.

'Lord Vernon Beauchamp,' Vernon said to Daniel. '*Brother* to the Duke. And you are Daniel Markham.' He gestured at Thea. 'We thought you dead. Your sister has been distraught. How the hell could you be so insensitive, and put her through such needless agony?'

Daniel stepped closer, almost toe to toe with Vernon, and thrust his chin forward belligerently.

'I was protecting her,' he growled. 'Unlike you. How the hell could *you* be so irresponsible as to allow her to jaunt around the country dressed like… like *that*?'

Vernon stood his ground, ready to deal with him if the other man became physical, but otherwise careful to make no move that might set that particular fuse alight. Fighting with his future brother-in-law was not wise.

'Have you *ever*,' he said, 'attempted to stop your sister doing anything she set her mind to?'

Their gazes held. Then Daniel blinked and his glare softened. He stepped back and lifted his arms sideways in a hopeless gesture.

'Why do you think I didn't tell her what I'd seen?' he said, through gritted teeth. 'When I knew I would be away from home for a while I wrote to Mama, but I swore her to secrecy. She was *supposed* to tell Thea I was visiting friends so she wouldn't worry. What do you imagine Thea's reaction would be if she found out that bas—*he*—' he gestured at Mannington, still prone on the floor '—was still alive? Do you think she would sit quietly at home and leave me to bring him to justice? Hah!

'And *you*…' this directed at Cordelia '…whoever you are, will you please put that da—*blasted* gun down?'

Cordelia glanced at Vernon, who nodded. Daniel scowled, then paced across the room and back again.

'You will have to marry her,' he said. 'I shall accept no less.'

Behind Daniel, Vernon saw Leo suppress a grin, stoking his irritation.

'I know my obligations,' he said. 'Of course I will marry her. I would not see your sister suffer.'

'And do I get a say in all of this?'

Vernon turned. Thea was on her feet, fists on her hips, her curls in a wild halo around her head: a hissing, spitting, fluffed-up kitten.

Chapter Twenty-Three

'First of all—' Thea strode to Daniel and poked him in the chest '—no letter from you arrived. I thought you dead. And second—' she whirled to face Vernon '—*I*, and only I, will make the decision about if, when and who I will marry. And… and…' All her fight appeared to drain away. She sucked in a long, juddering breath, her eyes huge, haunted. 'What *happened*?'

A sob exploded from her, followed by another. Vernon wrapped his arms around her and gathered her to him. 'Shh…' He half-carried her back to the sofa and sat with her tucked close to his side, his arm around her. Mannington, at his feet, was beginning to stir.

'Markham,' he said. 'Cover him with the pistol, will you? This scoundrel—whatever his real name is—has a lot of questions to answer before he goes off to jail.'

Cordelia handed the gun to Daniel, then looked around.

'I suggest you come over here and sit with me in the audience,' Leo said, patting the sill next to him. 'This promises to be most entertaining.' He raised an innocent brow in response to Vernon's glare.

'Who is *that*?' Thea whispered to Vernon as Cordelia did as she was bid. 'I saw him at the Crown.'

'My brother.'

'The *Duke*?'

She wriggled away from him, leaving at least six inches of empty sofa between them. Vernon frowned. He wanted her close to him. Touching him. So he *knew* she was safe, beyond all doubt. But maybe this was not the time and place to explain how things would be in the future. Once this charade was played out, however, he would tell her in no uncertain terms. She was his. And they *would* be married.

'One fact I have established,' Daniel said, 'is that his name is definitely Jasper Connor.' He nudged the man with his toe.

Jasper groaned, his hand going to his jaw. 'It's broken. You've broken it!'

'Good,' Daniel said. 'You deserve worse. Far worse. And I have no doubt you'll get it.'

Jasper rolled on to his side and pushed himself into a sitting position.

'You can't prove a thing,' he spat, speaking remarkably well for a man with a broken jaw.

'We can prove enough. We have witnesses.'

'What witnesses?'

'You'll see. Watch him, will you?'

Daniel went to pass the gun to Vernon, who rose to his feet and waved the gun away.

'I don't need that.' He formed a fist with his right hand and smacked it into his left palm. Jasper winced.

Daniel left the room and soon returned with four people—two men and two women—two of whom were strangers and two of whom Vernon recognised: Horwell's niece, Annie, and the Gipsy he had seen at the camp. A gasp burst from Jasper and then the second woman was flying across the room, fingers crooked into claws as she launched herself at Jasper Connor.

'You devil, you! How could you do it? Abandon me and our children?' She raked his face with her nails, drawing blood, as he tried, unsuccessfully, to fend her off.

The older of the two men rushed to her and pulled her away. 'Now, now, Gladys. This will get us nowhere. Allow the law to deal with him. I'm sure they'll not see you and the children penniless.' She turned into his chest, sobbing.

Vernon stared at Daniel. '*Children?* Are they…? Is she…?'

'His wife. Yes. And this is her father, Mr Morgan. He is a merchant in the town of Aberystwyth, on the Welsh coast.'

A whimper sounded from the sofa behind him.

Vernon sat down again and put his arm around Thea. She shrugged him off and stood up.

'How did you find them, Daniel?' Thea planted herself in front of her brother, hands again on her hips. 'How did you know he was married?'

'I didn't know it. Look, let us sit down and I will tell you what happened.'

Thea ignored the space next to Vernon and marched over to an armchair and flung herself into it, crossing her arms. 'Go on.'

'First, allow me to introduce Annie Horwell, who works here as a maid, and Absalom Gray, the Romani who saved my life by hauling me from the river after I fell in.'

'So you did fall,' Vernon said. 'You were not pushed?'

'Not pushed, but I had little choice. It was either the river, or his knife,' Daniel said bitterly. 'I had crossed over the bridge from the city when I saw him riding towards me. I hauled him off his horse and we fought. I had the upper hand, too. I intended to take him back home and press charges against him. But he broke away and ran to the riverbank. I chased after him and grabbed him and then he pulled the knife. I released him, thinking he would run again, but he did not. He came at me. I had the river at my back and no time to get my pistol from my pocket. I went in deliberately.'

'We were told the current was ferocious that day.'

'It was. More powerful than I could ever believe. And so fast. It tossed me about as it pleased and I could do nothing but try to keep catching my breath every chance I got.' He shuddered. 'Then I surfaced and I found myself in a sort of whirlpool, close to the bank. And, thank God, Absalom had seen me and stretched out a branch. I caught hold just when I thought I could fight it no longer and would be sucked under for good. He managed to pull me on to the bank.'

Daniel smiled at Absalom who stood to one side, watching. He acknowledged Daniel's smile with the slightest of nods. Thea leapt from her chair and went to Daniel, hugging him.

'Thank you,' she said to the Gipsy. 'What happened then?' she asked Daniel.

'Absalom's people were camped by the river, not far from where he rescued me, and he took me to them to recover. I racked my brains about how I could bring Connor to justice... I needed proof the man calling himself Henry Mannington was actually Jasper Connor and that he had swindled our father. I also wondered who had been killed in the fire in which Connor had supposedly perished. I had written to the Duke about his cousin, but I did not have much hope he would respond.

'And then I remembered Connor talking about the beauty of the Welsh coast, and about Aberystwyth, and I wondered if someone there might know him, or have information that might help. Sheer desperation drove me there, little believing what I would find.

'Absalom agreed to watch Connor. He enlisted Annie's help and then found out, through her uncle, that Connor was targeting the Americans and, later on, that a viscount was asking questions about Connor.'

'But why didn't Horwell tell me this when I asked if he knew you?' Vernon asked.

'Only I and my people knew that the man who had been swept away had not drowned, or that his name was Daniel Markham.' It was the Gipsy who spoke. 'Horwell never knew Daniel's name, or that he was alive, or that Connor had anything to do with it.'

'I swore them to secrecy,' Daniel said. 'My biggest fear was that Connor would find out I was still alive and disappear again.'

He turned to Thea. 'I *did* write to Mama. I would never have left you thinking the worst, even though I did not dare to tell you the truth.' He paced the room again, stopping in front of her. 'And I have been proved right, haven't I? The minute my back was turned, you... *Look at you!*'

He reached to grasp a handful of curls and Vernon tensed, ready to intervene but, with a groan, Daniel wrapped his arms around Thea and pulled her close.

'What have you done to your beautiful hair? Foolish, impetuous woman.'

Thea wriggled free. 'Never mind that now, Daniel. It will grow again. What happened to your letter?'

Daniel looked at Absalom, who shrugged.

'I gave it to a passing group of Rom,' he said. 'They were heading north. They'll have delivered it by now, I expect.'

'Bickling made no mention it,' Vernon said. 'My groom,' he added in response to Daniel's querying look. 'He came to Worcester from Stourwell Court three days ago.'

Daniel grimaced. 'Why would my mother mention a letter to a servant, particularly someone else's servant? Anyway, when I arrived back in Worcester, with Mr Morgan and Gladys Connor, Absalom told me that you...' he directed a hard stare at Vernon '...were staying at the Crown and had been asking about me, that you and the Temples were guests at this house party and that the Duke had arrived at the Crown. What I did *not* know was that you were the Duke's brother and that your *"nephew"* was my sister, whom I thought safe at home with our parents.'

'You must take the blame for your sister's panic and her subsequent actions,' Vernon retorted. 'If you had been less secretive—'

'And allowed this villain to get away with it? As soon as he had a sniff anyone knew the truth of his identity he would have vanished just as effectively as he did at Yarncott.'

'Speaking of which… Leo, I cannot believe you decided to make those enquiries yourself.'

'I confess to a certain amount of curiosity as to what convinced you to remain up here to search for a stranger.' His gaze settled on Thea for a moment and his mouth twitched. 'And, as Rosalind and I were escorting her grandfather to Birmingham, it was not too great a detour to travel via Oxford and Worcester.'

'What news from Yarncott?'

'I spoke with the former innkeeper and he confirmed that there were two guests at the inn the night it burned down: Jasper Connor and Henry Mannington. They evidently spent much of the evening playing cards and, from what he remembers, one man lost heavily to the other. He is unsure which, however…' He stood up and walked across to where Jasper sat sullenly on the floor, still cradling his jaw. 'Because after the fire—which began, incidentally, in Connor's bedchamber—he at first thought it was Connor who had somehow survived. But then the man who escaped the fire told him he had muddled the two men and that he was, in fact, Henry Mannington.' Leo leant down and took hold of Jasper's chin, tilting his face and moving it from side to side. 'There is a certain superficial likeness; it is not hard to understand why the innkeeper fell for your lies.'

'Stop! You're hurting!'

Leo jerked his jaw again. 'Dear me, how clumsy of me,' he murmured before releasing it. 'You may console yourself, Connor, that however painful your bruised jaw might be, it is as nothing compared to the agony of being burnt to death.'

'He didn't burn to death…he was already de—'

Vernon crouched down in front of Jasper and grasped his neckcloth, twisting. 'How did he die?'

Jasper shrank from him. 'I don't know.' He coughed and spluttered as Vernon tightened his grip. 'He just did.'

'In *your* bedchamber?'

'No. Yes.'

Holding the man's terrified gaze, Vernon said, 'Markham? Get the women out of here will you? We need a *private* chat with Jasper here.'

Daniel began to usher the women, plus Mr Morgan, to the door. Thea broke ranks and rushed to crouch next to Vernon, glaring at Connor.

'Tell them! You owe me that much. You are not going to wriggle out of this one…why make it harder for yourself?'

Jasper, sheer terror in his eyes, nodded. Vernon released his neckcloth and regained his feet, pulling Thea up with him. He nodded at Leo, then towed Thea out of earshot.

'You did not really believe I would use physical force on him, Thea?'

She stuck her nose in the air. 'I am sure *I* do not care what you do, Lord Vernon, but you cannot want Cordelia to think you capable of such barbaric behaviour.'

'*Cordelia?*'

She hunched her shoulder and pulled free of his grip. 'Do not try to pretend. I *saw* you embracing her. Now, I want to hear what that villain has to say for himself.' She took one pace towards where Leo continued to interrogate Jasper before spinning back to stare up at Vernon. 'Don't you?'

'No.'

Her mouth opened in silent surprise.

'Leo will fill in the details later.' He reached out and fingered a curl that dangled provocatively over her ear. '*You* are my priority now.'

Vernon's voice deepened as he spoke, raising a delicious shiver that danced across the surface of Thea's skin. His green eyes darkened as they bored into hers, as though he could see deep, deep inside her and knew her every thought.

Her every desire.

Her pulse quickened and she tore her eyes from his, disconcerted by the immediate response of her treacherous body.

Can I trust him? Is he playing a part?

Would he uncomplainingly sacrifice his freedom and his future because he was a gentleman and she was hopelessly compromised? He had been embracing Cordelia—she could not mistake the evidence of her eyes. Her restless gaze swept the occupants of the room.

Daniel: he had made his expectations of Vernon clear.

Jasper: she had trusted him and he had jilted her, humiliated her and almost destroyed her family.

The Duke: he, surely, would object to his brother marrying a woman so far beneath him?

She caught the eye of Absalom Gray, standing apart, once more watching the proceedings without taking part. *He* knew his place. *He* knew where he belonged. The only surprise was that he had involved himself in Daniel's affairs in the first place. Most of the gipsies Thea had met liked to keep themselves to themselves.

Absalom's eyes narrowed and Thea realised, with a start, that she had been staring at him. She felt the heat build in her cheeks and swung her gaze back to Vernon. His hand rested lightly on her shoulder. Not detaining her if she wished to go, but keeping that connection between them.

'How can *I* be your priority?' she said. 'I have my duty to my family; you have your duty to yours.'

His fingers tightened. 'You cannot mean that. What about...?' He put his lips to her ear. 'What about the way I feel about you?'

'What about Cordelia?'

She watched him closely. His astonishment appeared genuine, then his brows drew together.

'That is the second time you have mentioned her. Whatever you think you saw, you are wrong. I told you before, I have no interest in her: she is too young, too tall, and her hair...' he spread his fingers and pushed them through her curls '...is *far* too boring. And besides...' he curved his fingers around the back of her skull and pulled her closer even as he tilted her face to his '...she is not you.'

Her lids lowered and her lips parted as desire coiled in the pit of her stomach.

A loud cough interrupted them. Embarrassed, Thea pulled away. However many doubts her brain raised, it seemed her body held no qualms. Her feelings for Vernon were too complicated...she could not think straight, not with everyone here, and so she focused on the practicalities.

She spoke to her grim-faced brother. 'What about all the guests?'

'That girl, the American, she's gone to tell them their host has been taken ill. They will soon be gone. And then you and I, Sis, will be having a chat.'

She went to him, lay her hand on his arm.

'Not here,' she whispered. 'Not in front of the Duke.' She glanced over her shoulder to where he still interrogated Jasper Connor, having hauled him up to sit on a chair. He scared her. She had never met anyone quite so high-born before.

Except Vernon. He is of the same parentage, only younger. You are not scared of him.

She brushed away that errant thought. Whatever happened, she did not want it to be here, in this house.

'How did you get here?' Daniel said.

'On Star. She is in the stables.'

She caught Daniel's scowl as he eyed her legs. 'You will return in the post-chaise with Mrs Connor and Mr Morgan.'

'She will not.' Vernon had joined them. 'Thea will be with me, in my curricle. The Temples will need transport back to town, so they can go in the post-chaise. Leo?'

Vernon's brother looked around, raised a dark brow and sauntered across the room to join them, his silvery-grey gaze on Thea, making her feel like squirming. She firmed her lips and elevated her chin, and he smiled. She narrowed her eyes at him. He was as bad as Vernon.

'You called?' The Duke executed a mock bow.

'How did you get here? Carriage?'

'As it happens, no. I rode out from the Crown, in company with the charming but somewhat uncommunicative Mr Gray. And you will be pleased to hear that the ever-obliging Horwell is sending the constable out to take charge of Connor.'

'Good. I wondered how we were to transport him back. Markham?'

Daniel looked his query. 'You may ride alongside my curricle if you so wish, but your sister is coming with me.' He grasped Thea's arm and started for the door. 'We will see you all back at the Crown.'

Thea hung back. 'Do I not get a say?'

Vernon looked at her. 'No.'

Chapter Twenty-Four

❧❧❧❧❧❧

Thea huddled at one end of the curricle seat, her arms folded tightly across her chest, brooding. She was happy…she really was…that Daniel was safe but, at this moment in time, she wished she could consign all men—and, in particular, these two bristling, belligerent specimens—to Hades.

Vernon handled the reins and his whip with relaxed skill, but his profile appeared to have been carved from rock and he had spoken not a word since handing her into the curricle at Crackthorpe Manor. Daniel, astride Bullet—who, she had learned, had been tracked and caught by the gipsies after Daniel's rescue—and leading Star, rode beside the curricle, casting black looks at Vernon and Thea alike.

So much for gratitude. You'd think he'd appreciate us coming to search for him.

Back at the Crown, Vernon handed his blacks over to Bickling and, holding Thea's arm, he marched her into the inn. And stopped dead, cursing under his breath, as an attractive, finely dressed lady standing at the foot of the staircase turned and smiled.

'Good afternoon, Vernon,' she said. Her shining golden-brown hair was swept into a smooth chignon. 'Did Leo find you?'

Her words confirmed she was the Duchess. Thea swallowed nervously, tugging the peak of her cap lower over her eyes.

Vernon's fingers tightened around Thea's upper arm. 'He did and good afternoon to you, too, Rosalind. I understand you are escorting Mr Allen home to Birmingham?'

The Duchess's hand went to a silver locket that hung on a simple chain around her neck.

'We are, although he is only going back to collect his belongings. I don't know if Leo told you, but Grandpa has agreed to come and live with us at Cheriton Abbey. It is time he retired.' Her gaze settled on Thea and her brows twitched. 'Are you going to introduce us?'

The front door of the inn opened behind them and a quick glance over her shoulder confirmed that Daniel had entered the Crown. Vernon, too, had seen Daniel and he tugged Thea closer to his side.

'Not just at this moment, Rosalind,' he said, as he manoeuvred Thea in the direction of their private parlour. 'Please forgive me, but there is a matter that demands my urgent attention.'

Thea did not dare look at the Duchess as Vernon towed her past. He threw open the door to the parlour but, before he could shut it, Daniel barged in behind them.

'You are not needed, Markham,' Vernon bit out. 'Your sister and I have matters to discuss.'

Daniel crossed his arms. 'I go nowhere without Thea.'

Vernon thrust Thea behind him as he faced Daniel, who cocked his head to one side. 'Do *you* have a sister, Beauchamp?'

Thea marvelled at Daniel's bravery in confronting a member of the aristocracy even as she resented them both for taking control and talking about her as though she weren't even there.

'I do,' Vernon growled. 'What does—?'

'Would you allow *your* sister to remain even one minute, unchaperoned, in the company of a man who had already thoroughly compromised her?'

Vernon's rigid back relaxed somewhat but, far from relieving her, that made Thea more nervous. Matters were tricky enough without Vernon and Daniel forming an alliance against her. She pushed past Vernon.

'Neither of you has the right to *allow* me to do anything.'

'Now, Thea—'

'Do *not* "Now, Thea" me,' she hissed at Daniel. 'I—'

He put his arm around her. 'We only want what is best for you.'

'You…both of you…seem to think me incapable of deciding what is best for myself,' she said, wriggling to free herself. Daniel tightened his hold. 'You are wrong,' she hissed. 'I have a brain. I can decide my own future.'

'Markham?'

She felt Daniel stiffen. 'Beauchamp?'

'Might we leave this discussion until later?' Vernon moved forward and, somehow, Thea was free of Daniel's grip and Vernon was ushering her towards the door. 'Your sister is tired and she has suffered a huge shock. Allow her to rest. We can discuss this later.'

Thea glanced back at Daniel, who looked as dumbfounded as she felt. How had Vernon managed to manipulate them so smoothly? He opened the door for Thea. She walked out of the room, but Vernon remained inside.

'Go and sleep. I will see you at dinner.'

'Promise me you will not fight with Daniel.'

'I promise. Now, go.' He shut the door.

At half past five that evening Vernon knocked on Thea's bedchamber door. He heard a muffled 'Come in' and he opened the door. It had taken some doing, but he had persuaded Daniel Markham to allow him time to prove to Thea he was not marrying her because he ought to, but because he wanted to. It was the one thing the two men had agreed upon: Dorothea Markham could not be forced to do anything. She needed to make up her own mind.

As he stepped through the door he blinked in surprise. Sitting at the dressing table, dressed in a pale primrose silk gown, was Thea, frowning ferociously above a mouthful of hairpins. Vernon closed the door behind him as she pulled another curl straight and jabbed a pin through it. The end sprang up again. Thea sighed and scooped the pins from her lips, scattering them across the top of the dressing table.

'It is hopeless,' she declared. Her eyes sheened. 'It's even harder than before to make them lie flat.'

'But why do you want to flatten your curls?' Vernon wandered over to stand behind her and skimmed his fingertips across her nape and along her shoulder to the edge of her neckline, watching the skin pucker in response to his touch. 'They are beautiful. I love your curls.'

Their eyes met in the mirror. 'You do?'

He fingered one curl and tugged it gently before releasing it to spring and bounce back into shape. 'I do.'

She sighed. 'I will look an utter fright next to Cordelia and the Duchess.'

He dipped his knees and brushed a kiss to the sensitive spot below her ear. 'You will outshine the pair of them.'

She stretched her head to one side, exposing more of her neck for him to nibble and kiss. She sighed, her lids fluttering closed, but before long her eyes sprang open again.

'What will the Duchess say about me? Will she be *very* disapproving?'

Vernon paused in his ministrations. '*Rosalind?* Disapproving? Thea, sweetheart, if that is what you are worrying about, let me tell you that Rosalind is the least judgemental person I know.'

'Oh. And what about the Duke?'

Vernon grinned at her reflection and saw an answering smile quiver at the corner of her luscious lips. Lips he longed to kiss.

'Rosalind has worked wonders on him since their marriage. He is learning to have more fun and to take himself less seriously. Being a duke can be lonely, but he finally has someone to share the burden.'

'But…how long have they been married? I thought they have adult children.'

'A month. And Leo *does* have adult children. Three of them. Their mother died when they were young. Thea… I have not come here to discuss Leo and Rosalind, I have come to talk about us. But, first, where did that gown come from?'

'Malky got one of the maids to pack a bag for me. Bickling brought it with him.'

He had not known. He was pleased, for Thea's sake, she had a gown to wear this evening. He could not care less what she wore, but she had already proved to him that she *did* care.

'I like you in that colour. It suits you.'

She blushed. 'I'm sure anything is preferable to what you are used to seeing me wear.'

'*My* preference,' Vernon said, 'is to see you naked. Although maybe not until later this evening.'

Thea, her cheeks fiery red, grabbed at a velvet drawstring pouch and withdrew a pearl necklace and a pair of pearl ear drops. Vernon reached over her shoulder.

'Allow me.' He opened the clasp and draped the single strand of pearls around her slender neck, admiring how the lustre of the pearls complemented her flawless skin. 'Perfect,' he breathed.

She held his gaze in the mirror, then her lashes swept low to veil her thoughts as she fitted her ear drops to her lobes.

'I want to talk to you about Cordelia,' she said.

Vernon frowned. He thought he'd dealt with that misunderstanding.

'What about her?'

'Do you care for her? Because, if you do, you owe me nothing.'

'No! I—'

She rushed on: 'You must not feel obli—'

He hauled her from her chair and into his arms. 'Foolish Dotty. Will you just let me speak? Is that not just like you…rushing full tilt ahead without listening first?'

Thea stood rigidly in his embrace. 'I saw you embracing her.'

'It wasn't an embrace. Not as you mean it.' He slid his hands down her arms to take her hands, drawing them into his chest. 'I was comforting her after I told her the truth about Mannington's identity and that he was responsible for that man drowning in the river.'

'Oh.'

'She was upset.'

Thea stared at the floor between their feet. 'Oh.'

'Thea.' She looked up. He traced the line of her brow with a gentle finger. 'You saw us and yet still you rushed in to help us, even though you were hurting—'

'Angry! I was angry.'

'Angry. Of course.'

'But I was angrier with Jasper.'

'And now you know the truth of what you saw, are you still angry with me?'

She searched his face. 'No. Not angry.'

'But…?'

'Scared.'

'Thea, you are the most courageous woman I've ever met. What are you scared of? Me?'

'I am scared of the future. Daniel said you must marry me and I know you will, because it is your duty and because you are an honourable man. But you will regret it, because your family will not approve and society will not approve. I am not of your world. I could not bear to be an…an *embarrassment*.' Her voice choked on that final word.

'Thea…you could never be an embarrassment.'

She snatched her hands from his and spread her arms wide. 'Look at me! Of course I will be an embarrassment. You need a real lady. You need someone tall and elegant and smooth and sophisticated and—'

Vernon held his hand aloft and, miraculously, Thea halted her tirade of self-deprecation.

'When you have *quite* finished telling me what you think I *need*, Dorothea Markham,' he said, 'please allow me to tell you what I *want*. Or, to be accurate, what I do *not* want.

'I do *not* want a real lady, if by that you mean a female born into the aristocracy. I have met any number of them since my youth and not one of them has wriggled her way into my heart the way you have.

'I do not want someone tall.' He reached for her shoulders and pulled her into a gentle hug, propping his chin on top of her head, her curls tickling his jaw. '*You* are the perfect fit for me.'

He set her back again, and looked her up and down. 'You look beautifully elegant to me, so I *will* accept I need—and want—an elegant wife.'

She was watching him closely, a slight crease

between her brows, but the light of hope beginning to dawn in her eyes.

'Smooth? I do not even know what you mean by smooth. If you mean your hair... I *adore* your hair and I'll have you know that many society ladies spend hours trying to get their hair to curl or to fall in ringlets. You will be the envy of all.'

'But it is *red*!'

'It is the colour of a fine sunset and of an autumn leaf. It is warm and happy and perfect, and I would not have it any other colour.

'Now. What else? Oh, yes: sophisticated. You, Thea, are an intelligent and knowledgeable woman. You are stylish—maybe not when you are dressed in breeches, but...look at yourself, sweetheart.' He turned her to face herself in the mirror. 'You are the exact degree of sophistication I want and the exact degree of sophistication I need.'

He turned her to face him again. '*You* are the one I want and the one I need, Thea. You and only you. I love you.'

He lowered his mouth to hers. He had no more words to describe what he felt, so he poured his heart and his soul into that kiss, desperate to show her the deepest yearnings of his heart. She responded, melting into him, her fingers clutching at his shoulders and her tongue stroking his.

Conscious of the passing time, Vernon ended the kiss. 'Thea, I love you. Please do me the honour of being my wife.'

Her face was serious as her eyes searched his. 'I love you, too, Vernon. But I…'

His heart cracked. Surely she would not refuse him? What could he say to convince her? He searched desperately for the words, but they would not come.

'I need time to think,' she continued. She caressed his cheek, then averted her face. 'After Jasper, I swore never to trust another man.'

'You do not trust me?'

She captured his gaze again. 'It is my own judgement I do not trust. Give me time. Please.'

'How much time?'

'Does it matter?'

Yes, he wanted to roar. *It matters. I want you with me always, starting now.* He swallowed his pain.

'You may take as much time as you need,' he said. 'Although your brother might not prove so amenable. It seems impatience is a family trait.'

Chapter Twenty-Five

Dealing with her brother would be easy compared to summoning the courage to accept Vernon's proposal. She wanted to. She really wanted to. She had become so attuned to Vernon's feelings she could feel his suppressed pain and she hated that she was the cause. But something held her back from saying 'yes' there and then.

'You have often said I am impulsive,' she said, trying to lighten the suddenly sombre mood. 'You should be happy I am considering my answer seriously.'

'Happy is not how I would describe it,' he said, 'but I accept your right to answer in your own time.' He proffered his arm. 'Come. It is time to go downstairs. We have all been invited to dine with the Temples in their private parlour tonight, as it has a bigger table.'

'All?'

Thea took Vernon's arm and they left the bedchamber, heading for the staircase.

'You and your brother, and me and my family.'

'What has happened to Mrs Connor and her father?'

'There was no room for them to stay here and they declined to join us this evening. They are weary after their journey and also, I believe, in a state of shock at what Jasper has done.'

'What will happen to him?'

'He's been arrested and will be kept in jail until he stands trial at the next assizes. There's little doubt he killed Henry Mannington and set the fire to cover up his crime and it was only by the greatest of good luck Daniel survived. I'm afraid he will almost certainly be sentenced to hang.'

Thea swallowed. He deserved to be punished, but it was hard to think of him dying in such a way. They had reached the door of the small parlour they had used during their time at the Crown.

'We have arranged to meet the others in here before we join the Temples,' Vernon said. 'I shall introduce you formally to my brother and his wife—who will have conveniently forgotten they have ever set eyes upon my supposed nephew, Theo—and to Rosalind's grandfather, Mr Allen.'

He opened the door for Thea. Three pairs of eyes turned to look at her and her stomach roiled violently and her mouth dried as she took in the figures of the Duke and Duchess and Mr Allen.

What will they say? What will they think of me?

With a flash of insight she realised that here

was the 'something' that was holding her back. *They* were the reason she had not accepted Vernon straight away. It was not that she didn't trust him. She did. And she loved him, but part of loving him meant she would also protect him. During the past week she had learned that the Beauchamps were a close and loving family and she could not bear to be the cause of conflict between them. Their acceptance of her was crucial.

Yes, it is crucial. But I can still fight for him.

Vernon's hand was at the small of her back, large and reassuring, urging her forward. Thea swallowed, rolled her shoulders back, raised her chin a notch and walked forward.

Vernon made the introductions and Thea dropped a curtsy.

'Oh, there's no need to bother with curtsies,' the Duchess said, with a smile. 'To tell you the truth, I still haven't become accustomed to all that formal nonsense and I doubt I ever shall. Have you ever been to London, Miss Markham?'

'Why, no,' Thea said.

'Do not worry about it. If I can adapt to it, I am sure you will have no difficulty.'

'But I am not—'

Vernon was by her side in an instant. 'Thea has yet to agree to marry me, Rosalind,' he said, with a warning note in his voice.

'Oh!' The Duchess's cheeks washed pink. 'I am so sorry… I assumed…that is…'

'Hush, my sweet.' The Duke was quick to protect the Duchess's embarrassment and Thea warmed to him, although she still felt rather overawed in his presence. 'I am sure Miss Markham will agree to overlook your…er…eagerness to enrol her into the family.'

Thea studied both of their expressions, but could detect no hint of insincerity. The Duke smiled at her—not the amused, slightly cynical smile she recalled from Crackthorpe Manor, but a genuine, friendly smile.

'You do quite right to keep him guessing, Miss Markham,' the Duchess said. 'These Beauchamp men are far too accustomed to having females fall at their feet.' She dipped her head closer and whispered, 'But do not delay too long, will you? I can see you are besotted with one another and it will be pleasant to have a fellow newcomer in the family.'

They seemed welcoming enough. But what of her birth? What had Vernon told them? She wanted answers, but she knew no one in that room would be impolite enough to address such a vulgar question. She decided to tackle it head on.

'My father is a manufacturer, your Grace,' she said to the Duke.

He raised a dark brow, looking so like Vernon for a moment that she gaped at him.

'I am aware of your parentage, if that is what is bothering you, Miss Markham. Stour Crystal, is it not? Very fine lead-crystal glassware…you should be proud.'

'I *am* proud,' Thea said.

'There's nothing amiss with working for a living, bab.'

It was the first time Mr Allen had spoken and he did so with the flat Midlands accent Thea had been familiar with her whole life.

'I've been a silversmith all my life,' he went on, his chin jutting belligerently. 'Nothing to be ashamed of.'

The Duke grinned. 'Quite right, Grandpa. Not a thing to be ashamed of.' He then said to Thea, 'Mr Allen is my wife's paternal grandfather.'

'And my son, her father, was a common soldier,' the old man said. 'Leo here, he came and found me before he married my Rosalind and took me to London for the wedding. I hadn't seen her since she was six years old, but I never forgot her and she never forgot me. And now, I'm going to retire and spend the rest of my days with my grandchildren and, God willing, my great-grandchildren.'

The door opened and Horwell came in to announce dinner was about to be served. Daniel was already in the larger parlour, chatting to Cordelia, who seemed smitten with him. Thea noticed she barely glanced at Vernon when he entered the room. There was little chance for Thea to join in the conversation at dinner. Samuel Temple was so enthused about having a real-life 'dook and duchess' as his guests that he dominated the conversation, questioning Vernon's brother about almost every topic under the sun and not holding back with his own opinions. The Duke did not appear to object, but answered him patiently, exchanging loving smiles from time to time with the Duchess.

Thea watched. And thought. And reached the conclusion she had been fretting about nothing. She appreciated Vernon giving her time to consider what she wanted and was grateful neither he nor Daniel were harrying her to accept him. It was important to her, if she married, that her husband would respect her opinion. Any residual doubts about Vernon and Cordelia had vanished. Cordelia only had eyes for Daniel, and Vernon… Thea shivered in pleasure as his hot gaze lingered on her neckline.

She waited until there was a lull in the conversation.

'Vernon.'

A sudden hush fell over the table and Thea's courage nearly deserted her. Then she braced herself. Everyone here knew Vernon was waiting for her answer. She owed him this.

'Do you recall that question you asked me?'

He pursed his lips, his eyes dancing with merriment, the absolute devil.

He knows what I am going to say.

'I do,' he said.

'May I give you my answer now?'

He nodded.

'My answer is yes.'

A huge grin split Vernon's face. He shot to his feet and thrust his arms high in the air, as a cheer arose around the table. Before she realised he had moved, he was by her side and pulling her to her feet.

'Ladies and gentlemen,' he said. 'Oh…' with an ironic bow in his brother's direction '…and your Grace. Allow me to introduce the future Lady Vernon Beauchamp. The woman I adore. The love of my life.'

He kissed her soundly on the lips to a chorus of congratulations and a loud, 'I'm pleased *someone* has managed to talk some sense into her' from Daniel, which brought forth much laughter.

Horwell popped his head around the door to investigate the noise and added his best wishes to the happy couple.

'Horwell…two bottles of your finest champagne,' the Duke said. 'This calls for a toast.'

Later that evening—her head pleasantly swimming from the effects of the champagne and her heart full and happy and content and excited—Thea undressed to prepare for bed. She washed at the basin and slipped on her shift, then sat at the dressing table to brush her hair. She could not wait for it to grow properly.

She froze as a movement in the mirror caught her eye, her heart leaping into her throat as she realised the door behind her was opening. But her terror lasted only a second. Vernon—in open-necked shirt and trousers—slid through the opening. Their gazes fused in the looking glass and she saw the heat in his, and that recognition stoked such a fire in her blood she could barely sit still. But she forced herself to remain seated as Vernon padded across the carpet. He took the brush from her hand and drew it through her curls, a look of total absorption on his face.

'I adore your hair,' he murmured, his deep voice melting through her.

He knelt behind her, pushed her hair aside and kissed her nape, then feathered kisses along her shoulder, pushing the neck of her shift aside to allow him access.

'I adore your skin.' She looked up at him, over her shoulder and he gently flicked the tip of her nose. 'I adore your freckles.' He reached around and cupped her. 'I adore your breasts.'

She shuddered, pushing into his touch, wanting more.

He rose behind her and urged her to stand, kicking the chair out of the way. His hands were on the hem of her shift, lifting, and she raised her arms, and then she was naked, her torso from thigh to neck reflected in the mirror. His hands were on her arms, holding them aloft, and he groaned—a deep, heartfelt sound that vibrated through her.

She could wait no longer. She wriggled and

turned, tugging his shirt from his trousers and over his head. She stroked eager hands over the heavy muscles of his chest and shoulders, then fumbled at the fall of his trousers. He eased away from her and then he was as naked as she.

He cupped her chin and kissed her, hard.

'And I adore your impatience. And your impulsiveness. And...*you*!'

This time the kiss lingered, explored, feasted, as did their hands.

Vernon swung her into his arms and carried her to the bed, following her down.

Later, as she floated in the aftermath of their lovemaking, Vernon raised his head, suddenly serious.

'I love you, Dorothea Markham. I love you with all my heart and soul, and I swear to you now that I will make you happy.'

She stroked his lean cheek and along his jaw, relishing the scratch of his whiskers against her fingertips. She kissed him then, her heart bursting with all the love she felt.

'And I love you, Vernon Beauchamp, and I cannot wait to walk down the aisle and see you standing at the altar, waiting for me.'

'No doubts? You trust me?'

'I do.' She leaned up and kissed him again, pouring her heart into it. 'I do.'

* * * * *

*If you missed the first book in
Janice Preston's*
THE BEAUCHAMP BETROTHALS *trilogy,
check out*

CINDERELLA AND THE DUKE

*And look out for the last story in the trilogy,
coming soon!*

MILLS & BOON®

 HISTORICAL

AWAKEN THE ROMANCE OF THE PAST

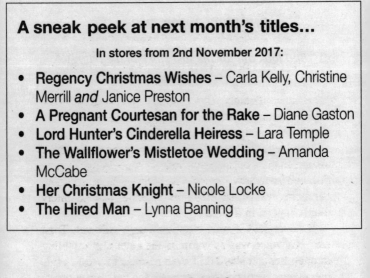

A sneak peek at next month's titles...

In stores from 2nd November 2017:

- **Regency Christmas Wishes** – Carla Kelly, Christine Merrill *and* Janice Preston
- **A Pregnant Courtesan for the Rake** – Diane Gaston
- **Lord Hunter's Cinderella Heiress** – Lara Temple
- **The Wallflower's Mistletoe Wedding** – Amanda McCabe
- **Her Christmas Knight** – Nicole Locke
- **The Hired Man** – Lynna Banning

Just can't wait?
Buy our books online before they hit the shops!
www.millsandboon.co.uk

Also available as eBooks.

MILLS & BOON®

EXCLUSIVE EXTRACT

Unhappily betrothed to each other, Lord Hunter agrees
to help Nell convince another man she's a worthy
bride. But their lessons in flirtation inspire desire
which has Hunter longing to keep Nell for himself...

Read on for a sneak preview of
LORD HUNTER'S CINDERELLA HEIRESS
the first book in Lara Temple's linked Regency series
WILD LORDS AND INNOCENT LADIES

'This most certainly isn't a waltz.' Nell laughed as he
swung her out of the way of a portly couple who were
clearly interpreting the music as a reel.

Her laugh collapsed into a gasp as her attempt to
avoid stepping on his boot brought her sharply against
him and somehow his leg slid between hers, straining
her skirts against her thighs in a manner that definitely
didn't happen in a waltz.

'I never said it was. No, don't pull back yet. Trust
me.' His voice was as warm as the cider still tumbling
through her and she didn't even manage to scoff at this
outrageous demand, too stunned by the sensation of
being held there in the middle of the chaos, just swaying
gently against his thigh, his head bent next to hers.

She had ridden astride more times than she could
count; she knew what it felt to have something firm and
muscular between her thighs, the pull of fabric over that
sensitive inner flesh. But not this. They continued to

move, with no regard to the rhythm, his leg shifting between hers, hard and muscled, scraping and pressing in a way that should have been thoroughly uncomfortable and it was, it was, just not in any way that she wanted to stop. It made her skin heat and tingle and begin to shake and for one mad moment, still misted in the fumes of the cider, she thought it might be the return of that horrible fear, but that thought passed immediately. It wasn't that kind of shaking. It was... She was coming apart and reforming around a completely new heat at her centre, that burst of sun had sunk from her chest and stomach and settled between her legs, insistent and aggravating and in a dialogue with his body she could barely follow.

He bent his head, his mouth beside her ear as if talking to her, and perhaps he was, if talking was that gentle slide of breath over the curve of her ear and every now and then his lips brushed its tip and the heat between her legs would gather in and prepare to shoot up through her to capture that caress and out into the heavens.

Don't miss
LORD HUNTER'S CINDERELLA HEIRESS
By Lara Temple

Available November 2017
www.millsandboon.co.uk